A
Season
of Grace

Books by Lauraine Snelling

UNDER
NORTHERN SKIES
3

A
Season
of Grace

LAURAINE
SNELLING

BETHANYHOUSE

a division of Baker Publishing Group
Minneapolis, Minnesota

© 2018 by Lauraine Snelling

Published by Bethany House Publishers
11400 Hampshire Avenue South
Bloomington, Minnesota 55438
www.bethanyhouse.com

Bethany House Publishers is a division of
Baker Publishing Group, Grand Rapids, Michigan

Printed in the United States of America

Library of Congress Cataloging-in-Publication Data
Names: Snelling, Lauraine, author.
Title: A season of grace / Lauraine Snelling.
Description: Minneapolis, Minnesota : Bethany House, a division of Baker
    Publishing Group, [2018] | Series: Under northern skies ; 3
Identifiers: LCCN 2018019153 | ISBN 9780764218989 (trade paper) | ISBN
    9780764230639 (cloth) | ISBN 9780764230646 (large print) | ISBN 9781493416097
    (e-book)
Subjects: LCSH: Domestic fiction. | GSAFD: Christian fiction.
Classification: LCC PS3569.N39 S34 2018 | DDC 813/.54—dc23 LC record available
    at https://lccn.loc.gov/2018019153

Scripture quotations are from the King James Version of the Bible.

This is a work of fiction. Names, characters, incidents, and dialogues are products of the author's imagination and are not to be construed as real. Any resemblance to actual events or persons, living or dead, is entirely coincidental.

Cover design by Dan Thornberg, Design Source Creative Services

Author is represented by the Books & Such Literary Agency.

18 19 20 21 22 23 24   7 6 5 4 3 2 1

Chapter 1

AUGUST 1910

The rocking chair on the porch made all the difference.

Nilda Carlson grinned at her sister-in-law and best friend, Signe. "There's no furniture inside yet, but now this house looks more like a home."

Signe smiled. "Pinch me. I must be dreaming."

Nilda did as she was told.

"Ouch." Signe rubbed the spot on her arm. "You didn't have to do it, you know."

"I know, but it's not often I get an offer like that. But believe it—you are moving into your very first brand-new house that you and my brother own! I can't wait for the housewarming party tomorrow. Our hours of hard work are not over, but tonight you will sleep in your own bed in this very house."

"And still eat and cook at Gerd's house until our cookstove arrives." Signe sat down in the rocking chair, shaking her head. She looked up at Nilda. "I have an idea, something that has been mulling in my mind."

"I think I know what you are thinking." Nilda laid her hand on Signe's shoulder. "Moving Gerd in with you."

Signe nodded. "How did you guess? It makes so much sense. I cannot bear to take Kirstin away from her. She can have the bedroom off the kitchen so she needn't climb the stairs. Rune agreed. Said he was thinking the same thing."

"Then it makes sense to move her furniture over here too, or at least part of it. When will you tell her—er, ask her?"

"Probably tomorrow, if we can wait that long. Maybe tonight."

That leaves only Ivar and me living in Gerd's house.

They watched Bjorn, Signe's oldest, halt the wagon that held the rope bed from the attic, along with the bedding and the trunks Signe and Rune had brought from Norway not much more than a year earlier.

"So much change in so little time." Signe leaned her head against the back of the chair.

"So much change in just the three months Ivar and I have been here. Let's go help unload the wagon and get the beds made for tonight. Although yours is the only one that will take any time. Throwing the boys' pallets on the floor won't take but a minute."

"Which room do you want?" Rune called as he and Ivar, Signe's younger brother, carried the two-by-ten boards for the bed frame up the stairs. Boards waiting to be hung for the walls took up space in all the bedrooms and in the hall. Bare studs enclosed the rooms. Finishing the interior walls was a good job for stormy days and wintertime.

Nilda smiled at her best friend as they stood in the upper hall. "You get to choose a room!"

"I-I . . ." Signe looked from doorway to doorway.

Rune and Ivar were both shaking their heads.

"I . . ." Signe sucked in a deep breath and pointed to the east room. "I want that one so I can wake up to see the dawn. I've always loved seeing the sun come up."

"How would you know?" Rune asked. "You are always down in the kitchen by that time."

"Why, Rune Carlson, you just made a joke." Nilda shared a grin with Ivar. "We'll let you two get your job done and start hauling up the rest of the wagon load."

While the men bolted the bed frame back together, the two women emptied the wagon. What had seemed like a lot in the wagon felt like very little in the empty rooms. They set the trunk from Norway under the window at the opposite end of the hall from the stairs and laid out the boys' pallets and bedding in the room beside Signe and Rune's.

"Mor?" Leif called from downstairs. "We got the beans picked and snapped. Tante Gerd said to tell you that Kirstin is missing you."

The two women left their cleaning bucket and returned to the other house to help get the beans on to can and make sure Kirstin did not get to the screaming stage, something she rarely did. But when she did, the whole township might hear her.

Kirstin was back to her happy self, the boiler of beans was steaming, and Signe was packing beans in more jars when Gerd called a halt for dinner.

"The bed is finished," Rune said as they sat down to eat. "I was hoping to have the others made by now too, but . . ."

"But you are still doing the finish work inside and outside at the house." Gerd gave him a stern look. "Be careful you don't get obsessed with finishing the house like Einar did with felling trees."

All of them stared at Gerd. Nilda made sure she closed her mouth. Tante Gerd Strand did not say a whole lot, but when she did, the wisdom she'd kept in hiding peeked out. Since her husband, Einar, had died so suddenly about six weeks earlier, she had become a different woman—one none of them realized had been inside her.

"Takk for the reminder, Tante Gerd," Rune said while nodding. "I guess all the things I wanted to get done before the housewarming might be good to do, but aren't necessary."

Nilda glanced at the loaves of bread rising in the pans. There were beans in jars on the stove, beans ready to cook with bacon tomorrow for the party, and a haunch of smoked venison waiting to be put in the oven in the morning.

"This afternoon I think you need to take a nap with Kirstin, Tante Gerd. You've been pushing as hard if not harder than the rest of us," Signe said gently.

"We've never had a party at this place before. It is about time." A faraway look crept over Gerd's face. "I always dreamed of having neighbors come to our house, to visit together like we did at home, but at first Einar and I were working too hard and then . . ." Her voice drifted off. She heaved a sigh and nodded. The look floated on by. "But now is different."

They all watched her while they ate.

She nodded more firmly. "Now we—I—can start over again."

The silence lengthened, as if no one even wanted to breathe, they were so focused on her. Kirstin set her chair to rocking and babbled at her fingers.

Leif turned to Tante Gerd sitting beside him. "And we can have a party with lots of good food."

"And music and dancing." Ivar nudged his brother. "Maybe even your far will dance," he said to the boys. "He always said he had two left feet and they liked to trip each other."

"Do you know how to dance?" Leif asked Tante Gerd.

She nodded. "I used to. If I try, will you dance with me?"

"If you teach me how."

She held out her hand. "Deal."

They shook. "Deal." Leif gave a little bounce on his chair. "This is going to be a real good party."

I just hope people are not afraid to come. Einar had made many enemies; in fact, just about no one liked the Strands. Nilda prayed that would change soon. She was careful to keep any doubt from her face. Sometimes memories were hard to dispel.

That evening after the chores and supper were done, and the lightning bugs were starting to twinkle in the dusk, the boys were raking around the new house while the adults enjoyed a last cup of coffee on the porch of the old house.

"Tante Gerd, Signe and I have made a decision, and we hope you will agree with us," Rune said.

Gerd paused playing with Kirstin. "What might that be?"

"We would like you to come live with us in the new house. You would have the bedroom off the kitchen so you needn't climb the stairs and, well, this is just what we would like to do."

"We think it would be easier," Signe added softly. "And better."

"I-I—but that is your house."

"Not really. It seems more to us it is *our* house, like you said this one is *our* house. Not the Strand house or the Carlson house, but our houses. Maybe the old one and the new one, but both are ours."

Nilda waited for Gerd to answer. *Please,* she pleaded silently. *This would be for the best.*

Gerd's voice shimmered with tears. "I . . ." Another pause lengthened, broken by her blowing her nose and sniffing. "Could we have Kirstin's bed in that bedroom too?"

"If you would like, though you know how she wakes sometimes during the night."

At nine months old, Kirstin sometimes woke in the night and

stood in her crib, shaking the bars and chattering until her mor took her to bed with her and nursed her back to sleep. They laughingly called her their night owl.

"I can't give her all she wants, but I do know how to call for help," Gerd said.

"Is that a yes?" Rune asked.

"Ja. I can't begin to tell you how grateful I am, that—that after all that has happened since you came, you really want me to live in your new house with you. I have a perfectly good house here, and like you said, I would see this baby every day and . . ." She sniffed again. "Takk, tusen takk."

Signe bobbed her head. "Good. Then on Sunday we will move you and your bedroom over to the new house along with whatever else you want to bring."

Gerd brightened. "If I move over there, we could set up the loom and spinning wheel here. Nilda and Ivar can live here, and if Gunlaug ever comes, she can live here too. That way we can have a women's workshop here and add on to the one by the barn for Rune to make skis and furniture in the winter." She nodded emphatically as if adding an exclamation point.

Rune smiled. "Sounds like you have it all planned out."

The boys skidded to a stop at the porch steps. "Is there any cake left? We're hungry. And then we're going to the new house, right?" Knute and Leif tripped over each other's words.

Nilda lit the kerosene lamp in the kitchen and set it in the middle of the table. "More coffee?"

"Nei, the stove is nearly out. How about buttermilk?" Signe suggested. "Knute, please get the crock from the well house while we cut the cake."

When they were seated at the table, Rune looked around at each member of his family. "I think the way we are going, we will soon need a bigger table."

"Well, good thing the kitchen in the new house is bigger, then." Ivar grinned. "We'd better get to building, Rune. You think the lumberyard has enough walnut or maple? Or would you rather use pine?"

Gerd nodded. "I think you should use pine. It seems fitting, even though it's a softer wood. I remember when Einar hired a portable sawmill to cut up one of our pine trees for use around here. We built the chicken house and machine shop from that and a lot of the fencing. Isn't there still a pile of lumber behind the machine shed?"

"We used some of it for adding to the pigpen. All those babies needed room to run and grow in." Leif sneaked a bit of his cake down for his half-grown puppy, Rufus, who had latched onto Leif like a long-lost brother. The Bensons had given them the white puppy with black and brown spots after Einar died. Leif grinned when he caught his mor's look. Somehow the rules of not feeding the dog at the table and the dog sleeping on the porch were sliding into oblivion.

When the cake was gone, Rune and his family gathered up what they needed and trooped out the doorway.

On the porch, Gerd hugged each of them as if they were heading out on a journey. "I know, I know, this is silly, but . . ."

Signe laughed. "Not silly at all. We are the silly ones to want to sleep in our new house before it is really ready and before the housewarming. No stove or sink or anything. But we have beds, at least ours and Kirstin's."

"See you in the morning, Tante Gerd." Leif waved before he and Knute charged off toward the newly painted house that glowed white against the dark of the pinewoods.

"We need to remember to ask Reverend Skarstead to bless the new house before the party tomorrow," Nilda said as she followed Gerd back into the kitchen. "I will do the dishes first thing in the morning."

"It seems awful quiet here now." Gerd headed for her bedroom. "'Night."

"'Night." Nilda put the plates and glasses in the dishpan on the stove. The reservoir was still hot enough to do the dishes, but instead she followed Ivar up the stairs to their bedrooms in the attic. A sheet hung across the middle to make two rooms. One day soon, they would finish the attic, but they needed beds first.

She lay down on her pallet and felt sleep creep over her. *Ah, peace.*

"Nei, nei! Leave me alone! Nei! Not again!"

Nilda shoved against his chest, hammering with one hand while the man clenched her other wrist. He backed her against the wall and fumbled at her bodice. Twisting her head away, she kicked at his legs.

"Oh, I love a feisty one," he growled in her ear. "I've been patient, but now I am tired of waiting."

"Nei!" She panted against the weight of his body pressing her into the wall. "God help me, I can't bear this! Nei!"

"Nilda, stop. It's all right. It's only a dream." Ivar's voice broke into her scream. He was shaking her shoulders.

Nilda struggled against the sheet wrapped around her, her breath ripping at her throat. The darkness of the attic room was safe. No one was tearing at her.

"You kept screaming. What were you dreaming?" Ivar asked.

"Dreng. Dreng Nygaard was attacking me. I couldn't break free of him." She gulped in air.

"It was a nightmare. He is not here. Nilda, he'd never find you. You're safe."

"But he said he would get even."

"He is all threats and bombast. He's probably starved to

death by now. After all, he doesn't know how to work, and his far refused to give him any money. He paid the ticket, put Dreng on the ship, and he was on his own."

"Are you sure?"

"We threatened to tell everyone what had been going on. Mr. Nygaard was furious that his son had acted like that to young women."

Nilda sucked in a deep breath and let it out slowly. A bad dream. A horrible dream, but so real. Surely he wouldn't really be able to find her.

Stretched out on her hay-stuffed pallet, she stared out the window at the stars and tried to find that peace again. So much change already. What would the coming months bring?

Chapter 2

"They're coming, they're coming!" Leif skidded to a stop at Signe's side.

Nilda and Signe settled the last of the sheets over the sawhorse tables set up to hold all the food, knowing everyone would bring plenty. Benches made of boards laid across timber rounds were grouped for easy visiting. Ivar arrived with the cart bearing food from the other house.

"Let's put the desserts on that table." Nilda pointed to the smaller one. "Knute!" She shook her head at his guilty look as he sucked a bit of frosting off his finger.

"It was an accident."

"Of course. Why don't you go show the folks where to park their wagons?"

"Far is doing that. He said to come help you."

"I see."

"You go get your far so we can greet people as they come." Signe nodded for Knute to do as she asked.

The Bensons were the first to arrive and stopped their buggy to help carry food over. "I think most of Benson's Corner is on their way here. We've not had a party like this in far too long a time," Mrs. Benson said. They set baskets on both tables before

Mr. Benson drove off to park the buggy. "I made something new—a baked corn casserole that we could not get enough of when I made it for us."

Signe lifted the lid off the casserole dish to take a sniff. "Smells wonderful. Are you sharing the recipe?"

"Of course." Mrs. Benson pointed to a large flat pan that was covered with a dish towel. "The smoked venison you told me about?" At Signe's nod, she continued. "You know, Bjorn could earn himself some money bringing in deer. Has he ever brought down a moose?"

"Not yet, but he has hopes."

"Where would you like us to put the presents?" Reverend Skarstead asked Rune when he met them on the porch.

"Presents? We don't need—" Rune stopped when their guest shook his head.

"Housewarmings mean presents, so where?"

"In the big room, I guess. There's nothing else there yet, not even a table."

"That'll do fine. It's hard to believe you even got this painted."

"All of this is thanks to so many of the people who are driving up. Last Saturday, four people showed up to help us paint. They even brought their own paintbrushes. How do we begin to thank everyone?"

"Just be part of a work party for someone else. I heard your names on the list for helping the Skagens get their hay in before the rain, so you'll be fine. As soon as everyone is here, we'll say a blessing over your house and then have supper."

Rune nodded. "Takk. Tusen takk."

Signe saw big, burly Petter Thorvaldson dismounting his horse. That would please Nilda. Where was she? Ah, over there by the food tables. Petter went over and spoke to her specifically. Signe smiled.

The English teacher, Fritz Larsson, rode into the yard on horseback. His thatch of brown hair always looked like it could use more combing, but it was especially windblown today, as he was not wearing a hat. He dismounted and unhooked a big, lumpy burlap bag from his saddle. Straight as an arrow, he crossed the yard to Nilda. They spoke. Smiling brightly, she nodded and pointed toward the house. Fritz handed her his horse's reins and went into the house, but moments later he came back out, still carrying the loaded burlap sack. They talked, smiling and nodding. What were they saying? Signe was dying to know, but she had a party to host. She would try to bring up the subject with Nilda later.

Someone, or several someones, had brought chairs, and a bench held more gifts. Signe was stunned by the sheer number of people gathering here. And to think she had worried that no one would show up.

Petter was talking to Reverend Skarstead, and he suddenly let loose a piercing whistle. Reverend Skarstead waved, and folks made their way to the back porch of the new house. The reverend asked Rune to gather his family and raised his arms for silence.

"We are gathered here tonight to celebrate this family as they move into their new house and make it a home. As Rune said, so many of you have helped build this house, and for that, we all offer thanks. This is what the family of God can be for each other as we walk in love as He first loved us. First we will bless the house—if you have not gone inside yet, feel free to do so. Then we will bless the food, and the party begins. I hope you brought your dancing shoes, as I know we will have dancing music later. Rune, did you want to say a word or two?"

Rune swallowed and cleared his throat. "Takk. Thank you for all your help in building, roofing, even painting. We would not have been able to sleep in our new house last night if not for your generosity, which now includes that pile of gifts in there." He paused for a moment that Kirstin, in her mor's arms, decided to fill with her happy chatter.

When the laughter died down, Reverend Skarstead raised his arms again. "Gracious heavenly Father, we thank thee for this special day so filled with joy and gratitude. We cannot thank thee enough for all you have given us, but one way we do is to share what we have with others. We ask you to bless this house and all those who will live within these walls. Let love bloom here in this season of grace, give good health and wisdom and a desire in all of us to seek your will and learn from your word. Set up a guard around this place so that all that is done here may be done for your glory. In the name of the Father, and the Son, and the Holy Ghost."

And everyone shouted, "Amen!"

The people shouted and laughed and clapped. Then they quieted again for the table grace, which those who knew it said together in Norwegian. "*I Jesu navn gär vi til bords.* . . . Amen."

"The tables are set up on the other side of the house, so bring your plates and eating utensils and enjoy yourselves," the reverend announced.

Signe smiled and nodded, feeling like she was overflowing with a stream of joy that rose up through the soles of her feet and covered everyone. She almost feared her cheeks would crack from it. She and Nilda wove their way through the groups of people, offering drinks and answering questions. Gerd sat on a chair with a quilt in front of her for Kirstin and two other babies to sit or lie on. Two young girls played with the babies. The lines continued on both sides of the tables as everyone served themselves and found places to sit on benches, chairs, or the ground.

"Can we go play in the haymow?" Leif asked, two other boys beside him.

"Ja, you can, but don't let the hay slide out the door," Rune said.

"We won't."

That group of boys ran off, and Knute appeared at Rune's side. "Can we play ball? Mr. Larsson brought the balls and bats from school."

Ah, so that was what was in his lumpy burlap sack. Signe smiled.

"Of course," Rune said. "How about out in the front pasture? That's not been used recently. You might ask Ivar and Bjorn to round up some of the older boys. You can use old feed sacks for bases."

Soon the shouts from a ball game echoed back to the women cleaning up from the meal. Most of the men had followed the ball game and could be heard playing and cheering. As the sun sank closer to the distant treetops, the crickets struck up their song, and the musicians began tuning their instruments.

"I noticed Mr. Larsson watching you," Signe whispered to Nilda as they put lids back on pots and pans.

"Don't be silly."

Mrs. Benson leaned closer. "No, it was Petter Thorvaldson who was paying her the most attention."

"Enough. You're going to embarrass me."

"There are other single men here too," Mrs. Benson continued. "I know that nice Mr. Kielund needs a mother for his two little ones. You caught his attention right off."

"I swear, if you two keep this up, I will go hide in the attic and not come out until everyone is gone."

Signe shrugged and made her way over to the quilt, where she picked up Kirstin and nuzzled her cheek.

Mrs. Engelbrett picked up her little boy. "She sure overcame that rough beginning, didn't she?"

"Thanks to your help."

"I was so grateful I could do that for her. I sure rejoiced when Mrs. Benson told me your milk had come back in. Such grand news. I have a few dresses my Lacy outgrew. I kept them for another baby, but Arnie here won't take to wearing dresses much longer. Now that he's crawling, he tangles up in the shifts."

"Tante Gerd made Kirstin some short shifts. They make crawling easier, and she sure can scoot across the floor now. Every time she sees one of the cats, she makes a beeline for it, and Rufus thinks she is the best thing next to a dog. He just moves away when she pulls his tail or his ears. The other day I found him sound asleep beside her on the quilt in a patch of sunshine. What a picture they made."

"If you like, I will keep the little ones up at the other house so you can enjoy the party," Gerd offered. "Perhaps a couple of the older girls would like to help me."

Mrs. Engelbrett smiled. "That is a fine idea, Mrs. Strand. I remember we used to put all the children lined up like cordwood on the bed when they grew tired."

Several of the mothers, including Signe, joined Gerd on the walk to the other house and settled their little ones in after nursing or a bottle. Two girls helped take care of toddlers and small children, even helping them go to sleep on pallets on the floor.

Meanwhile, down at the party, after the musicians tuned up their instruments, the baseball game closed down and the folks all gathered around the dance area.

"We'll start out with a polka tonight to get everyone in the dancing mood," Mr. Garborg on the guitar announced. "A-one and a-two . . ."

Petter grabbed Nilda's hand, and they joined the others, fast-stepping to the beat. While the night was cooling, the heat that rose from the dancers had everyone mopping their foreheads after a couple of dances.

Mr. Kielund asked Nilda to join in a square dance, and the slim, graceful Mr. Larsson lucked out in a waltz. As he twirled her under his arm, Nilda smiled up at him. Signe caught the smile as she and Rune turned in front of them.

"They are good," she whispered to Rune.

"Nilda has always been a graceful dancer, don't you remember?"

"Ja, and I never really was." She flinched as she set her foot in the wrong spot. "Oops."

"Sorry. Hope I didn't hurt your toes."

"Wouldn't be the first time." She caught Nilda smiling up at Mr. Larsson again. They did make a nice-looking couple.

When the musicians called for a break, Signe sat down beside Nilda. "You look to be having a fine time."

"My feet are screaming at my shoes." Nilda dabbed her face with the edge of her skirt.

"Well, you are the belle of the ball, and I expect you to enjoy yourself."

Nilda watched the gathering for a few moments, a somber look on her face. "None of these young men are like Dreng. They're polite. Well-mannered."

"You mentioned something about a young man in Norway making inappropriate advances, but you didn't say much about it. That one?"

"Ja." Nilda sucked in a breath. "I guess he frightened me more than I realized. I still think about him sometimes." She added hastily, "Not in a nice way."

"I would have been terrified."

20

Nilda nodded. "I was, ja. His mor called me awful names, of course, but later his far sent him off to America. Dreng blamed me and threatened me."

"He's here?"

"Surely not here. America is vast. But he's somewhere. I pray I'll never see him again. And I burned the note he sent swearing he would get me."

"Oh, dear. I didn't know it was that serious."

Nilda firmed up her voice. "It's all behind me. I must dismiss it. I see that someone brought punch. You want a glass?"

As if by magic, two glasses appeared in front of them from the hands of Petter. "Thought you might appreciate these about now."

Signe took one of the glasses. "Thank you, that was most kind."

He sat down on the other side of Nilda. "You're welcome. Thank you for hosting such a grand party. Even in Blackduck there are not a lot of dances."

When the music started again, he and Nilda were the first couple out. Signe noticed that Mr. Larsson did not look happy, but then, he didn't smile a lot anyway. When she danced with him later, she realized he did not talk much either, only *please* and *thank you*. But he was a marvelous dancer.

They danced polkas and waltzes, schottisches and traditional Norwegian dances, square dances and round dances. Small boys danced with their mors, and fars danced with their little daughters, who stood on top of their feet. But as the younger children succumbed to sleep, both in the house and on the porch, families began to gather up their children, the kettles and baskets they'd brought, and head out.

Signe and Rune made sure to thank each person both for coming and for helping at some point on the house.

"If you need someone to nail up walls, just let me know," Mr. Garborg, their neighbor to the west on the lake, offered. "My boys are pretty handy with hammers too."

"Thank you again, and for taking the boys fishing too. They had such a good time."

Mr. Garborg smiled. "Always more fun when you catch fish. We need to do it again one day. School's going to be here before we know it."

When everyone had left, Leif looked up at Signe. "I didn't get to dance with Tante Gerd."

"Well, maybe next time." She patted his shoulder. "You need to get to bed. Morning will come early."

"It always does."

"Ah, this bed feels good," Rune whispered a few minutes later. "That was some housewarming."

"I think Nilda wishes for a pan of hot water to soak her feet."

"Watching her and Mr. Larsson dancing together made me wish I had learned more."

"Some people are cut out to be dancers, and some are not."

Rune nudged her. "Are you saying I am in the 'not' category?"

Signe smiled. "Perhaps it's implied, but all your other good assets more than make up for it."

"I think that was a compliment."

"It was indeed." She paused to listen to Kirstin snuffle and wiggle in her bed, then settle back down. By that time, Rune was snoring gently. A breeze from the open window blew cool air over her skin. What a party indeed.

Chapter 3

Counting stars, let alone sheep, was not working.

Nilda rolled onto her right side and let the dancing fill her mind. Never had she enjoyed an evening more—never laughed more, never danced anywhere near that much and especially with so many different men, most of whom she'd not met before they asked her to dance. And such interesting conversations, several where all she had to do was nod and smile. Like the young man who wanted to go on fishing boats in Duluth but his parents wouldn't let him. They said he was too young. As far as Nilda was concerned, he should still be in school.

She rolled onto her left side. Mr. Kielund made her sad. He so desperately needed a wife to take care of his two small children; his wife had died in childbirth along with the baby. He made his living with his draft team, hauling logs or doing farm work like haying and harvesting for other farmers. Nilda knew for certain that although he seemed like a good man, she was not cut out to be his wife. Not that she had any idea who her future husband might be, but after tonight, she felt certain she would find the right man. Someday.

She flopped onto her back. The two men she already knew

had managed to dance with her the most often. Petter Thorvaldson, their blond friend from the ship, made her laugh the most. He wanted her to encourage Ivar to spend the winter in a logging camp, like he planned to do. She had a feeling that with any encouragement she would see Mr. Thorvaldson far more often, even if he did live and work in Blackduck.

Winter in a lumber camp screamed of danger. Cutting down their own trees was dangerous enough with one falling at a time, let alone many. While she'd thought of hiring on as a cook's helper, after the stories she'd heard, she would only do so as a last resort. She got the idea that a lumber camp was not a great place to meet future husbands.

Heaving a sigh, she threw off the sheet and went to kneel in front of the window to feel the cooling breeze. It felt so good, she dragged her pallet over and lay back down.

Mrs. Benson had teased her about all the attention and warned her to be careful and, above all, patient. And Mr. Larsson would make a fine husband. She'd managed to slip that idea in several times. Nilda simply grinned at the ceiling. The slight, trim Mr. Larsson was a wonderful dancer, but he was a better teacher than conversationalist. From their encounters, she had come to believe he loved teaching more than anything else. How his eyes lit up when someone finally understood what he was trying to explain.

Her eyes drifted closed. The waltz she had danced with Mr. Fritz Larsson—now that was something to remember.

Sunday morning was like other Sunday mornings—chores, cleanup, breakfast, and getting everyone in the wagon before Rune hollered the second time. As always, Kirstin managed to need a diaper change just as they were about to leave. Leif closed the door after his mor so that Rufus would stay in the house and not follow them. They heard him barking as they drove down the lane. Gerd in the wagon with them—that was the biggest change.

"You could have put the dog in one of the stalls in the barn," Bjorn said.

"They're all full. I moved the last of the hens and her chicks into one this morning. That hen got me good." Leif showed the raw wound on his hand. "At least it quit bleeding."

Kirstin reached for his hand, jabbering at him, drool running down her chin. He let her guide his finger to her mouth and chew.

"Ouch. You know how to use those teeth now." He jerked his hand back. "Bad enough the hen bit me, but now you too?"

His little sister frowned at him, sniffed, and worked into crying.

"You don't have to yell at her," Knute said with a frown.

"I didn't yell. She bit me hard." Leif shook his head. "Sorry, K, you didn't mean to hurt me, I know." He reached for her, and she snuggled into his arms for a moment, then grabbed his hair to help her stand up, knocking his hat off and giggling when it fell. He picked it up and set it on her head. Looking up at the brim, she waved her fist in the air and fell into his arms.

Nilda watched them play and watched Gerd turn and smile down at them from her place on the wagon seat. This was one well-loved baby, with the sunniest of dispositions, unless she didn't get fed on time.

As usual, Mrs. Benson met them at the door to claim Kirstin for her customary cuddle and hug. To Signe's obvious relief, Kirstin fell asleep soon after the service began. Mrs. Benson needed grandchildren, but she sure was enjoying the Carlson children for the time being.

Ivar nudged Nilda and nodded to Fritz Larsson, who had left the organ bench and taken a seat for the duration of the sermon.

"Enough," she hissed back, shaking her head. But she'd caught Mr. Larsson glancing at her earlier. What would happen if she smiled back?

After church as Nilda was leaving, Mr. Benson motioned to Leif. "I heard you might be in the market for some sheep."

"Who, me?" He stared at him in surprise.

"Your mor said you are taking care of the hogs, so I should talk with you."

Leif grinned at Signe. He nodded. "Ja, we've talked about buying some sheep this fall. You know of some for sale?"

Mr. Benson nodded. "I do. I thought perhaps you might like to trade some of your young pigs for sheep."

Leif looked from his mor to his far. "Me? I mean, I can trade?" When they both nodded, he looked at Mr. Benson. "How many are there?"

"Three ewes and a young ram of different bloodlines."

"What kind?"

"Hampshire. You know, the ones with black faces and legs. Big. They've been shorn for this year, so no wool, but you will have plenty next year."

"And at least three lambs." Leif turned to his far. "Do you think a pig for a sheep is a fair trade?"

"You can ask."

"But what if they want more?"

"Then it's up to you how badly you want the sheep." Rune laid a hand on his son's shoulder. "Do you want to go look at them tomorrow? Or perhaps this afternoon?"

Leif turned back to Mr. Benson. "Where do they live?"

Mr. Benson pointed to a man and wife who were just getting

into their buggy. "That's Mr. and Mrs. Wilson. Why don't you go talk with them?"

Leif looked up at his far. "All right?"

Rune nodded. "You better hurry."

Nilda and the family followed him over to the Wilsons' buggy. Leif stopped beside the man who was helping his wife into the seat. "Mr. Wilson? Mr. Benson said you have some sheep for sale."

He turned with a smile. "We do. And who might you be?"

"I'm Leif Carlson, and I wondered if we could trade feeder hogs for your sheep."

"How big are the hogs?"

Leif glanced up at Rune. "Thirty pounds?"

Rune nodded. "About that, give or take a bit."

"They're growing fast," Leif added, "and should be ready to butcher in late November."

Mr. Wilson nodded. "Never thought of that, but I think . . ." He looked at his missus. "Do you want ham this year?"

"I do. What is a fair trade, do you think?" she asked Leif.

Leif cleared his throat. "Uh, a pig for a sheep?" Nilda watched him; this was one nervous young man, but she was impressed he was able to have this whole conversation in English. She noticed that Rune was smiling, looking amused.

Mr. Wilson looked rather amused too. "Four pigs. We could keep a gilt or two for breeding. I always liked having pigs around. And since we won't have sheep grazing that pasture down to nubbins any longer, we could build a fence for pigs instead." He held out his hand. "Deal?"

Leif did the same, flashing his far a big grin. "Deal!"

"How about I load the sheep in the wagon tomorrow, deliver them, and haul the hogs home?"

"You can pick out the ones you want."

"Very good. See you in the morning. Looks like I might be building a fence today." He waved as he climbed up in the buggy and backed his horse up so he could head north.

Leif stared up at Rune. "I didn't ask Tante Gerd if I could do this. What if she says no?"

Rune shrugged. "Remember, she was the one who mentioned sheep. I think she'll be very proud of you and grateful."

Leif told Gerd what he had done as the rest of the family climbed into the wagon.

Nilda smiled at her older brother. "So you are raising a businessman?"

"Ja, he is the real farmer, he and Knute. I like farming, but I've learned I would rather make things like skis and furniture in the shop. It's a good thing there's plenty of work for everyone and of all different kinds."

Nilda watched Gerd put her hands on Leif's shoulders and nod. At the grin on the boy's face, she knew Gerd had agreed with him. No wool this year, but four fleeces next year. Spinning and weaving—how Nilda enjoyed that, just like her mor, Gunlaug, did.

In the wagon on the way home, Gerd raised her voice. "Do you think we might be able to trade more of our hogs for a bred heifer or another milk cow? Leif just gave me all kinds of ideas. One thing I know for sure, we don't want to butcher twenty hogs this year. Sell, trade—those pigs are like money in the bank."

"Or on the hoof," Bjorn added, shooting Tante Gerd a grin.

When they arrived home, Bjorn hopped out of the wagon to help Gerd down from the seat. She moved toward the house, Nilda close behind her, dinner on their minds.

"What in the world?" Gerd stopped in the kitchen doorway as Rufus tore past her to leap around Leif and then greet the others, yipping and nearly wagging his tail off.

"What is it?" Rune joined her just inside the doorway.

"The broom. Rufus chewed up the broom. And look, part of the broomstick."

"Guess we won't be leaving him in the house while we're gone." Rune raised his voice. "Leif, you have a cleanup job here and no broom to sweep with."

"Bad dog," Leif yelled at the slinking hound. "Look what you did."

"He's a puppy yet, and puppies chew, just like babies do. We should have thought of that." Gerd shook her head.

"There's a broom at the new house. I saw it in the stack of gifts." Nilda tried hard not to laugh. It was amazing how much space a well-chewed broom could cover.

"You'd think he'd have a mouth full of slivers." Leif swept the kitchen while the women got dinner on the table, including warming the biscuits they'd baked that morning.

"There sure wasn't much left on that haunch of venison," Bjorn said when he dished the last of the meat from the platter. "Anyone else want some?"

"I'll take another biscuit." Knute looked in the bowl. "Er, the last biscuit."

"There were hardly any leftovers from last night," Nilda said.

Ivar leaned back in his chair. "Someday we should roast a pig for a party here. I heard down in Texas they roast whole steers over a trench of coals. They put it on a frame with a handle for turning."

"A whole steer? How can they do that?" Bjorn stared at Ivar. "How would it ever get done?"

Ivar shrugged. "Don't know. I just saw a drawing of it. The article said the meat tasted really good."

"Where did you see that?"

"In a magazine on the ship when I was helping in the main

salon. Texas seems like a place I would like to visit. They have ranches of thousands of acres, run thousands of head of cattle. I asked a man on the ship to read me the article. He'd been to Texas, but he thought he was going to die on the ship."

Nilda watched her little brother. He had a knack for finding unusual information, and he was curious about everything. She thought about Fritz, who also had that strong streak of curiosity. Ivar and Mr. Larsson would likely make good friends.

"So, Tante Gerd, are you ready for us to move your bed and chest of drawers to your new home?" Rune stretched his arms over his head and grunted. "All that dancing last night must have been hard work."

"Nilda is the one who should be tired." Ivar mimicked Rune, so the boys did too.

"You better be nice to me. I'm the one dishing up the cake." Nilda waved the pancake turner in the air, then pointed at the bowl of whipped cream she would be spooning over the pieces of cake.

Rufus whined at the screen door. Leif started to get up to let him in, caught the look from his far, and settled back down.

"You really mean it?" Gerd passed the plate of cake to Leif to pass on around.

"Of course," Signe said. "Unless you would rather stay here until we are more moved in over there. Walking back and forth all the time might be hard on you."

"It might be good for me too. We could set up the loom immediately. I have not worked a loom since I came to America. We will need to buy supplies for it. I wonder who might have wool for spinning now." Gerd paused. "Hmm. I wonder if the people who sold us the sheep might have a fleece or some wool left over to sell." She looked at Rune. "Have you ever put looms or spinning wheels together?"

"No, but I figure it can't be too hard. They're rather simple. Besides, both Nilda and Signe used to use them. I'm sure they can put them together."

"Don't worry, Tante Gerd," Signe said. "We'll manage. If we had any rags, we could do a rag rug, but we use everything till it's gone. One of the best rugs Mor ever wove was from strips of leftover men's pants for the weft. It lasted forever. She used heavy cord for the warp."

Nilda looked from face to face. Family. What a wonderful thing. She missed their relatives in Norway, of course, but her family here was just as close and caring.

"My mor used to braid rugs. I have always liked an oval or round braided rug." Gerd wore a faraway look. "So many things we could do." She nodded and looked at Rune. "Today would be good. The sooner we turn my room into a workroom, the better."

"What other furniture do you want us to bring?"

Gerd's stare moved from Rune to Signe. "I, ah, what would you like to bring? Perhaps the sewing machine, but it would be good here with the loom." She nodded. "I think the sewing machine would be good here, but the trunk in the parlor could go in my room. Do you think we might use the sofa and chair? We rarely do here. We all just stay in the kitchen where it is warmer. Even the few times we've had company."

"We're going to have lots more company at our new house." Signe nodded emphatically. "Benches can be built faster than chairs."

"Or perhaps we can order a table and chairs from the Sears Roebuck catalog. After all, if people can order houses in a kit, perhaps we can order furniture too."

"Next time I'm in Blackduck at the lumberyard, I'll ask about such things." Rune pushed his chair back. "Come on, let's get going. The next thing someone is going to suggest is moving this house closer to the other."

Eyes round, Nilda and Signe stared at each other and then at Rune. "You know, that might be a very good idea," Signe said. "The cellar is the only problem."

"Other than moving this entire house. Why, a snap of the fingers." He did as he said. "Come on, boys, let's go. Give these women time to think up new schemes."

"As if we need permission." Gerd's eyebrows arched. "We can all go with you and put away those gifts waiting for you. Do you have shelves up in the cellar yet?"

Rune shook his head. "We don't have shelves in the bedrooms, let alone the cellar, and no cabinets in the kitchen."

"You can buy those from Sears Roebuck too, you know. I saw a picture once."

Shaking her head, Nilda set to washing the dishes at the stove. So far they didn't have dishes over at the new house either. Or kettles. Actually, moving the old house might just be easier.

Wait until she wrote to her mor about all this.

Chapter 4

I can't believe this," Rune said at breakfast the next morning. "I'm getting restless to get out in the woods again."

"You said we would get real beds first," Nilda said.

"I know, and we're working on beds today. I just thought it surprising. I know we have plenty to do around here first. With all three of us working in the shop, maybe we'll get them all done. Knute, you and Leif work on the woodpile. We need to find another dry tree."

"We still have plenty to cut up in the piles of branches. The earlier piles are dry." Knute looked up from his oatmeal. "It's a shame Onkel Einar burned so many."

"He said the ashes would help build up the dirt. He was disappointed that the soil that grew those huge trees really isn't very good for raising crops." Gerd toasted more bread over the open fire. "We need to churn today and do the wash."

"You boys can take turns at the crank too." Signe buttered the toast and passed the plate around. "We never run out of work to do, that's for sure."

"You should go see how the pigs dug up their new pen," Leif said. "In one of those books I'm reading, in other places they let pigs run wild in the woods so they don't have to feed them all summer. Do you think there is enough for ours to eat out there? What if they run away? Or some animal gets 'em?" He looked at Rune, who shook his head. "Did you know they like acorns?"

"I think pigs like whatever they can dig up or find in the feed trough. Did you let them out already?"

"Nope. I figured it would be easier to catch 'em in a smaller pen. I let the sows and the boar out."

"We better get at it, then." Rune pushed his chair back. "Come get me when Mr. Wilson gets here if I don't hear the dog barking. That Rufus, even if he did chew up the broom, is already a good watchdog."

"Where are we going to put the new sheep?"

"In the small corral by the barn for now. Let them settle a bit, and then you can take them out to graze. Stay with them for a while. Talk to them so they get to know your voice."

"The pigs know my voice. They hear me call and come running."

Rune smiled at his youngest son. Not even ten, and look at all he was doing. Rune's own far would be so proud of these grandsons of his. What a shame he refused to come to America. Mor would so love to come.

When Rune stepped off the porch, he had to stop and shade his eyes. The glare nearly blinded him. Today was looking to be one of his bad eye days. The pain didn't let up when he rubbed them. Pulling the brim of his hat down to shade his eyes, he headed for the shop, grateful Ivar and Bjorn could do the measuring and sawing. When he squinted with his good eye, the forest of big trees beyond the barn was only a blur rising up from the land. What would he be able to do if his sight went entirely?

"We'll cut all the frame boards first, then drill the holes, making them all the same size. We need four beds minimum; Knute and Leif can share. How many boards, Bjorn?"

"Sixteen," Bjorn replied immediately. "And the end pieces are five inches shorter than the sides, with four holes drilled per side and three on the ends. It seems to me that if we drilled more holes and put the rope closer together, it would make a better base for the mattresses or pallets."

"Good reasoning, but I can tell you that the way we have it is comfortable, especially compared with a pallet on the floor. We won't have enough rope for the beds if we drill more holes."

"One of these years, I hope we will need to make a bed for Mor too," Ivar said. He slid the first board onto the sawhorses, followed by another. Bjorn was doing the same thing on the other pair of sawhorses.

Rune watched as the two young men measured, marked both sides with the end of a nail, and then used a schoolhouse ruler to draw the line to make sure the pieces were all accurate. From the beginning, Rune demanded accuracy rather than speed, reminding them that they were building furniture rather than fences—not that he didn't require perfection on fence boards too.

They had the boards all cut and were drilling holes when Rune heard Rufus barking. The jingle of a harness further announced the arrival of a wagon.

"Come on," Rune said, "let's go see our new sheep."

Leif was already up on the wagon seat, showing Mr. Wilson where to go. He stopped the team right by the corral gate and greeted the others.

"Fine morning we have. Your boy is mighty excited about his big trade." Mr. Wilson stepped to the ground and shook Rune's hand. "You ever raised sheep before, son?"

"We had sheep in Norway." Leif studied his four sheep, which huddled as far from him as they could in the wagon box.

"So you know how to hang on to them?" Mr. Wilson asked.

"Ja, neck and rump. How long ago did you shear them?"

"A little over a month. You'll need to keep the ram separate until you breed them. We liked lambing in early spring, so they need to be bred around the first week of November. Do you have a place to winter them?"

"Ja, we plan to add on to the lean-to off the barn and build another corral. We'll keep our four sows over there and the boar too."

"It looks to me like you're going to need more animal housing by winter." Mr. Wilson let the rear gate down slowly. "Now move in easy, son, and keep talking to them. I'll bring out the first." He motioned for Rune to guard the exit and walked slowly up the ramp, pausing to talk to the skittish critters before moving in. He grabbed one by the neck and rump and guided it down the ramp, and Leif copied him perfectly. "I got the bell sheep, she leads the flock. You did well, even when he tried to leap away from you. One thing with sheep—moving slow and easy keeps 'em calm. Once they get frightened, it takes time to calm them down again." As he spoke he snagged the next ewe and held steady until Leif had the last. With all four sheep in the corral, already crowding at the far side, Mr. Wilson nodded again. "Just remember that sheep can actually die from fright. It seems strange, but I seen it happen once when a coyote got in the flock. He killed one, but the other that died had not a mark on him. I see you got a young dog—be real careful with him and these here critters."

"I will. Far said to keep 'em in the corral and spend time with them." Leif hung on the corral bars, nodding. "We really have sheep. Mor is—oh, Tante Gerd wondered if you have any wool or a fleece you might sell us?"

"I'll ask the missus and bring it to church on Sunday. Now, let's move on to the hogs."

"It's not going to be as easy," Rune said. "If you could back up to the gate there." He pointed to the pigpen.

Bjorn clapped Leif on the shoulder and nodded. "More chores."

"I don't mind." With all of them at the pigpen, Leif opened the gate to let his brothers and Ivar into the pen. "Far, please pour that bucket of mash and sour milk in the trough. We'll each grab a pair of back legs and wheelbarrow the pig into the wagon."

Rune grinned both inside and out. His young boy had figured out how to load the pigs without even asking for help.

"You see any you like?" Leif asked Mr. Wilson.

"You already cut 'em, I see. Did you leave any of the males intact?"

"Not this time."

"Well, I want two gilts for sure. That one with the black spot looks good."

As soon as the pigs lined up at the trough, Leif pointed one out for Bjorn. "Grab her quick and hang on."

Bjorn rolled his eyes. Rune knew he was thinking that they'd caught hogs before and usually much bigger than these. Bjorn guided his hog up the ramp and grabbed the board Rune handed him to help keep the pig in the wagon. Ivar followed with the gilt of Mr. Wilson's choice, but she squealed and tried to twist away.

"Hang on!" Mr. Wilson said around a snort.

Knute grabbed a pair of legs but ended up on his rear when another pig banged into the backs of his knees. "Ugh! Pigs smell bad."

"You keep these in, and I'll get another," Ivar said. Bjorn stuck the board in front of an escaping pig's snout just in time.

While they changed places, Ivar grabbed a third, looked for the buyer's agreement, and drove that gilt up in the wagon, where the two men were helping Knute keep the others from escaping back to the melee in the pen, as the trough was already empty.

"One more. Your turn, Bjorn."

"See that one over in that corner?" Mr. Wilson said. "He looks real good, not that they all don't."

The four boys formed a line and let the other pigs go, keeping their attention on the chosen one—who got by in spite of them. Amused snorts from the two men encouraged the catchers.

"Just get whichever one you can," Mr. Wilson called. "They all look good."

"You wanted that one, you get that one," Bjorn said.

The pig got by them again. And again.

"Get what you can before these get loose," Mr. Wilson said.

"It's getting pretty hot out here too," Rune called.

Ivar finally managed to grab one that tried to dart by him, and with the line of boys keeping the others in the wagon, they loaded the last pig and slammed the gate into place.

Mr. Wilson shook hands with all of them. "You did a fine job, boys. Now to get these critters into some shade. I'll do like you did, Leif, and make a mudhole to help them stay cool. My missus is more excited about these hogs than I am. Sheep for shoats. What a good trade."

"Shoats?" Leif glanced at the pigs. "That's a different name."

"An old English word for young pigs. My grandpa always called them that. He came to America from England when he was a young man." Mr. Wilson stepped up the wagon wheel and settled into the seat. "Good doing business with you. You going to be selling those others come cold weather? I could tell some of my neighbors."

Rune nodded. "That would be good of you. If we could sell

38

them local, we'd be pleased. By the way, do you know anyone who has a milk cow or bred heifer for sale?"

"Not right off, but I'll keep my eyes open. The bulletin board at Benson's is the best place to look, and some people advertise in the Blackduck paper." Mr. Wilson clucked his team forward. "Thanks again."

Rune and his crew stood watching the dust kick up from the wagon going down the lane. "Anyone else in need of a cold drink or a sluicing from the bucket by the pump?"

They all stared at Knute, who looked down at his dirt-crusted pants with a frown, then brushed at his legs, earning snickers from the others.

"Leif, you grab the buttermilk crock from the well house while these others clean off at the pump. Surely everyone could use some time to sit down about now." Rune pumped water as the boys stuck their legs and bare feet under the running water and then doused Knute from the waist down. "We probably should just throw your pants in the wash, since that's the big thing for today."

Knute wrinkled his nose. "Pigs stink."

"Well, their pens do, especially when wet and stirred up." Rune had a hard time keeping from laughing at the frown on Knute's face. "At least your feet are clean."

"And cold. Maybe we should just stick our heads under the pump to cool off."

"At home we'd go jump in the creek," Bjorn said.

Knute shivered at the memory. "The water there was always cold. You know that creek where I water the horses out in the big timber?" Rune nodded. "Maybe we should dig a hole in it for swimming. There's sort of a deeper place already. I waded in it last summer."

Rune studied his soaking son. "Now would be the best time to do such a thing. Unless it is spring fed. How about we go find the source on Sunday? We can look for trees to cut for stove wood at the same time and find out where the survey markers are, get an idea how many big trees are still out there." He nodded slowly as he spoke. "What a fine way to spend a Sunday afternoon." The thought of really looking over the land made him nod again. He wondered if Gerd had ever walked the property lines. Surely Einar had before he bought it.

Knute perked up. "Onkel Einar said there is a lake out there somewhere. Maybe we could go fishing."

Rune strolled to the house along with his workers.

Gerd was hanging clothes on the line, and Signe and Nilda were at the washing machine. Kirstin lay on her belly, jabbering at the cat seeking safety under the rocking chair.

"Can you use a buttermilk break?" Rune asked. "It's hot out here."

Signe wiped her forehead with her apron. "Ja, we can do that. I think there might even be cookies in the jar." She looked at their wet pant legs. "You sit here on the steps, and we'll bring it out to you."

Basket on her hip, Gerd wrinkled her nose as she climbed the porch steps. "It's easy to forget how pig manure smells."

"Mr. Wilson really likes his pigs." Leif handed Nilda the buttermilk crock. "I really like the sheep. We need names for them."

"Loading pigs is a mess." Knute looked at Rune. "Will we have to haul all those others in a wagon to sell them? And we're only keeping four? That's a lot of pigs to load."

Gerd sat in the rocker and lifted Kirstin onto her lap. "We might use some of the others to trade like Leif did."

"Mr. Wilson said he would bring what wool he could to church on Sunday," Leif told her.

"How kind of him."

"He also said he didn't know of anyone with a cow or heifer for sale, but he'll keep an eye out." Rune swallowed half his glass of buttermilk in one long drink. He held the cool glass to his forehead with a sigh. "What a morning. You missed all the excitement."

"Are you saying doing the wash is not exciting?" Signe passed the plate of cookies. She sipped at her buttermilk and nibbled on a cookie. "It seems you didn't invite us to share the excitement, but you are kind enough to share the stink of it all."

Leif snorted, spraying buttermilk out of his nose.

Rune patted him on the back, chuckling with the others. They had come so far since laughter had been forbidden. *Thank you. Lord God. We never realized what we were missing, and now you have given us this. Please remind me to be thankful all the time, like your Word says. Praise in all things.* He sipped his buttermilk this time. *Today is easy. But I'm sure there will be times again where thankfulness does not come easy, or even come at all.* He finished his buttermilk and rested his elbows on his knees, hands dangling. *Lord, how do I be thankful for my failing eyesight? And the pain?*

Chapter 5

We all have real beds."

Signe smiled at Rune and then at each of his helpers. "We need a celebration."

"Like with a pie?" Leif's eyes widened.

"For breakfast?" Knute nudged his brother, giving him a disgusted look.

"Dinner perhaps?" Leif asked.

"Maybe supper." Nilda shook her head. "How come you like pie better than cookies?"

Leif screwed up his face, then shrugged. "Don't know, it just popped out." He grinned at Signe. "You need to come meet the ladies—well, and Mr. Ram too. They really like oats. They came up to me and ate right out of my hand. And they only got here yesterday. I think Mrs. Wilson liked her sheep a lot."

"'The ladies'?" Bjorn cocked one eyebrow and shook his head. "They are sheep, not people."

"They are people to me. So are Rosie and the cows and the big pigs. They all have names."

"Rufus has a name—does that make him human too?"

"They aren't human, like we are, just people. There's a difference." Leif mopped the egg yolk off his plate with the last of his biscuit as if the others were not staring at him.

Bjorn shook his head again. "Maybe you should ask Mr. Larsson about that."

Leif shrugged and drained his glass. "Can I be excused? I have work to do."

"If you like." Signe looked at Rune, who was fighting off a smile. She watched her youngest son go out the door without a backward glance.

Leif called back. "I'm going to take some corn suckers out to the ladies, and we are going for a walk out in the pasture."

"And what will the rest of you be doing?" Nilda asked with raised eyebrows.

"Well, I hope someone will be baking a pie." Rune pushed his chair back. "Ivar and I are going to work at the house. Knute and Bjorn will saw branches down at the big tree piles for firewood. Leif will help them when he finishes his chores. Any other suggestions?"

"I wonder what kind of pie I should make," Signe said.

"How about one custard and one chocolate?" Rune took his hat off the hook. "Come on, guys, before they find something else for us to do around here." He stopped on the porch. "Could you send Leif out with dinner so we can keep on working? It'll be good when we have the cookstove in. Just think—we ordered it out of the Sears Roebuck catalog. Who would have ever dreamed such a thing?"

"Only in America," Nilda mumbled. "And to think, we will get a catalog of our own with the stove when it comes."

"Catalogs work good in the outhouse, I heard once." Gerd started on the dishes. "Are you baking bread today or tomorrow? I think we should leave a full row of the beans for drying now, along with others later. I'll go out in the garden and see how the carrots are doing. I've been wanting carrots." She plucked the baby's sunbonnet from a hook on the wall and leaned over to pick up Kirstin. "You come with me, K. You like the garden as much as I do." Gerd flinched as she straightened.

Signe saw it. "Gerd, that baby is too heavy for you to pick up anymore."

"We manage. I'll be more careful. She likes riding in the wagon."

Signe shook her head as Gerd and Kirstin went out the door. "Stubborn."

"Runs in the family." Nilda got out the yeast and other ingredients for bread. "There's enough cream to churn again. How about going early for class tomorrow and taking butter and eggs to the Bensons? I have a letter to mail. Do you?" She stared out the window. "How I can ever feel homesick, busy as we are, is beyond me."

"I did and still do at times, just not so much since you and Ivar arrived. And while I hate to say it, life is so much more, more . . ." She searched for the right word.

"Happy?"

Signe nodded. "I kept hoping Einar would change, would be . . ."

"Polite? Kind? Perhaps not kind, but not mean either. It seems to me he deliberately worked to make others miserable." Nilda paused. "You know how Reverend Skarstead talks about forgiving others? I can't forgive Einar. Not for hurting me, but for the way he treated you. And the boys." She shook her head. "I can't."

"When he says that, I agree with him, but then I think, he really did not know Einar. You know where Jesus says for those who hurt these little ones, better that a millstone be hanged

around their neck? Some things in the Bible are confusing."
Signe measured lard for the piecrust into a bowl with flour and
salt and then crumbled it together before adding water. "Maybe
sometime I will ask him."

When a cool breeze lifted the curtains, Signe glanced out the
window. Sure enough, the sky was graying over and turning
black on the horizon. Distant lightning stabbed the darkness.
The thought of her boys working down in the big trees brought
back painful memories of Bjorn and the lightning strike that
took his hearing—only for a time, but certainly a frightening
time—and broke his arm.

She cut the dough in two and patted it into two rounds before dusting off her hands and going to help Gerd bring Kirstin
back inside. Stepping out on the porch, she inhaled the cooling
dampness.

"We're coming," Gerd called. "This feels like a bit of heaven."
The first sprinkles pocked the dust as she reached the steps.

Signe met them and lifted her daughter. "Feel that, little one.
Rain, blessed rain. Our garden will soon be dancing for joy.
All the plants and trees will be." She spun in a circle, making
her daughter chortle and squeal. "We should dance too." She
hustled up the steps and called, "Come on out here. We can
dance in the rain."

"Almost done with the bread dough," Nilda called back. "I'll
get the eggs and towel."

"You're going to wash your hair?" Gerd asked from the rocking chair, where Kirstin now sat on her lap.

"Yes, what a shame to waste the falling rain. You come too.
We'll tie her in the chair."

"I-I—no, I don't think so."

"Have you ever washed your hair in the rain?"

"Not that I remember."

Nilda brought out the eggs and towels. "Come on, Tante Gerd. There's nothing like it."

"I use the water from the rain barrel after it heats in the reservoir."

"Of course, but this is far better. We'll help you. We'll get our dresses clean too." Nilda held up a bar of soap.

Thunder rumbled closer.

"Hurry, or it will be too late." Signe and Nilda ran down the steps. "Come on, Gerd."

Shaking her head, Gerd did as they insisted.

As the rain drenched the earth, it soaked them all, streaming down faces and over shoulders. Signe cracked an egg on Nilda's head and vice versa. Then she looked Gerd in the eyes, smiled, and broke the egg, then with both hands rubbed the egg into Gerd's streaming hair. The three of them laughed and scrubbed their heads, the egg frothing like a bar of soap. As the rain rinsed their hair, they shared the soap and rubbed the spots from their faded dresses and aprons. Thunder rumbled around them, and the rain blessed them in sheets as they stood with their faces lifted skyward and water puddling around their bare feet.

When the shivering sent them back in the house, they stripped to the skin, rubbed themselves dry, and donned clothes just washed the day before and still smelling fresh from the sun. After they wrapped their hair in towels, Signe brought Kirstin in from the porch, and Gerd fed the fire and pulled the coffeepot to the heating part, all the while shaking her head.

"Come on, admit it," Signe said. "You enjoyed yourself out there, just like we did."

"Ja, at least I am clean again." Gerd hung her rain-washed dress on a hook behind the stove along with her underthings and the apron. "Easier than running the washing machine and wringer." She unwrapped her hair and used her fingers to comb out tangles and fluff it dry in the heat.

"Here, use this." Nilda handed her a big-toothed comb. "Ivar made that for me one Christmas. It works good on wet hair like this. I've used it ever since." She stuck her fingers in her hair and gave it a shake. "Good thing the guys were not here. Some things are better women-only."

Signe twisted her long hair and wrapped it around her head, tucking the ends underneath the heavy coil. "Oh, I hope the hairpins are still on the porch." With one hand holding her hair in place, she pushed open the screen door. "Right where we left them."

Inserting the pins, she stared out across the garden and fields. The horses and cows had not bothered to seek shelter and were still out grazing, probably enjoying the rain beating on them as much as she had. She shivered as the breeze scattered the remaining raindrops.

"I sure hope Rune thought to shut all the windows. Good thing you did that here, Gerd, or we would have a lot of mopping to do." Handing off the rest of the pins, Signe slid a clean apron over her head and returned to her pie dough. While she finished that, Nilda beat up the eggs for the custard, and Gerd handed her the pitcher of milk. Signe slid the custard pie in the oven to join the other crust. The chocolate pudding would go in a baked pie shell. "Just think, perhaps one of these years we will have apple pie filling canned."

"And strawberries for jam and canning," Gerd added. "Those few raspberries we planted this year will yield plenty next."

"We need strawberry starts. I'll ask Mrs. Benson if there are wild strawberries somewhere around here."

"Chokecherries will be ripe soon," Gerd said. "First of August or so. I picked them over by Chippewa River a couple of years ago. Someone mentioned juneberries. All these things grow up after the big trees are cleared away. Some you find in natural clearings. The Indians really know all the wild things we can eat. They've been living on them for centuries." She paused. "Einar never had a good word to say about Indians. As far as he was concerned, they're lazy, shiftless, and dirty. Drunkards too. I never saw it, though. We are not too far from several of the reservations, Red Lake especially."

Signe and Nilda both looked at her and then at each other. Gerd never talked this much.

"My pie crust!" Signe jerked open the oven door and, using her apron as a hot pad, pulled the pan out. "Pretty brown."

"But not burned." Gerd set a hot pad on the table. "You want me to make the chocolate pudding?"

"Ja, while I go skim the pans and bring the churn up to warm."

Trundling the wagon behind her, Signe strolled to the well house. The fresh air made her stop to take a deep breath. The rain-soaked dirt squished up between her toes and stuck to her feet. Even that felt good. She'd need to wash them before going in the house, but who cared. A bird called from one of the blades on the windmill that creaked in the wind. Another answered. Barn swallows dipped and circled, catching bugs to feed their second clutch of babies. No wonder there were so many barn swallows around.

The chickens were back outside—they did not like rain— and scratching in their pen. Rain brought bugs and worms to the surface, and the chickens feasted. Pigs squealed in the pen. Others grunted. They were all most likely enjoying the mud puddles. Signe splashed her own feet clean in a puddle.

Water still dripped off the roof of the well house, forming miniature water lines in the ground from the runoff. She looked back at the house, where they had rain barrels at two corners.

48

Someday they would plant shade trees around the houses, an orchard, more gardens, and perhaps even some flowers. What if Gunlaug came? She might bring some of the irises from her mor's garden and even some seeds.

The sun peeked out, turning the drops to sparkles and drawing steam from the ground. The grass in the pastures would be green again in a short time. The cornfield glistened green. Hopefully the oats were not beaten down, as that field would soon turn gold for harvest. If they were indeed to build a dairy herd, they'd need a lot more grain and hay to feed the animals, and more housing for winter. Was that Rune's dream now, or was that only Einar's dream? Signe could not remember. If they had more cows, she could make cheese.

When she pushed open the door to the well house, a rush of escaping cold air caught her by surprise. Scrubbing her feet on the doorsill, she stepped down onto the stone floor, leaving the door open so she had enough light to see to skim the pans.

Setting the full churn in the wagon, she made sure the sun reached it and then set to skimming. After she skimmed the pans from the night before, the cream went into crocks to set in the tank of cold water. The skim milk went into milk cans to haul down to the barrel by the pig troughs to sour for both hogs and chickens. Right now, the growing hogs were keeping the barrel low. And it would get worse. Could they really raise that many pigs to butcher size? Plus the steer would be large enough to butcher this fall.

After washing the pans, she threw the soapy water on the floor and used the wide broom to sweep the water to the lower corner, where a short piece of pipe drained any spills out of the well house. Einar had done a good job building this necessary place, or perhaps Gerd had more to say about this than she let on.

Einar really had been good at most anything he undertook—cutting timber, building a house, and finishing the barn and the machine shed. He just didn't finish beyond the absolutely necessary. Like the stairs to the cellar. She thought about this as she left the churn waiting in the sunshine and went to look at the sheep. Leaning her chin on crossed hands on the top rail of the corral, she watched them race to the far side, huddle, and turn to face her, ears forward and sniffing the air.

"I know, I know, I am a stranger to you, but no need to fear. I'm as glad to have you here as Leif is. I hope you enjoyed the corn suckers."

The ram stamped his foot and, eyes on her, took a step forward.

"If you are this brave now, what will you be like when you are fully grown?"

He snorted and flicked his ears.

"Never mind, I'm leaving, but you better get used to me too. I'll be back."

The blue sky had returned, along with fluffy clouds fleeing before the wind. As had the heat. By the time she'd pulled the wagon to the house, the steam rising in the sun had made her forehead sweat. Such a different day.

She lifted the churn up onto the porch and climbed the steps.

"You hungry?" Nilda asked. "We missed dinner, you know."

"Where's Kirstin?"

"She and Gerd are napping on a pallet in the bedroom. I suggested the parlor, but she was concerned K would fall on the floor. We need to keep a pallet here for them. That way we could close the door. What took you so long?"

"Oh, I swept the floor and went down to introduce myself to the sheep. Mr. Ram seems to take his job seriously. He snorted and stamped at me. I was really scared."

Nilda rolled her eyes. "Let's eat out on the porch." She handed Signe a plate with pieces of fried bread and butter. "Buttermilk or coffee?"

"Need you ask?"

"Take the big wagon and the old team to Benson's Corner," Rune said after dinner the next day. "We need feed for the pigs. Joe Benson said he would load it while you two are at class. I'll need to make a run to the lumberyard soon too."

"Have you thought of a corn crib?" Gerd asked. "With the added acreage, there will be too much to store in the barn. Einar kept saying each year he'd do that as we planted more corn."

Rune blinked at her. "Are you serious?"

"I am."

"I hate to say this, but we don't have money for a corn crib."

"I saw one in the Sears Roebuck catalog. I have enough cash in the box to pay for it."

"But then what do we do for cash?"

"We sell some pigs. I figure five or so ought to do it."

"But—"

"I know." Gerd raised a hand. "But you see how much they are eating. Five less will eat a lot less and still give us plenty." She turned to Signe. "Put up a sign on the bulletin board at Benson's. We'll see what happens. We need to develop a market for next year too, if young Leif is going to keep on with his hogs."

Later that afternoon, Nilda flicked the reins and clucked the team into a slow trot. "There is more going on in that woman's head than she is telling us. She said to remind you that school will be starting soon and both boys have outgrown or worn out their boots. Also, Einar used to have a cobbler's bench for when he repaired his boots. Probably out in the machine shed." Eyebrows arched, she shrugged. "I know, it caught me by surprise too. But I've been thinking—the way Rune is going, he'll need to enclose that whole building for a shop. And build a new shed for the machinery."

Signe shook her head. "You certainly have learned to dream big. Now all you need to do is figure out how and when to build and where the money will come from."

At the store, they turned in their list and left the wagon to head to the church for their English lesson, taking their chairs just in time.

Mr. Larsson's gentle face was smiling. "Welcome, everyone. Remember, tonight for the last half of the class, we will speak only English. I hope you've been practicing all week."

The groans from the others told Signe they weren't the only ones who'd not practiced a lot. They dutifully repeated what Mr. Larsson said, practiced their vocabulary words and phrases, and turned to each other to talk with words to be used daily. They greeted, introduced, asked questions, prepared answers, and found themselves laughing along with the others.

At the break, Signe muttered to Nilda, "He's had his eye on you much of the class time."

"He has not. He smiles at everyone and encourages everyone the same."

Signe raised her eyebrows and slowly shook her head. "You are either blind or stubborn—or both."

"Most likely both. Stop, you are embarrassing me." Nilda stood up and stretched.

Conversation slowed considerably when they had to speak only English. Pauses lengthened as people searched their minds for the right words, then chuckled when someone else filled in for them.

"This is harder than haying," one of the men said in Norwegian.

"But not as sweaty," one of the women countered.

Larsson raised his hands. "English, folks, please." He repeated what they had said in Norwegian and then stated the phrases in English. "Now repeat after me." They all did. "The more you repeat it, the more you will remember the words. Repetition. Repetition. You are all to be applauded. You are doing well."

As they rose to leave, Mr. Larsson motioned to Signe. "Please wait a moment." When he had answered one last question and the class members were moving toward the door, he picked up two flowerpots from the floor and handed one to Signe and one to Nilda.

He spoke slowly in English, enunciating each word. "My aunt Gertrude Schoenleber in Blackduck sent these rose starts home with me for you. This way there will be a rosebush at each house." He smiled at Nilda. "She asks about you every time I see her."

"Really? She was such a charming hostess. I'll never forget her."

"Well, she has not forgotten you either. She said these will bloom next year. You will need to cover them with straw or hay when the deep freezes start. She said even pine branches and needles could be used."

Nilda asked, "They will really live through the winter here?"

He shrugged. "You see roses blooming in Blackduck, and the lilacs in June make the entire town smell sweet."

Signe smiled. "Please tell her thank you. Do you have an address for her?"

"Just address it to Mrs. Schoenleber, Blackduck. She will get it."

Nilda smiled. "Thank you for being the messenger."

"You are most welcome." He licked his lips. "Uh, let me get this straight."

"Straight?"

"In this sentence it means *correct*. Signe Carlson is your sister-in-law and her husband is your brother, is that right?"

"Ja. I mean, yes. Rune is my brother. So *sister-in-law* means the woman my brother married." Nilda frowned. "The opposite: the man my sister marries—brother-in-law?"

Mr. Larsson broke into the broadest, sweetest smile. "Miss Carlson, you are so quick!"

Nilda frowned again. "Quick. Fast?"

"Oh dear. One of the problems with English is that one word may mean many different things. *Quick* means fast, you are correct, but it also means fast mentally. Fast thinking." He tapped his head. "Oh, and it also means the core or deepest part of something, but not something material. When I say 'you cut me to the quick,' it means you hurt me deeply, but not bodily. Physically." And now he was frowning. "Does that make sense?"

Signe almost giggled, but she kept her peace.

Nilda smiled. "No, it does not really make sense at all, but I understand what you are saying. Thank you."

"Again, you are most welcome. I will see you next week?"

"Ja, and on Sunday too," Signe put in for good measure, making sure her grin did not show.

Back at the store, Signe asked, "Could you please pin this to the bulletin board? It is for selling some of our young pigs." She held up the sign Gerd had made.

"You go ahead. There are pins stuck in the corner. I hear you're looking for another milk cow." Mrs. Benson handed several packages to Signe. "A widow outside of town is leaving her farm to move in with her son in Duluth. She has to sell off all her animals quickly at half market price. If you're willing to buy a cow sight unseen, Mr. Benson can bring it out to you."

"Oh. That *is* quick!" Signe did not have to think for long. "Yes, we will buy the cow."

"I'm glad. He'll bring her out in the next few days. That sure was a marvelous party at your house. We need to do that more often." Mrs. Benson leaned over the counter with a smaller bag. "This is for those boys of yours. When Leif asked me to dance . . ." She chuckled and shook her head at the same time. "He is one smart young man. You should have heard him bragging about his herd of pigs. And how he loves that puppy. Rufus is a perfect name for him."

"Thanks to you and Mr. Benson. Oh, I forgot. Do you have brooms for sale? That Rufus chewed up our broom when we were in church last Sunday."

"I do." Mrs. Benson fetched one and handed it to Nilda. Then she walked out with them and untied the horses as they climbed into the wagon. She looped the lead rope over the hames and waved as they left.

The horses leaned into their collars and dug in to get the wagon moving through an especially soft spot before they reached the road.

"I'll be glad when the Ladies Aid meetings start up again." Signe sighed. "Even the few times I was able to go, I was starting to make friends. I never realized how much I took friends in Norway—well, family too—for granted." She patted Nilda's hand. "I guess we all do that."

"Ja, me too. I don't know how you stood it this last year, as bad as things were. And you never complained. We had no idea living with the Strands was such an awful thing. Not the work—hard work never hurt anybody—but the meanness."

"It made me all the more glad when we learned you were coming sooner than we had ever dreamed." Signe swatted at a mosquito buzzing around her face. "But thinking back makes me even more grateful for now. And tomorrow we get to plant rosebushes. Can you believe that? Mrs. Schoenleber must be a real special woman."

"She is. I wish I could think of something to do in return for her kindness."

"You never know. Something will come up."

Chapter 6

"How is it, milking the new cow?" Gerd asked Leif.

"All right. Tante Gerd, she wanted the far stanchion and wouldn't go anywhere else. I'm going to name her Bossy."

"Three cows in the barn now leaves only one more stanchion. I guess we won't look for another for a while." Gerd set a platter of pancakes on the table. "How are your new boots?"

"Okay. They take some getting used to. My feet sure grew this summer."

"All of you did. Pants too short, shirts too short, and Knute, you pretty much wore your clothes out. I have a lot of patching to do so Leif can wear them."

Rune glanced around the table. "It looks to me like they all grew a lot. Bjorn, you're nearly as tall as Ivar. The two of you could be twins." He put two more pancakes on his plate. "It's hard to believe how much that wood stack has grown."

"It's hard to keep ahead of the cookstove." Knute reached for his milk glass. "Maybe we should miss school until we get those two dried trees hauled in and—"

"And maybe not. School starts tomorrow, and that is that."

"But we really need more wood."

"True. But you need school, so . . ." Rune spread butter on his pancakes and stared down his son. "So we will all go out to bring in those trees. We'll use the teams to drag them out of that swampy area."

"All of us?"

"All the men." Nilda grinned at her nephews. "We women will stay here and burn as much wood as we can. After all, keeping that boiler going is what is filling the cellar with food for the winter."

"Be careful," Signe admonished as the men left the kitchen a short time later.

"Maybe we can have fried bread when we get back," Knute called over his shoulder.

"Just because I had started bread." Signe found herself shaking her head in amazement a lot lately. Things seemed to be moving much too smoothly. Other than the new cow kicking over the milk bucket the first time Knute sat down to milk her, but she didn't mind Leif at all. But then, Leif got along with all animals better than any boy she had ever seen.

Nilda said wistfully, "I wish Far and Mor could see these boys now. They'd never say anything, but they would be so proud. I've been thinking about them a lot lately. Mor would be shocked at how much we've canned and stored in the cellar. By the time we get the root vegetables dug and in the bins and the squash in . . ."

"And more pickles. We should finish the beets today." Signe stretched her arms over her head. "I'll slip the skins while you slice."

"And Kirstin and I will finish that shirt for Knute. I'm glad we bought some clothes. That sewing machine and I spend a lot of time together." Gerd had cut around the holes in one of Einar's shirts to make one for Knute, but Ivar and Bjorn just rolled up the sleeves on his others.

Like well-oiled machinery, the women set to their tasks for the day. With beet-stained hands, Signe dumped beet skins in the slop bucket, which was filling rapidly. Soon the boiler, full of jars of beets, bubbled on the stove, and Gerd and Kirstin had gone to the garden to dig up more. After they scrubbed what they had, the next biggest kettle held raw beets. The temperature in the kitchen rose, even with all the windows and doors open.

Nilda wagged her head. "To think I nearly froze my feet on the way to the outhouse this morning. We might have to start wearing shoes again. At least we haven't outgrown ours."

When they sat down at noon to a meal of fried egg sandwiches, Signe admired the rows of purplish red jars of beets. "I'd do all beets pickled if I had my way."

"Buttered beets are hard to beat," Nilda said.

"Good, 'cause we're having them for supper—again."

"Better than rutabagas," Gerd said. "It's a shame the turnips got wormy."

The jingle of a harness announced a visitor. The two younger women smoothed back their hair and checked the cleanliness of their aprons while Gerd shook her head.

"Tsk. Such primping."

Signe scowled. "Easy for you to say. You don't have a beet-decorated apron."

"It just shows that you've been working hard."

Signe waved from the door. "Mrs. Benson, what a nice surprise. Come in, come in."

Mrs. Benson climbed out of her cart, basket on her arm, and climbed the steps. "Look at all those leather britches you got drying. Why, I've not seen a sight like that in a long time." She motioned to the pairs of string beans drying over lines on the porch.

"We had so many beans, we decided to do some this way.

All the rest on the vines we are letting dry." Signe held open the screen door.

Mrs. Benson inhaled deeply. "Mmm, pickling beets?"

"And you're just in time for fresh bread and butter."

"I brought a jar of apple jelly, the first of the year." Mrs. Benson set her basket on the counter. "I had a delivery to the Garborgs, so I treated myself to a stop here. The apples are nearly ripe on the trees, but the jelly is from windfalls. I chased another deer away. They sure like apples. Mr. Benson shot a spike out there the other morning, so we'll have venison."

"Bjorn will probably want to plant apple trees sooner rather than later when he hears that." Gerd pulled the coffeepot forward to heat. Apron cushioning her hand, she opened the oven door. "The bread looks ready to me." She tapped the nearest loaf. "Sounds ready too. Sit down, sit down."

Mrs. Benson pulled an envelope out of her basket. "This came in yesterday. I was going to wait for you to stop in, but when the trip to the Garborgs' came up, I figured I'd kill two birds with one stone." She patted Signe's arm. "This is for you. I know it has been some time since you had mail from Norway, so I hope it is good news." She set a small bag of peppermint sticks on the table and reached over to tickle Kirstin under the chin. "Soon, little one, you'll be able to enjoy peppermint too. My goodness, as fast as you are growing, you'll be in school before we know it."

Gerd carefully sliced one of the loaves of hot bread, being careful not to squash it any more than necessary. Laid on plates, the slices seemed to return to their original shape as the butter melted. "Mor always said to wait two hours before slicing bread, but you miss out if you do that."

The bread disappeared about as fast as if the boys were eating it. The sipping of coffee took a bit longer.

Mrs. Benson stood and picked up her basket. "Well, I better get back to the store. Takk for the time and good food. By the way, I am putting our name on your list for a butchered hog. Mr. Benson is really looking forward to pork chops and ham. He says he will do the smoking."

They waved good-bye and went back to their chores, and the afternoon flew by.

Signe read the letter at the supper table that night.

"'Dear Signe and family,

"'I apologize for taking so long to write, but you know what summer is like—all the canning, so many up at the *seter*, and the long days that entice us outside. I am sure you are doing the same.

"'We had a tragedy. A boat went down in the North Sea, taking everyone aboard with it. Rune's cousin Nels now rests in the arms of our Lord, and his mor and far are heartbroken. As is his wife. Their little son is too young to understand. He was the eldest, as you know.'"

Signe paused, shaking her head. "So very hard."

"Did you know him well?" Gerd asked.

"No, but still, his poor mor and wife." She returned to the letter.

"'Gunlaug told us all about Nilda and Ivar's trip over. That Nilda writes a very entertaining letter. I am so grateful we all share the letters that come from America.

"'Greet everyone from all of us here. And please try to write more often. I know you are busy, but we so enjoy your letters. On another note, Mrs. Nygaard has been bragging about how well Dreng is doing in America. What's strange is that he never says where he is living now or what he is doing. She thought he was going to be a lumberjack.

"'With love,

"'Your Mor and all of the
rest of your family'"

Signe sniffed and folded the letter. She glanced up to see horror freezing Nilda's face.

Nilda's voice trembled. "What if he were to come here?"

"There are hundreds of lumber camps, Nilda. That Dreng has no idea where you are, and besides, he has most likely forgotten all about you by now." Signe stood up to start clearing the table. "Make sure you have those books you borrowed ready to take with you in the morning," she reminded Knute and Leif, who both nodded. Tomorrow was the first day of a new school year.

"I made cookies for your dinner pails," Gerd offered.

Leif sighed. "They should start school later, like October. Right now I got too much to do here."

"And—and I could work out in the big trees too." Knute heaved a sigh.

"The work will wait for you," Rune said. "We will work as long as we can in the evening, just like we always have."

"But we will have to do homework." The final word turned into a wail. Knute shook his head. "It's not fair. Bjorn gets to work in the woods."

"He is older." Signe took Kirstin from Gerd. "Come now, let's go to the other house. Morning will come fast."

"We're going back out to the big trees?" Bjorn asked the next morning at breakfast.

"You still have plenty to do on your house," Gerd answered before Rune could.

"I know, but I said I would go back to the woods when school started." Rune blinked and rubbed his eyes. No, not rubbed. Massaged. If only there were a way to help his eyes. Signe had mentioned pain medicines, but he'd said no, because they made him sleepy and he couldn't work. She watched him squeeze his eyes shut and then open them several times.

Gerd chided, "But back then we did not know all we know now about what money we would have. Will a few more trees still standing make that big a difference?"

"I am a man who keeps his word."

"I know you are. You needn't prove it again with the trees." Gerd sat down. "Now, let's have no more about this right now. Once the weather really turns cold . . ."

"We will be butchering hogs."

Gerd nodded, a smile trying to break through. "Exactly."

"Gerd Strand, you are not the same woman I met when we came here."

"You are right. Then I was in bed, and now I am out here. Then I slept all the time, and now I have opinions. Strong opinions." She took a bite of her biscuit. "Please."

Rune shook his head and chuckled. "Oh, all right."

A couple days later, Signe heard Leif shouting from the lane. "Mor, there's another letter from Norway! This time for Far." He bailed off Rosie with the dinner pails. Knute rode on to let Rosie out to pasture. Leif leaped up the back steps. "I'm starving."

"Change your clothes."

"I will. Did you check on the sheep and the pigs?"

"And the chickens and the garden and—"

"*Mooor.*" He unbuttoned his school shirt and grabbed his old small one for chores. "We beat the other team at ball today, and I hit the ball."

"The teams remain the same?" Signe set some bread with butter and sugar on the table, along with two glasses of milk. "You can take a moment to eat."

He buttoned his shirt as he drank the milk. "Are the ladies in the corral?"

"Ja, they were out in the pasture for a couple of hours, then came back in."

"Really? I told you they're smart. Only three days of school, and they know to come for grain when I get home." Bread in one hand, he just missed running over Knute in the doorway.

Knute looked over his shoulder, shaking his head. "How come he's in such a hurry?"

"The ladies are calling for him. Far and his helpers are at the other house. Change your clothes."

"I will." Without sitting, Knute drained his glass and grabbed the remaining slice of bread.

Signe asked, "Homework?"

"Of course." He puffed out his cheeks. "I'd rather be working in the woods."

"So I hear. But the others are working at the house."

"That would be fine too. Anything you want me to take to Far?"

"Nei. I mean, no."

As he went out the door, Signe picked up the letter from the table. Addressed to Rune, not Nilda. All the other letters from Gunlaug had been to Nilda. Signe set the letter up against the salt cellar on the table. Nilda had gone to the other house to help there for a change, since they had quarts of sliced carrots steaming on the stove now.

When everyone gathered for supper, washed up, and sat down, Signe handed the envelope to Rune.

He looked at it. "Let's have supper first. These men are famished." He laid the envelope back on the table.

When they had all finished eating and had passed their plates around, Rune picked up the envelope and sliced it open with the blade of his knife, leaving a dab of butter on the paper. He cleared his throat as he unfolded the single page.

"'My dear faraway family,

"'This is the hardest letter I have ever written. Your far passed away in his sleep on the fifteenth of August, from what we believe was a heart attack. He had not—'"

"Far! Oh, Far!" Nilda pressed her hands to her face. Ivar clapped his hand over his mouth as his eyes brimmed over. Rune continued.

"'—had not been feeling like his usual self for some time, but there did not seem to be anything specific wrong. We went to bed as usual, and when I woke in the morning, he'd been gone for some time. It is so hard to believe that something like this could happen and I was not aware of it.

"'We buried him in the family plot at the church, next to his far.'"

Rune stopped reading. He rubbed his eyes and sniffed. "Sorry."

Signe walked around the table and laid her hands on his

shoulders, feeling him shudder. Resting her cheek on his head, she let her own tears fall.

"That means Farfar is in heaven now?" Leif leaned into Gerd's arm, which was wrapped around his shoulders.

"Ja, he is gone to be with his Lord." Nilda wiped her eyes and blew her nose on her apron. "Too soon. He was not old enough to die yet."

"I always thought maybe they would come here." Knute stared at his far.

Rune nodded. "Me too." He picked up the sheet again and continued to read.

"'While some people think I am making decisions too quickly, I want to come to America to be with all of you. Perhaps the others will come too, eventually. I can only hope.

"'Your cousin Selma and her little boy want to come with me if we can find the money for tickets. Since her husband was lost at sea, she says she has no reason to remain in Norway. He had wanted to emigrate too but decided one more season on the fishing boat would give them the money for tickets. We are all ready to start new lives, like you have.'"

They sat in silence, except for sobs now and then.

Finally, Gerd spoke. "I will sell enough hogs for her ticket." Her tone brooked no argument.

"I—we can pay part of one." Rune looked to Signe, who nodded. Not that she was sure they had that kind of money.

Ivar heaved a sigh. "I don't want Mor coming alone. She is just stubborn enough to do so. We should find a way to bring Selma too."

Rune nodded and returned to the letter.

"'I pray you are all well and that we will hear from you soon.

"'May God bless us all,

"'Your Mor, Gunlaug
Carlson'"

Signe leaned over and hugged Nilda, who wrapped her arms around her neck. "Such horrible news."

Ivar propped himself against the back of his chair and stared at the ceiling. "I wish I had some way to earn money immediately."

"We will manage," Gerd said. "Remember, you all told me we are a family. There is no *mine* or *yours*, but *ours*. We'll sell some of those trees early if we have to. Perhaps we should ask Mr. Kielund to haul a load in."

Rune reminded her, "We can haul trees. We have four-up now, strong enough to pull a loaded wagon."

"Four horses is all well and good, but can the wagon carry that much?" Signe asked.

"Selling hogs is easier." Gerd pushed back her chair. "All we need to do is find a buyer. Rune, why don't you ask around when you go into Blackduck tomorrow?"

"I will write Mor a letter tonight." Shuddering a sigh, Nilda pushed back her chair. Then she paused and slowly sat down again. "Wait. I have an idea. You said Mr. Kielund lost his wife. And Selma lost a husband. . . ."

Signe stared at her. "An arranged marriage? Is that what you're thinking?"

Nilda bobbed her head. "In this country they call it mail-order brides. It's done a lot, I hear, especially farther west. If Mr. Kielund could help with the passage money, Mor and Selma can come right away."

Rune snorted. "I agree they could. But who is going to ask Mr. Kielund?"

Chapter 7

"When you go into Benson's Corner, ask Reverend Skarstead to talk with Mr. Kielund."

Nilda blinked at Gerd. "Of course. Bless you, Tante Gerd. Tonight when we go to class, we will ask Reverend Skarstead. Surely he will talk with him."

Nilda thought back to her brother Johann's wedding, when her cousin Nels and his wife, Selma, both good friends of Johann, had come to celebrate with the family. That thought led to another. Selma had once worked for the Nygaard family. Had she been accosted by Dreng too? But then, Selma was older. Perhaps he'd been too young then. Nilda had been feeling safe out in the Northwoods of Minnesota, but now the fear had reared its ugly head again.

Right now she wished she knew what the men in Norway had done to Dreng to help him "rethink his ways," as they put it. His own far was the one to banish his spoiled son from Norway. Out in the garden, she stabbed the fork into the dirt with a vengeance and leaned on the handle to release the carrots from the earth. It was a beautiful day with fall in the air, and Dreng was back on her mind. Why couldn't he have been the one lost at sea? Not a fine man like Nels! But then, Dreng figured he was too good to work like others. He would never be on a fishing boat.

She broke another carrot from the soil. Going down the row, she stabbed and pushed to lift. With each stab, Dreng disappeared further into the back of her mind. Several crows flew overhead, their cries grating on her nerves, as if they were scolding her.

Turning, she kicked the basket ahead of her as she pulled the carrots free and knocked them together to dislodge the dirt. When the basket was full, she took it over to the windmill and gushed water over the carrots, raising her face to the sun as she pumped. When she inhaled, the tang of fall made her smile. What made the air change dresses like that?

Back on the porch, she finished scrubbing the dirt off the carrots with a bucket of water and a brush, including the tender skins. These would sure be appreciated in the winter when those stored fresh in the cellar were gone. Together she and Signe sliced the carrots on wooden cutting boards and packed them in jars. They needed to buy jars again too; they had put up far more food than Signe had the year before. Of course, there were more mouths to feed.

When they loaded the eggs and butter in the cart that evening, they added a rabbit carcass as a gift for Mrs. Benson. Every time Knute moved his snares to a new area, they had fresh meat again.

"We need to can five or six of those young cockerels. Chicken potpie will taste real good this winter. At least we can butcher one or two as we need them. A couple of the older hens would be fine too." Nilda stepped up into the cart and flicked the reins. "I sure hope Reverend Skarstead is at home."

They dropped off the butter, eggs, and their list of what they needed at the store, then drove to the house next to the church and knocked on the door.

"Coming." The call came just before the door swung open. "Why, Mrs. Carlson, Miss Carlson, come in, come in." Mrs. Skarstead stepped back. "I assume you are here to talk with my husband?"

"Yes, if we may."

"Come on back to the kitchen, and I'll put the coffeepot on."

"Thank you, but we can't be late for our English class," Nilda said.

"Surely you have time for coffee. It will be ready in a couple of minutes." Mrs. Skarstead motioned them to the table, pulled the coffeepot forward, and went out the back door.

Signe looked out the window. "Sometime I hope to have a garden and yard like theirs. A shade tree, bushes, and flowers."

"You will. But you might need a fence to keep the wild critters out."

Signe shrugged. "I don't know. Gerd doesn't have a fence."

"Gerd doesn't have anything growing around her house other than the rosebush. And the garden is fenced."

"True, but I want blooming flowers and birds and—"

"Well, well, to what do I owe the honor of this visit?" Reverend Skarstead's smile preceded him. He shook each of their hands and pulled out a chair. "I know you are on your way to class, so how can I help you?"

Signe cleared her throat. "First the news. Thor Carlson, the father of Rune, Ivar, and Nilda, died recently in Norway."

"Oh, I am so sorry! Please accept my condolences."

Nilda nodded, and Signe continued. "Their widowed mother wants to immigrate, but we hate to see her travel alone."

Nilda added, "A cousin of mine lost his life when a fishing

71

boat sank. He left a wife, Selma, and small son. Mor wants to come to America to be with us, and we hope Selma can come along."

"I see."

"You know Mr. Kielund."

"He is widowed. . . ."

"And in search of a mother for his children."

Skarstead nodded, his smile widening. "So you want to play matchmaker."

Signe smiled too. "If possible. I know Selma. She is a fine wife and mother, and she loved my cousin dearly. But she wants to start new here, and what better place than with . . ."

"Mr. Kielund, who loved his wife dearly and has two—"

"Darling childen," Mrs. Skarstead said. "I think this is a perfect idea."

"We hope you can go talk with him," Signe said. "See if he might be willing to pay for Selma's ticket or at least help with it. We do not have enough cash available to buy both passages. It would be something like a mail-order bride."

Nilda hastily added, "But tell him that if he and Selma don't like each other or something, we will repay the cost of the ticket. Probably next spring when we sell the trees."

The reverend leaned forward. "Let me get this straight. You want me to get him to pay for the ticket."

"If he can. She would come more quickly that way." Nilda gave him a hopeful look. "Tante Gerd is paying for Mor's ticket by selling hogs."

"What a story this is turning into." He looked to his wife, who nodded. He wagged his head. "I can't promise anything."

"We know."

"I am certain this is going to work out." Mrs. Skarstead set a plate of cookies on the table and poured coffee into their cups. "Now eat and drink quickly. Mr. Larsson does not like his students to be late, be they children or grown-ups."

Reverend Skarstead chuckled. "Just like he does not like church to start late. When that organ calls, I hustle."

"Cream or sugar?" Mrs. Skarstead asked.

"No, thank you." Signe dipped a cookie into her coffee. "Thank you, this is delicious."

"You better hurry. I'll make sure I talk with Oskar in the next day or so and let you know. For sure there are not many single young women around here." He grinned. "You know any other young women in Norway?"

"As a matter of fact—"

He laughed. "Let's deal with this one first. I can just see a newspaper headline. 'Local Pastor Promotes Mail-Order Brides.'"

"Thank you." Nilda tapped Signe on the shoulder. "Come on, we cannot be late."

They slipped into their seats at the church just as Mr. Larsson finished a conversation and moved to the front of the class. At least they were not late.

"I think this is getting easier," Nilda said as they stood up to leave over an hour later. "It really is."

"Keep dragging me along, then. Perhaps one day I'll feel the same." Signe said it in Norwegian because neither of them knew what "drag along" was in English.

"Miss Carlson?" Mr. Larsson stopped in front of Nilda. "You are doing splendidly, Miss Carlson," he said in English. "You are capturing English very well. In fact, you seem to master syntax easily."

"Syntax?" That was a new word.

Mr. Larsson spelled it, then explained. "How the words fit together and follow each other. I would like to loan you these textbooks that children in French-speaking areas of Canada use to learn English. Look through them and see if anything there would be helpful for you." He pressed three books into Nilda's hands.

"Oh my. Thank you, Mr. Larsson. That is very . . ." How did one say *generous*? She had no idea. But she knew another word. ". . . very kind of you."

He dipped his head. "I will see you next week, I trust."

"Yes, uh, thank you. Yes." Why was she suddenly tongue-tied? She turned and led Signe out the door.

As they climbed into the wagon, Signe said smugly, "I told you. He really does smile more in class when he looks at you."

"Oh, stop it." But Nilda felt her cheeks grow warm.

One of the books was mostly a French-English dictionary and of little use, since Nilda knew no French at all. But she found the reading exercises in the other books very helpful. She and Signe made a concerted effort to use English for the rest of the week.

Sunday after church, Mr. Kielund stopped to talk with Rune. Nilda and Signe tried to watch without anyone noticing. As soon as they were all loaded in the wagon, Signe whispered, "What did he say?"

"He said he is willing to give it a try," Rune answered. "He will get the money for the ticket this week."

Gerd nodded. "I will go to Blackduck with you. There is money in a bank account there."

They mailed the tickets off on Thursday.

"We get to see Mor again." Nilda stared at her brother when Rune and Gerd returned home with the news. "I dreamed of this, but never that it would happen so soon."

Ivar nodded. "I always prayed that Far would change his mind and come too. And now . . ." His voice trailed off.

Nilda sniffed back the tears that hovered whenever she thought of her far. Sometimes death seemed to come so easily, but was so unexpected until people were old. Her far was getting up there, but he wasn't really old yet.

That Sunday when they made their way to their seats before church, Nilda nearly stopped and gasped. Petter Thorvaldson smiled at her from a pew farther back. She returned his smile and ignored Signe's nudge when they sat down. Now, that was a surprise. Petter had come clear out here to go to church. Keeping her mind on the service took more concentration than she could dig up. Why had he come? Surely he wouldn't ride or drive out here for church when there were several churches in Blackduck. He never had before. Curiosity could be nearly life threatening. She could feel his eyes on her back. The sermon seemed excessively long.

"How good to see you again," Ivar said, shaking hands with Petter after service. "Welcome to our little church."

Petter nodded and grinned at Nilda. "Good day. You look lovely as always."

"Th-thank you." She could feel the heat rushing up to her face. "What brings you out here?" *What a dumb thing to say. Surely you can do better than that.* Scolding herself did not help.

"I'm on an errand." He greeted the others, and they all moved toward the exit.

"Well, well, Mr. Thorvaldson, good to see you again," Reverend Skarstead said. "Welcome to our church. We have coffee downstairs if you would like to join us." He included the whole family in his smile.

"Thank you, Pastor, but we are using every minute we can on getting the house ready for winter." Rune eased his family forward. "And thank you for taking care of that bit of business."

"You're welcome. I do hope it all works out." He turned to

Gerd. "It is so good to have you here with us. By the way, I told another family about your pigs for sale, and they are planning to talk with you." He nodded to a couple who waited near the steps. "I'm not sure if you have met the Tengvolds."

Rune and Gerd walked over to the couple. "I hear you are looking for pigs to grow out," Rune said.

The others walked toward their own wagon. "Surely you can come out to the farm for dinner," Signe urged Petter.

"Thank you, I would be delighted. I'll ride beside the wagon." He pointed to a saddled horse tied to the hitching rail.

"Three more pigs sold," Gerd announced from the seat of the wagon as they left the churchyard. "Leif, you have done a fine job."

"There's still a bunch to sell," Leif said. "When are they coming for theirs?"

"Tomorrow, so you better not let them all out in the big pen."

"I won't."

"Maybe we better stay home to help catch them," Knute offered.

"I think Ivar and Bjorn can handle that job," Rune said over his shoulder. "Especially if there are fewer in the pen. Mr. Tengvold said he wanted one gilt for sure."

As they clattered into their yard, Nilda tried to sort out her feelings about Petter. And then thoughts of Fritz Larsson pushed themselves to the front of her mind. When she and Ivar had come to America, she had not anticipated all this.

"You want to see how our new house is coming?" Ivar asked Petter.

"Don't be too long. Dinner is in half an hour or so." Signe handed Kirstin off to Nilda while she climbed out of the wagon. "She sure is busy today."

Nilda tickled the little one under the chin to make her giggle. "Busy and happy. You were such a good girl in church."

"Ja, she slept through the sermon, so I could listen for a change."

The men returned from the inspection of the new house just as Nilda stirred the gravy one last time and poured it into the pitcher. Signe set the platter of food on the table and motioned for everyone to be seated.

"You can be real proud of that house," Petter said as he took the seat next to Ivar. "I'm amazed at how far you've come."

"We've had a lot of help, and there's still a long way to go." Rune waited for everyone to be seated before bowing his head to say the traditional Norwegian grace together.

"That was such a good dinner," Petter said later as he declined another helping. "Knute, there must be a shortage of rabbits around here by now."

"Good thing they have lots of babies, but now that I am setting my traps closer to the woods, something ate part of one," Knute said.

"Why don't you all go out on the porch?" Signe said. "Gerd and I will clean up here."

"I think the boys and I will go work in the shop." Rune nodded in that direction.

"But I thought Petter might like to . . ." Bjorn caught a look from his far. "Well, I . . ." He shrugged in puzzlement but did as he was told.

Out on the porch, Nilda sat in the rocking chair while tall, hefty Petter leaned against a post.

"So how do you like working at the lumberyard now?" Ivar asked from the bench where he sat with one knee bent to prop his arm. "Still dreaming of a lumber camp for the winter?"

"I have a good job, and ja, I still want to work in a camp. I keep hoping you will come with me. I think it would be easier if you knew someone."

Ivar shook his head. "I have plenty of trees to cut here. There's no need to go to a camp."

"But the pay is good."

"So I hear."

"That is not the main reason I came out here." Petter pulled an envelope out of his shirt pocket. "Mrs. Schoenleber sent you this." He handed it to Nilda. "For you both."

"Do you know what it is?" She slit the envelope with a fingernail, watching him smile at her. He had such a winning smile, she couldn't help but return it.

"I do. She is planning an evening social and wants you both to come. She said you could spend the night and perhaps go to church with her on Sunday morning if you like. Or you could come out here like I did."

"A social?" Nilda stammered as she read the note out loud. The handwriting was beautifully formed, but it was in English, and she struggled with the words.

"'Dear Miss and Mr. Carlson,

"'I am inviting you to join other young people at my home for a get-acquainted evening of games and refreshments to celebrate fall, two weeks from this Saturday. I would be delighted for you both to spend the night here, since I would not want you returning home so late in the evening. We can stable your horse with no problem. Please tell Petter you will attend and make this old woman very happy.

"'Sincerely,
"'Gertrude Schoenleber'"

The thought of going made Nilda's stomach clench. *If they all speak English instead of Norwegian . . . I won't know anyone . . . . What kind of games? Surely we can turn this down gracefully.*

"What do you think?" she asked Ivar, trying to make him see her hesitation.

"She wants the young people of the area to get acquainted; at least that's what she said. There aren't a lot of events, other than things at the churches." Petter leaned slightly forward. "I know she loves to entertain and enjoys having younger people around her. You know anyone else out here who might want to go?"

"Not really."

"If this goes well, I'm sure there will be others." His smile invited one in return. "Please say you'll come."

"Well, I . . ." Nilda looked to Ivar, who shrugged, palms out. *Come on, help me here.*

"Of course they will go." Signe pushed open the door with her hip, balancing a tray with glasses full of something on it. She indicated for Ivar to pull out the bench and she set down the tray. "I thought we'd have something to drink before you have to leave. Gerd took Kirstin down for a nap. Ivar, why don't you go get the others?"

Nilda half smiled at Petter, who grinned back and wiggled his eyebrows. There was that irresistible smile again. *But how can I do this? I do not have a dress fit for a social like that.*

Shaking her head, Nilda glared at Signe, who turned with a smile. "I'm sure you will have a grand time. Besides, it's about time for you to do something fun for a change. After all, what could it hurt?"

Chapter 8

F ar, Rufus just tore down the stairs!"

"I heard him. The pigs are squealing!" Rune jerked his suspenders over his shoulders and slammed his feet into his boots. "Bjorn, grab the rifle on your way out."

What in the world could be going on? He could hear Rufus's bark change tone. What had he found?

The boys pounded down the stairs right after Rune, the screen door slamming behind them.

"What can it be, Far?" Bjorn clutched the rifle and handed the shotgun to Rune. They ran toward the barn and the pigpen. With no moon, the stars yielded little light.

"Lantern?" Bjorn asked.

"Nei, we can see better without it." Rune stopped. "Rufus is after something. Hear his bark getting farther out? Call him, Leif. Whatever was big enough to stir up the hogs like this is more than he can handle."

Leif cupped his mouth with his hands. "Rufus! Rufus, come. Come on, Rufus."

Ivar arrived from the other house, sliding to a stop. "I heard Rufus go crazy."

"Rufus, come! Come, Rufus!" Leif turned to Rune, his eyes wide with fear. "He always comes when I call him."

"I know. Keep it up." Rune unlatched the gate and entered the pen. The pigs were grunting and panting now, no longer squealing. Whatever had disturbed them was gone.

"Knute, go get a lantern so we can see if any are injured. Leif, circle around the pen. I can't think of anything big enough to carry off a pig."

"Unless it was a bear."

"True. Look for blood." There would be no chance of tracks in the pen, and with no recent rain, the ground was pretty hard. *If only I could see decently.* Like the boys, he moved through the herd, murmuring, "Easy now, easy."

Knute returned with the lantern and handed it to Ivar, who could hold it higher.

"Over here, Far." Leif stood at the field side of the fence, which was made out of slab wood and boards buried down into the dirt to keep the pigs from digging out. When Rune saw what his son pointed out, he nodded. Something had hauled a pig over the fence, dragging it enough to leave skin and hair. The lantern showed blood too. They climbed over the fence and started to follow the trail dragged through the dew-wet grass.

They all listened but heard no more barking. Other than grunts and snuffles, the herd was settling back down.

"Do you think Rufus is all right?" Leif asked.

"Call him again."

Leif did so, his voice catching on swelling tears.

A yip answered him, and Rufus trotted into the circle of lamplight. Tongue hanging out, he kept looking back over his shoulder, his ribs heaving.

"Good boy, oh, such a good boy." Leif dropped to his knees

and held out his arms so his dog could lick his face and ears. "You're okay." He felt through the white fur, looking for any wounds. "You didn't get hurt. Oh, Rufus, you didn't get hurt."

"Good thing that critter got away," Ivar said, "or Rufus might have bled to death out there."

Bjorn dropped his voice low. "I heard there are wild cats, big ones like lions, out here! Pumas or cougars—I forget what they call them, but it seems strange one would attack now. There's lots of game out there."

"Ah, but a pen of pigs, far easier to catch something." Rune stared out into the darkness. Surely a bear couldn't have lifted that pig over the fence and gotten away that fast. "Maybe Gerd will have some ideas in the morning. A wolf could never lift an animal this size over a fence. If it is a big cat, I heard they do not hunt every day, but it knows now where the easy meal is. It will be back."

Ivar planted a fist on his hip. "And we will be waiting for it. Bjorn and I will take turns. Give it a couple of days. I'm thinking of watching from the haymow. As the moon gets toward full, we'll be able to see."

Rune waved an arm. "Check on the rest of the animals."

The horses and cows were right up at the barn, watching the line where field met forest, all stamping feet and switching tails. Leif and Knute moved among them, patting shoulders and murmuring gentle sounds. As the animals settled down again, Bjorn took the lantern back to the barn and blew it out.

"'Night," Ivar said as he headed back to his house and the others made their way back upstairs, Bjorn hanging up the guns before he followed the others.

"We'll get him," Bjorn said softly, patting Leif's shoulder. "If he does come back."

"At least Rufus is all right. I'll look all the pigs over good in the morning. See if any others are injured. How could a cat carry something that big—and over the fence?"

"Surely there must be someone around here who knows a lot about the wildlife. We've just got to find them and learn all we can. Nailing a big hide like that would take up a lot of the barn wall."

Rune returned to his bed, proud of the determination and fearlessness in his boys.

In the morning, Leif came up from chores. "One of the other pigs had big scratches on its shoulder. Should I put something on it, Mor?"

"Use a glop of tallow," Tante Gerd said. "Einar said he saw a big cat like that one time out in the woods. It stirred the horses up, but that was all. We didn't have a bunch of livestock then. I'm surprised it went for the pigs instead of the sheep. Once the pigs are bigger, they'll be safer."

That afternoon when the boys came home from school, Leif came looking for Rune. "Mr. Benson said Mr. Edmonds, who lives near Mr. Garborg, is the best hunter around and knows the most, 'cause his pa taught him. They homesteaded here earlier than most others. Besides him, he said the Indians know all about the animals that live around here, but he didn't know a name of an Indian to talk with."

"Then Mr. Edmonds it is. Come on, harness up, and we'll take the wagon over there so we can all go. It's good to learn all we can, since we live in this county and plan on staying."

Rune sat up in the box, but he let Bjorn drive. The road to the Edmonds' tunneled through half-grown trees too small to harvest. Was this what Gerd's property would look like in twenty years? Rune wondered how long it had taken these trees to grow this much. Had they been planted, or did they just sort of pop up, like the little runt-maples in Norway, more weeds than trees?

The narrow road opened out into a broad yard. The house, the barns, the sheds—nothing was painted. The buildings were all bare, gray, weathered wood.

A woman stepped out of the house onto the porch. Two boys and a small girl came running out behind her. "Leif! Knute!" Laughing, they greeted their classmates.

A grizzled fellow came out of one of the sheds. He sported a full beard that had a few gray strands in it. His face and hands were weathered from long years outdoors.

Rune slid down off the wagon and crossed the yard to meet him. Rune extended his hand. "Rune Carlson. You are Mr. Edmonds?"

The fellow did not offer to shake. He spoke Norwegian, but with a heavy American accent. It was clearly not his first language. "You're Einar Strand's ilk, right?"

Whatever Rune was going to say stopped halfway to his mouth. He stiffened and drew himself up straighter. "I am Einar Strand's kin, yes. But my family and I are not his ilk. We treasure neighbors, we care about others, and we're honest."

Mr. Edmonds stared at him. Rune held his eye. After a long moment, Mr. Edmonds nodded slightly. "I guess you'll do. What brings you?"

"Something went over a sturdy fence in our barnyard and carried off a large feeder pig. Snatched it right out of the sty. I'm told you know the local wildlife, and I'd like to learn more about it."

"You want to learn more about the wildlife." Mr. Edmonds stood there looking thoughtful, so Rune forced himself to wait patiently. Finally he turned and headed back toward the shed. "Come."

Rune and the boys followed. What a sad legacy Einar had left behind, that no one liked him. No one. He was despised, without honor.

They entered the shed. Mr. Edmonds struck a match and lit a lantern. "I'm a trapper and hunter. I make good money selling hides and furs."

"Oh, wow!" Bjorn stared around the shed.

Rune was staring too. Long poles stretched shoulder-high from one side of the shed to the other. Over them were draped bear skins, deer skins, raccoon skins, and animal hides Rune could not identify.

"This is probably your culprit." Mr. Edmonds swatted the draped hide of a fawn-colored animal six feet long, with a long cat-like tail. "Puma. Cougar. Out west they call them mountain lions. This cat can clear a tall fence in a jump, and can do it while carrying a pretty big animal in its mouth."

Bjorn pointed to another wall. "Are these furs you will sell?"

The wall held rows and rows of narrow shelves with strange boards propped on them. The bottoms of the boards were flat, but the tops came to a blunt, rounded point, like a bullet. Every board was covered with an animal skin stretched tight around it, the fur inside. Rune could see the dimples where the legs were.

"Ja, they are. Muskrat here, mink—don't find many of them anymore. Pine martens—these right here—are common, though. Hardly any wolverines, like this one, but bobcats. Plenty of bobcats. And weasels. We still have weasels."

Rune was disappointed that the fur was on the inside; all he could see was the ruffled fur on the edges, the mink very dark, the muskrats lighter.

"The round pelts on this wall are beavers. You stretch beaver pelts out round. They still use them for men's high hats."

Rune laid a hand on a bear skin, mostly to feel what the fur was like. It was long and coarse and rather stiff, with a soft underfur. "Would a bear take a pig?"

"They climb trees in a heartbeat, scurry right up, but not over a fence, and usually not with a heavy load in their mouth."

"Wolves?"

Mr. Edmond shook his head. "I don't have any wolf pelts left. Sold them all. Hardly any wolves around anymore. A few up north, I hear, but I do most of my trapping locally."

Knute was just as wide-eyed as the others. "You mean you get muskrats and mink out of that lake where we went fishing?"

"Ja, that one and a few other small ponds close by."

Ivar moved from hide to hide, studying them and gazing wistfully around the shed. "When I came to America, I was going to be a logger. Or a farmer. But now, looking at this, I want to be a trapper."

Bjorn nodded. "Ja, so do I."

Mr. Edmonds sniffed. "Well, I advise not. There's not enough animals to trap anymore. You wouldn't make a decent living, especially just getting started. You should have seen my sheds ten years ago—three, four times as many pelts as you see here. The place is too civilized now, the whole area. Clear-cut. These animals don't do well on farmland. They're forest creatures."

Ivar snickered. "I know a puma that's doing pretty well. It eats fresh pork."

Mr. Edmonds laughed. "Ja, but you won't get much money for his hide. Not much market for big cats. There used to be thousands of fur animals. The mink and sable bring high prices, but they're rare now. I haven't seen a sable in years."

"What's a sable, sir?" Leif asked.

"Dark chocolate brown, very dark. About this long, over twice the size of a mink or marten, but the same family. They look like really large mink. And their fur is amazingly soft

and thick. Know what I sell most of? Skunks. Skunks and rabbits. Women like their black skunk coats and stoles. Of course,
skunks with narrow white stripes sell better than skunks with
broad white stripes, because the furriers use the black mostly."
He blew out his lantern, so Rune led the way out into sunlight.

"Thanks to Knute, we've got lots of rabbit skins." Leif nodded. "All on the barn wall."

"Really? You could sell them, you know. I could show you
how to get 'em ready."

"You would?" Knute asked, eyes wide.

"Of course. That's what neighbors do." He nodded at Knute.
"You come back one day after school, bring a couple with you."

"Yes, sir. I will, sir." Knute's eyes shone. "I trap rabbits for
us to eat. We planned to make mittens out of the skins, not
sell them."

Mr. Edmonds stopped in the middle of his yard. "I forgot to
show you a lynx, a cat bigger than a bobcat but stub-tailed like
a bobcat. I still have one lynx pelt left. Lynx could probably
steal your pig; they'll even take down a small deer. But there's
hardly any of those left either. Farmers will shoot a lynx on sight
because they have a taste for lambs and calves." He led them up
onto the porch and into his house. "Mabel, we got company."

They entered the kitchen.

"Figured. Coffee's made." Mrs. Edmonds's brown hair
dropped in a long heavy braid down her back. She looked
humorless and stern, almost haggard.

Rune almost gasped out loud, because she had only one hand.
Her right hand was gone, and her right wrist was a round stub.

With her left hand and that stub end, she picked up a large
cookie jar and plunked it down on the table, no differently
than if Signe with her two hands had moved it. "Have a seat.
You youngsters get your cookies and go back outside." The

Edmonds children grabbed a treat and ran, so Leif and Knute followed.

Bjorn licked his lips. "Ma'am, may I stay here and listen?"

She looked at him and almost smiled. "Ja, you may."

"And may I too?" Ivar asked.

"Ja. You boys are looking to become mighty hunters, I'll wager." Her Norwegian flowed more naturally, and Rune figured he knew where Mr. Edmonds had learned his. She poured coffee for Rune, Mr. Edmonds, and herself, then sat down and dipped into the jar for her own cookie.

Bjorn glanced at his far, almost guiltily. Yes, that was exactly what he was thinking. Rune could tell.

Mr. Edmonds took a bite of cookie. "I make most of my income now from fishing. Pickerel and pike, trout, walleye, whitefish. People will even buy sunfish, would you believe it? Lakes full of fish, and they buy them in a store."

Rune sipped his coffee. Mrs. Edmonds made good, strong coffee. "Bjorn and Ivar here are talking about keeping watch from our haymow and shooting the pig thief the next time it shows up."

Mr. Edmonds nodded slowly. "Might work. Got a dog?"

"Yes, sir," Bjorn said. "His barking is what woke us. We'd keep him inside, though, at night. Would that puma take a dog?"

"Sure would. But people don't like the taste of predators. Cats especially. So if you get that puma, bring him to me, will you? I have a few places to sell the hide. The flesh is next to useless except to feed dogs."

The boys beamed as though he'd given them a hundred dollars.

Rune studied his coffee for a few moments. "You say the animals are becoming rare. I see the big trees becoming rare too; so many mature forests are being logged off." And he was having second thoughts about logging the trees left on his property and Gerd's.

"True. My parents came up from Ohio for exactly that reason. The forests there were all turning into farmland. We were the first white farmers in this area. Now it is happening here."

"I understand the value of farmland. Still, there is a great sadness to it."

Mr. Edmonds smiled. "Mr. Carlson, indeed you are not like Einar Strand. Not at all. I hope we become good friends."

The boys could have raced the horses on the way home. Bjorn clucked the team into a trot, still shaking his head. "I want to talk with him again. Just think, he offered to help Knute with all those rabbit skins."

"I'm not sure the oldest ones are still any good, but we will see," Rune said. "You just never know what good thing God is going to bring your way. The Garborgs took you boys fishing. Mr. Edmonds wants the puma."

"If he comes back, we will get him. I wonder what one would do with a puma skin?"

Rune shrugged. "Make a rug, I guess. There are bear rugs, and all kinds of animal hides are used for clothes and furniture, rugs, you name it."

"I want a bear hide rug on our parlor floor."

"Or by your bed," Ivar suggested. "Or on your bed. Might smell some, though."

"Far, we could use the steer hide for making a chair. Farfar had a leather chair, but one with the hair still on it, that would be really fine. Maybe we could use the hog hides too. And we got those deer hides. I need to learn to tan hides." Bjorn shook his head. "So much I never thought of."

When his son mentioned Farfar, Rune's heart wept a little. Thor, gone. He snapped himself out of it and slapped his son on the shoulder. "You have a whole life ahead, son. I'm glad to see you thinking on new things. Ja, who would have thought of all this?" A sigh slipped by him. *What would Thor Carlson say about my fading eyesight? I wonder, will I be able to tan hides when I am blind?*

Chapter 9

I can't go to a social like that," Nilda said with a deep sigh.

"Whyever not?" Signe sometimes wondered about Nilda's ideas.

"You haven't seen her house, the way she dresses. Mrs. Schoenleber has a staff, not just household help. Meaning a cook, maid, butler, and driver, and those are just the ones I know of. She is very wealthy, and from what I've heard, quite the society matron."

"So? She obviously likes you and Ivar and made a special point to invite you, sending a private messenger, even." Signe went back to pulling rutabagas. She broke off the tops, tossed the tubers in the wheelbarrow, and left the tops in the row. "We should have dug these when the ground was wetter so the dirt clung better." She looked around the fading garden, shaking her head. "We should make it bigger next year. It will take some work to fill that bin. And we need more jars to can these." She studied Nilda. "You're really serious, aren't you?"

"I don't have anything fit to wear."

"Oh. You have your dark skirt and—"

"And the one waist I have is looking worn. The lace is even falling apart."

"So we mend it very carefully."

"Signe! You know what I mean."

"Ja, I do, and I have nothing suitable you can wear either. We can brush the skirt and make it presentable but . . ." She rocked back on her heels, ignoring the dirt stuck to her apron. "I-I wonder if Gerd could sew you one? After all, you have more than a week." She stood and shook out her apron, brushing more dirt off the faded shift that hung below it. "And if she can sew you one, does Mrs. Benson carry finer fabrics there, or only flannels and such? I've not looked through her fabrics much."

"You really think we can do that?" Nilda reached down to grab Kirstin before she stuck a fistful of dirt in her mouth. "No, baby, you don't want to eat that. *Ishta*." She brushed Kirstin's hands together to get the dirt off and earned giggles and reaching fingers. "You sure do like playing in the dirty wagon." They had set some rocks and pine cones inside for her to play with, but everything went in her mouth. "You need a bath."

Signe grabbed the barrow handles and pushed the load of rutabagas up to the cellar door. "Uff da, that was heavy." She wiped her brow with her apron. "Here I thought it was cooling off."

"Mrs. Benson called this Indian Summer, one frost and then a few weeks of days like this. She said winter will probably come one night when we least expect it." She untangled baby fingers from the hair that had escaped her bun. "I should know better than to leave my hair unbraided. I'll be right back to help you, as soon as Gerd agrees to set her in the sink and bathe her."

"I wouldn't mind a bath myself. Remember the creek at home where we went to clean up in the summer? Not that the water ever got warm, but it sure left us clean."

"The boys talked about digging a spot in the creek out in the woods to swim in, but there just hasn't been time."

Signe pushed the wheelbarrow over the lip and down the ramp to the earthen floor of the cellar. Wheeling it to the bin set aside for this crop, she dumped the barrow on the mound already started and spread them out by hand, being careful not to step on any. One more layer, and she'd cover it with dirt and start the next. Then they only had carrots and potatoes to go.

Even in the dimness of the cellar, the shelves of canned goods seemed to glow. So much work, but the thrill of seeing the results like this made up for the hours. Her family would not go hungry this winter. And to think, Rune's mor would soon be here to see this. It would mean more mouths to feed, but they were ready for that.

She pushed the wheelbarrow back up the ramp and out into the sunshine. Mashed rutabagas sounded good for supper. *I wonder if grated rutabaga could be substituted for potatoes for pancakes?* She snagged a basket off the porch and went back to the garden for more rutabagas for the house. It had been a while since she'd tried something new like this. But then, perhaps it was not new at all.

Gerd had Kirstin in the sink, splashing water all over, her giggles making Gerd laugh too.

"I never thought I would hear you laugh like that." The words slipped out before Signe could catch them.

Gerd sobered some and nodded. "Nor did I." Turning back to the baby, she splashed water up on her belly.

Nilda and Signe grinned at each other. The whole kitchen laughed with them.

Gerd wrapped Kirstin in a sheet and drained the water. "Now we have a sweet-smelling baby who needs a diaper and a shift so she can get down on the floor and get all dirty again." She carried Kirstin off to be dressed.

Signe asked, "Nilda? Can you beat those eggs and add the cream for the squash pie? These crusts are about ready." She had two pie pans lined with crust and one waiting. Within minutes the pies were in the oven, more wood was in the stove, and the coffeepot had been pulled forward.

"Good thing the boys will be home any minute. The woodbox is calling," Signe said.

"Let's take the little princess out on the porch and have our coffee out there. Everyone says there might not be many more times we get to do that this fall." Nilda set cookies on a plate, poured glasses of milk for the boys to go along with chunks of corn bread and jam, and set the tray on the porch table. Gerd and Kirstin sank into the rocker. When Rufus leaped off the porch and tore down the lane, they knew the boys were home.

"He's better than an alarm bell." Nilda settled on the floor against the porch post, while Signe took the bench and leaned her back against the wall. Sighs and sips signaled their contentment.

"Are they out in the woods?" Knute called as he pulled Rosie to a stop for Leif to slide off.

"No, over at the house," Signe said. "Food is ready for you."

"Now, let's talk about the waist you want." Gerd rocked gently, Kirstin nodding off against her shoulder. "I can do the machine sewing, but I don't have any fabrics like that, and the one waist I do have would never fit you."

"But does Mrs. Benson have the materials and a pattern?" Nilda tipped her head back against the post. "What if I rode Rosie to Benson's right now, hopefully to return with all we need?" She looked at Gerd. "Do you really think we can do this? It's not like this is necessary."

Gerd and Signe both nodded.

Nilda stood. "I'll get Rosie. Do we need anything else from the store?"

Supper was on the table when Nilda returned. "She had lawn and a pattern." She held up a brown wrapped package.

"Lace?" asked Gerd.

"Not enough, so she'll order it. She said she could send it home with the boys in a couple of days. We can at least get started."

"All this because you want to look—" Ivar cut off his comment at a look from Rune.

Nilda finished it for him. "Acceptable? Yes."

The next morning Signe laid Nilda's worn waist on the table with the pattern and compared the two. "I hope you bought plenty of lawn. All these tucks down the front . . . I've never done something this intricate. What about you, Gerd?"

"Nei, but I can learn. I know how to do tucks. They're easy on the sewing machine. It's going to need a lot of ironing as we go. The flatirons are in the trunk. I haven't used them in a long time. You need to make sure there is no rust on them." She smoothed the pattern out, all the while shaking her head.

Signe held Kirstin on her hip. Could this really happen?

Life went on around her while Gerd studied the finished waist, the pattern, the cut pieces of lawn, and the instructions. Day three, she needed the lace. The boys brought it home after school, along with a letter from Norway.

Signe read it at supper.

"'Dear Signe, Ivar, and all our family there,

"'We will be leaving Norway in ten days, something I did not dream possible. I am gathering up what I can to bring along. And yes, I will bring starts of the irises you asked for, along with flower seeds. Selma says that one minute she is excited, the next terrified. What if she and Mr. Kielund cannot abide one another? I remind her that God loves all of them and is bringing their good into being. With all her suffering, I think she might be afraid to fall in love again, or that love cannot happen more than once in a woman's life. I trust that you think highly of this man and that your pastor does too.

"'I am praying for calm seas, as I have to confess, I fear I will be terribly seasick. Your accounts of the crossing make one tend to fear that way.'"

Nilda shook her head. "I'd be afraid of that too, but there were so many good things to come of it. The good outweighs the bad."

"How old is Eric, Selma's son?" Leif asked.

"I think he is nearly five." Nilda thought a moment. "Or perhaps only four. Little, anyway."

"But bigger than Kirstin?" At her nod, he continued, "So she will still be the baby."

The women nodded.

That night Bjorn and Ivar took shifts watching for the pig thief to return. The only thing they earned was exhaustion and hay in their hair.

Three days passed. The waist now looked like it should, with sleeves puffed at the shoulders and fitted from elbow to wrist. Lace edged the stand-up collar and the front tucks.

"Tomorrow I make the buttonholes and sew on the buttons." Gerd rubbed her eyes. "And we have enough fabric left for me to make a dress for Kirstin. I think I'll do tucks on the bodice for her too. Such tiny tucks."

"I was afraid you would never want to sew again." Nilda

traced a finger down one of the tucks. "It's so lovely. Gerd, I will never be able to thank you. You need to teach me how to use that machine. What a godsend."

No puma came for the next two nights. Sleeping in the haymow had lost its appeal for the boys.

"Maybe he found something else to eat," Knute offered at the breakfast table.

"What if it is a she and she has cubs to feed?" Leif said. "She'd probably come back more often, in that case. But if you shot her, the babies would die."

Signe shook her head. Leave it to her tenderhearted boy to think of that.

"Would you rather she killed more of our pigs? What about the sheep? Mr. Edmonds said bobcats like lambs and calves. We better build more stalls for the winter." Knute looked at the clock. "But right now we better get on Rosie and get to school. We're going to have to canter partway as it is."

The two boys grabbed their dinner pails and ran out the door, Rufus jumping and leaping with them. In the beginning he had tried to follow them, but Leif had trained him to stay home.

"That boy sure has a way with animals," Gerd said when Rufus jumped back up on the porch to wait, never taking his gaze from the lane. "How that dog already knows when it is time for them to come home is more than I can understand." She picked up the coffeepot. "Anyone for more?"

Saturday afternoon, Nilda and Ivar drove Rosie and the cart to Blackduck. "You watch," he said. "That puma is going to show up while we're gone, and Bjorn will sleep through it."

"Fine way to talk." Nilda glared at him.

He clucked Rosie to an easy trot. "Fine day to go for a drive.

Fine day to be working in the woods. Fine day for most anything, including a social this evening."

"Whoever would have dreamed something like this could come about because of a woman we met on the train who decided we needed feeding? Do you realize that the only other wealthy people in the whole world that we know are the Nygaards? Their house isn't as fine as Mrs. Schoenleber's, but they have help." She shuddered. "I don't know Mr. Nygaard, but his wife is a banshee and thinks she's better than anyone else."

"He's not a bad sort, I guess." He paused. "Why are we talking about them?"

"Good question."

"Tonight you'll see Petter again."

The flush started at her chest and flamed her neck and cheeks, clear up to her hairline. "He came to see both of us, remember?"

"Ja. But he has eyes for you."

"Ivar Carlson, that is quite enough." She poked him hard enough to get her point across. "Now when I see him, I'll be so embarrassed that I'll turn fifty shades of red, and it is all your fault."

They delivered the butter and eggs to Mrs. Benson and arrived in Blackduck, where they stopped at the lumberyard so Ivar could give Mr. Hechstrom, the clerk at the lumberyard, their list. At the mercantile, Nilda bought thread and a packet of needles for the sewing machine, then fingered the chintz she would love to sew into a dress. But the navy serge would make a fine skirt and be a much wiser purchase. She paid for the needles and thread and returned to the cart, where Ivar waited patiently.

"Good thing Mrs. Schoenleber said to come early, because we are."

"We'll go back to the lumberyard and then to her house," Ivar said. "Not that we have a lot that needs settling in."

The wrought iron fence announced Mrs. Schoenleber's house before they could see the lovely front yard. A maple tree flaming crimson and scarlet scattered leaves with abandon next to the brick two-story house with curtain-draped windows and a wreath on the carved wooden front door.

"Even her house looks friendly," Nilda said.

Ivar turned Rosie into the driveway and stopped at the walk from the drive to the front door.

"Welcome Mr. and Miss Carlson, glad you could come." George, the driver, walked up to Rosie and stroked her nose. "Mrs. Schoenleber is probably ordering tea and refreshments right now. You go on up to the door there, and I'll take care of your horse and cart."

"Thank you. Good to see you again." Ivar stepped down to assist Nilda, winking at her as he did so. He took their bags from the back of the cart.

"No, no, leave that to me," George said. "You just go and enjoy yourselves."

"If you say so." Ivar set their meager belongings on the path and did as he was told. He dropped the door knocker against the plate once and waited. The door opened after only a few seconds.

"Welcome," the man who answered said. "I am Charles, and Mrs. Schoenleber is waiting in the main parlor. Tea will be served, and the fireplace is burning in case you might be chilled." He half bowed and motioned them inside.

"Thank you." Nilda smiled at the butler, who managed to look formal and friendly at the same time.

He led the way down a walnut-paneled hall and opened the door into the same room they'd visited in before. Mrs. Schoenleber had referred to it as her favorite room. She stood and came toward them, both hands extended.

"I am so glad you could come. I know you live so far out, but you humored this old lady. Thank you, thank you." She took Nilda's hand first and then Ivar's. "You too look like living in America agrees with you."

"Oh, it does. More than we ever dreamed." Nilda returned the hand squeeze. "Thank you for inviting us."

"That Petter was thrilled to be asked to deliver the invitation. He said he has been out to deliver lumber and help build your brother's house. He'd never been to a house-raising before. 'Why, it went up in two days,' he said." She motioned to the chairs in front of the snapping fire. "I know we didn't need a fire today, but fall seems to call for fires, don't you think?"

Nilda could feel a bubble of delight rising in her middle. "In Norway, many of the houses still cook in fireplaces. I remember when Far and Mor were able to put a stove in our house for cooking."

A maid entered with the refreshments.

"Just set the tray there." Mrs. Schoenleber nodded toward the low table. "We'll be eating later at the social, but I thought you might like something before you go up to your rooms to get ready. Nilda, do you need anything pressed for tonight?"

"Really? Why yes, I was going to hang up my skirt and waist immediately."

"Never fear, Gilda will have them back to you in no time. Do you take milk in your tea? I know you are coffee drinkers, but tea is delightful in the late afternoon like this." While she poured the tea, the maid handed them each a plate and napkin, then held out the tray.

"Please help yourselves," the maid said. "Madam does not like anyone to go hungry. Or thirsty, for that matter."

"Are you Gilda?" Nilda asked. She studied the tray. There were so many choices, and for only three people. Ivar had better eat a lot.

"No, miss, I am Stella. Welcome to Schoenleber House."

Nilda and Ivar answered their hostess's many questions while they ate. Then they were shown to their side-by-side rooms. In her room, Nilda took off her shoes and flopped backward onto the high, canopied bed she had slept in before. Such comfort beyond imagination. If only Signe could see this.

A few minutes later, a knock at the door announced Gilda, who brought Nilda's skirt and waist in on hangers and hung them in the wardrobe. "Can I get you anything else, miss?"

"My name is Nilda. Please, can you call me that?"

"If you wish. We don't really stand on formality here as much as many. You remember we have running water, both hot and cold, and a bathtub in the bathroom. You have plenty of time to bathe, and afterward, I could help you with your hair if you like."

Nilda sat on the edge of the bed. "Are you sure this isn't a small bit of heaven?"

Gilda smiled. "I'm glad you think that. Now, may I start the bath for you? It takes time to fill."

Lying against the sloped end of the tub, bubbles frothing around her, Nilda heaved a sigh. How could she ever deserve such luxury as this?

Some time later, she made her way downstairs, one hand trailing on the railing. She might not have the fanciest clothes, but she felt like a princess anyway. Hearing laughter from the drawing room, she paused at the doorway. Petter spotted her immediately and crossed the room to greet her.

"I'm so glad you could come. I'll introduce you to the others. More people will be coming soon."

The knocker on the door announced another guest. As she entered the room with Petter, she could hear Charles greet the newcomer. For some strange reason, she paused long enough to hear an answer.

"I am a friend of Petter's."

Nilda froze. Surely this was not possible. It couldn't be.

Petter gave her a puzzled frown. "What's the matter? You look like you've seen a ghost. I was looking forward to introducing you to my new friend, Dreng Nygaard. He's recently from Norway too."

Nilda's worst nightmares were now reality.

Chapter 10

Run! Stay! Run!

With those words screaming through her mind, Nilda stiffened her back and raised her chin, hands fisted at her sides. How she would talk through such tightly clenched teeth was beyond her. *You will not run! You will not let him see your fear! Stand and smile! Now!*

The smile on his face did not reach his eyes. Wisely, he did not offer his hand. With an infinitesimal bow, he said in a voice that might have been sweet, had she not seen his eyes before he smiled, "Petter told me others here had recently come from Norway. How good to see old friends from home."

Friends? Friends! *Ivar, get over here.*

Instead of screaming, *How did you find me*, she said, her words clipped more sharply than the finest steel knife, "Really, such a surprise." Shock, more likely. She caught the puzzlement on Petter's face. "Whatever brought you to Blackduck?"

"Dreng said he is hoping to hire on at one of the camps, like I will," Petter explained.

"I see. I hope you get your wish." *And a big tree falls on you*. Immediately she fought to bury such thoughts. Hearing her mor's voice in her head brought back a measure of sanity. "Shall we go join the others?" She saw Ivar was engrossed in talking with two other young men. No help there.

"So, how are you and Ivar doing here in America?" Dreng asked politely. "You are with relatives, if I remember right."

How do you know that? Of course, others in Valders knew of their situation. She ignored his comment. She was not going to converse with him as if nothing had ever happened. *Behave yourself.* That voice again. *Be the lady you look to be.* If only she dared ask him how his banishment to America was going.

When could she beg a headache, the one pounding at her temples, and go upstairs?

Mrs. Schoenleber was making her way around the room, greeting and welcoming everyone to her home for the evening. Petter made the introductions.

"Welcome, Mr. Nygaard. So you are new in town?" Mrs. Schoenleber said.

"I arrived last week by way of Minneapolis. I've been in America for, surprisingly, almost half a year. How time flies, doesn't it, Miss Carlson?"

Nilda nodded, albeit stiffly, as if she wore a brace on her neck, probably the same one that was keeping her back rigid. She felt a glance from Mrs. Schoenleber.

"Well, I believe everyone is here, so let's get started." Their hostess clapped her hands for attention. "Welcome to our first social of this year. The first of many, I hope. I am so pleased you all decided to come. My purpose is twofold. To use the home God has given me as a place for people to gather and become friends, and to bring laughter to this house again, since my husband left this life for the next. I want the young people of Blackduck to gather, become friends, and have good times to look forward to. So, if you all enjoy yourselves, we will plan on gathering on a monthly basis."

Applause circled the room.

"I thought we could go around the room, and everyone can say your name and where you came from. Following that, the card tables are set up for whist and euchre, so take your pick. If you do not know how to play, those who do will teach you. After the first round of play, I'd like you all to change tables, with one person remaining at the table. This will help you get to know each other better."

How was Nilda going to avoid Dreng with something like that?

Mrs. Schoenleber continued. "A modest meal will be served later, but coffee, tea, and punch are available at the bar now. If you need anything, please feel free to ask me. Oh, and if you have a friend you would like to invite next month, please do so." She smiled around the room. "And now, let the introductions begin."

Of the twelve people present, seven were male. One could scarcely be heard, and another blushed clear up to his almost white-blond hair, but Dreng spoke clearly with complete self-assurance. He smiled, mainly at the young women, and nodded to Petter, who stood next to him. Nilda was next; surprisingly she knew she sounded assured as she spoke, even though her hands were shaking, more from being clenched than from being shy. They all spoke English. Most, like her and Ivar, with heavy accents, but at least they could be understood.

When they finished and began drifting over to the tables, Petter asked her, "Which is it, whist or euchre?"

"I-I—excuse me, please. I'll be right back." Nilda smiled, or at least she hoped she did. All she really wanted to do was get in the cart and go home. And never see Dreng Nygaard again.

"We'll save you a place," Petter offered.

"That's all right." She left the room without running but paused in the hall, leaning against the carved paneling, her hand at her throat as if to stop the pounding of her heart.

"Are you all right, miss?" Stella asked.

Nilda nodded. "I will be. I guess it felt a bit close in there. I-I've forgotten where the powder room is."

"Second door on the right. Are you sure I can't get you anything?"

"No, thank you. I'll be fine." Nilda made sure she smiled. There was no sense in letting everyone know how she wanted to run.

She used the necessary, washed her hands at the sink, and while drying her hands, stared into the mirror. *Pinch your cheeks, put a smile on that face, and get back out there. You will not allow Dreng Nygaard to destroy the pleasure of this evening. Just stay as far away from him as possible.*

Back in the drawing room, she ignored Petter's smile and took the last seat at another table. When the tables changed, she made certain she was with Ivar. "Stay close to me!" she hissed.

"This is a crowded room. He can't try anything here. And frankly, I'm avoiding him too. I despise him as much as you do."

"But it is not you he tried to . . ."

"No, but I was one of those on, shall we say, the disciplinary board." Ivar grimaced. "He hasn't spoken to me, and I am not speaking to him. I want to let it go at that."

Was Ivar afraid? Nilda couldn't imagine that. "Well, don't get too far away from me, anyway. I mean, you know, if I need you."

"You're safe."

The third time the tables changed, Nilda could not stay away from Dreng without making a scene. She smiled at the other two gentlemen and asked, "Who would like to deal?"

"I will," Dreng offered. He shuffled the deck and dealt the cards.

Euchre was not her favorite game, but there was no way to back out. Her mind refused to concentrate, so she stumbled on a couple of plays. "I'm sorry, I haven't played this for a long time."

"May I get you something to drink?" one of the men asked.

"Thank you, no. I'll be fine." *Pay attention*, she ordered herself as she forced a polite smile.

"Supper is served," Charles announced a bit later. Massive dining room doors opened to long, lovely tables set with fine china. Nilda chose a chair near the middle of the table. Making sure she was not by Dreng took every bit of ingenuity she possessed. There was nothing she could do about sitting across from him except make certain she did not look at him.

Had Charles said "supper"? And Mrs. Schoenleber had said "a simple meal." But servants entered from two directions carrying food on beautiful porcelain serving dishes. They paused by each guest as he or she put a serving on their plate. The servants then placed the bowls down the center of the tables so that those who wished could take seconds. When a bowl emptied, it was replaced with a full one. At the end of the meal, there was as much food on the table as ever. Nilda could not imagine so much food.

"Such a delightful time," Miss Croggin said beside Nilda. "How will we ever be able to thank our hostess?"

"I think the best way would be to attend next month too, and possibly bring a friend."

Miss Croggin dropped her voice to a whisper. "You'd think with this percentage of men, more young women would want to come."

"I agree. I know of several young women who want to come

from Norway in the worst way, but earning fare for a ticket is difficult."

"So I understand. We moved here from St. Paul nearly a year ago so my father could work in the mill. He is rather protective of his daughters, so this was a perfect opportunity to . . . you know."

"Yes. It is."

"Did I hear right that you knew Mr. Nygaard in Norway?"

"Yes."

"He seems so charming." Miss Croggin nodded slightly. "You are from the same area?"

"Same village." *Stay away from him!* How could she say that without sounding terribly petty or even jealous? Tonight he was showing the side that captivated women. Was he different with those who worked at his home in Norway? Had he learned his lesson and changed? Somehow that did not seem like a possibility. But wouldn't banishment from home and country be sufficient cause to change?

Her mor's old saying tiptoed through her mind. *Can a leopard change his spots?*

No, but people could change; after all, God was in the people-changing business, wasn't He? She wanted to rub away the headache that never had completely disappeared.

The evening couldn't end soon enough for her.

"Would you two care to join me in my favorite room and enjoy the fire for a bit before you go to bed?" Mrs. Schoenleber asked Nilda and Ivar when the last guest was out the door. "I have some questions I would like to ask, but they can wait until morning if you prefer."

"Of course," Ivar answered before looking at Nilda, who only shrugged, hoping he did not see the pain that was most likely showing in her eyes. The dimness of the hall lighting could help protect her.

"I'll order tea, unless you would rather have coffee or something else?"

"Tea sounds good." Nilda followed them into the cozy room and sank into one of the chintz-covered easy chairs in front of the welcoming fire. She sighed and let her eyelids drift closed. Such a peaceful place to be.

"If you would rather go right up to bed . . ." Mrs. Schoenleber said.

"No, but then, I might never move out of this chair either." Nilda smiled at Mrs. Schoenleber. "Thank you for a very nice evening." *And for letting us stay here.* The thought of making the long drive home at night made her want to shudder.

"I cannot tell you how grateful I am that you came. Thank you, Stella, that will be all." Mrs. Schoenleber poured the tea and handed them each a cup and saucer with a rolled cookie alongside it. "Now, do you have any suggestions on ways to improve our get-together?"

Ivar looked at Nilda, and they both shook their heads. "But you realize we have nothing of this sort to compare it to," Nilda explained.

Sipping her tea, Mrs. Schoenleber nodded. "But you think everyone felt comfortable?" At their nods, she continued, "I hope to have music another time. You know my nephew, Fritz Larsson. I want him to play the piano for a sing-along, especially in December, but then we'd have to meet on a Friday night. I don't want him riding back to his house in the night so he can play for church on Sunday."

"I hope he told you how much we appreciate the rosebushes," Nilda said. "They are both looking healthy. What a marvelous surprise that was."

"I start roses and other cuttings out in my greenhouse in the backyard. I will show you sometime. A hobby of mine.

109

Spirea and love-in-a-mist are really easy to start, as are geraniums. But back to thinking on this evening. I was surprised Petter invited Mr. Nygaard but pleased you could see someone from home."

Nilda stared into the fire. To answer or not?

Ivar just nodded.

Mrs. Schoenleber studied Nilda closely. "Why do I get the feeling you were not particularly pleased to see him?"

"It is a long story and one best forgotten," Nilda said. "Time will tell, as Mor always said when she was trying to make me see something I disagreed with."

"Hmm, this sounds more interesting all the time." Mrs. Schoenleber set her teacup on the tray. "Enough questions for tonight. If you think of something later, please let me know. Do you plan to attend church with me here in Blackduck or leave early for your own?"

Ivar scooted to the front of his chair. "I think we should leave early, if it is not too much trouble."

"Whichever is best for you. Breakfast will be ready at five. Someone will wake you if you want."

They both stood. "Thank you for giving us this gift." Nilda included the room, the tea, and the entire house in her glance. "We will see you in the morning, then."

Mrs. Schoenleber was sitting at the dining room table reading a newspaper when they entered the room the next morning.

"Good Sunday morning. I trust you slept well?" she said.

Nilda glanced at Ivar, who nodded also. "How could one not sleep in a bed like that?" Ivar pulled her chair out, which earned him a surprised grin, then sat down beside her.

"Now, tell Charles what you would like."

"We have bacon, eggs, biscuits, toast, oatmeal, fruit, and I'm sure Cook would make pancakes if you would rather." Charles waited patiently for their orders.

"Toast with bacon and eggs and fruit please," Nilda said, and Ivar nodded his agreement.

When their plates were served and admired, Nilda asked if Mrs. Schoenleber was going to eat too.

"Oh, I have already finished. But I have something I would like to discuss with you, Nilda."

Nilda laid her fork down, the better to pay attention.

"No, no, go ahead and eat. I know you need to get on the road. I would like to offer you a position here in my home as my assistant, two days a week."

Nilda stared at the smiling woman. "What could I possibly do for you?"

"Oh, I'm sure I will find plenty for you to do. Mostly things like errands that I do not like to do. Accompanying me to some meetings, all manner of things. I would like you to spend two nights of the week here, and I will pay you on the first of the month. Does this sound agreeable to you?"

"You don't mean cleaning, laundry, that kind of thing?"

"No, I already have a well-trained staff to do all those things. I can tell you learn quickly and do not succumb to vapors or fear. Oh, and I will provide you with a wardrobe appropriate for whatever I ask you to do. I really think it might be an adventure for you."

Nilda looked to Ivar, who raised his eyebrow with a slight tip of his head. Definitely an agreement sign.

"You don't have to decide immediately," Mrs. Schoenleber said. "Think on it."

Nilda already knew her answer. "Since my mor is coming

and could help out as necessary on the farm, I am honored to be offered such an opportunity. Thank you. I accept."

"Good. I was hoping you would say that. I have one requirement—that you learn to read and write well in English. I will see that you have instruction."

Nilda nodded. "Of course." But inside, her heart banged against her ribs. "When would I start? Could it be after Mor arrives in a week?"

"Yes, of course." Mrs. Schoenleber sat back just a tiny bit. "Wonderful."

After many thank-yous and good wishes, Ivar guided Rosie to the road to Benson's Corner. "Now, that was some surprise," he said.

"Ja, with Dreng Nygaard the only dark spot. The fear that came upon me. I could not believe it when I heard his voice."

"You have to admit, he has changed a great deal."

"I have my doubts but shall keep them to myself."

At least I don't have to have an acquaintance with him, other than last night. I imagine Signe will have something to say about this. And Mor. Mor might know more from the Nygaard family in Valders. Surely Dreng's mor would brag about whatever she had learned, if her son ever wrote home. He must have, to find out where Nilda was living.

She and Ivar slid into their seats at church just as the organ broke into the opening hymn.

"The puma came back," Bjorn announced the moment the service ended.

"And he missed." Knute gave his brother a disgusted look.

"What happened?" Ivar asked.

"I was dozing. The pigs squealing woke me up. I couldn't see where to shoot, so I fired into the air, and that cat was over the fence and across the field in a flash. They sure can run."

"Did it get another pig?"

"No, but a couple got scratched, and one had teeth marks on his neck. They can't get away, locked in that small space. Mr. Edmonds said pumas were really strong and fast." Knute shook his head. "We gotta get him."

"I'd like to ask Mr. Edmonds more questions. You think he would mind, Far?" Bjorn asked.

"He said stop by anytime, and I don't think he is a man to say something like that lightly." Rune glanced at Bjorn, who was driving the wagon. "Learn all you can. And if you get the puma, you can repay his time with the carcass."

Nilda knew Ivar was as interested as Bjorn in talking with the hunter again. It was surprising how interests could change when one was exposed to new things. She thought of the social the night before.

"So, how was the party?" Signe asked.

"We had a rather big surprise." That was one word for it.

"Ja, and what might that be?"

"Petter invited a new friend of his, someone else from Norway. He thought we would be pleased." Nilda shook her head. "I nearly fainted when I heard Dreng Nygaard's voice."

Signe gaped at her in shock. "Dreng Nygaard is in Blackduck?"

"In person, only this young man was so charming, if you didn't know better, you might believe he was a nice person. Ivar said, what if he has learned his lesson and changed?"

"And you believe that?"

"The other young women there were delighted with him. He was polite, smiling, and a model gentleman. He even charmed Mrs. Schoenleber."

"Did you say something to her?"

"No, if he really has changed . . ." Nilda gazed at the farm they were passing. "Then would it be fair to brand him with what he was before?"

"But what if he hurts someone here, and we knew about him and did not warn anyone?"

Nilda sighed. "Ja, there is that." She thought back to the way he had treated her at home. "Indeed, there is that."

Chapter 11

Rune rubbed his eyes. Sometimes the pain made him want to bang his head on a wall. "It's hard to believe that I will see Mor again this side of heaven. I never thought it possible."

"And we finally have our cookstove in the kitchen in spite of all the delays."

All he and his helpers had to do now was set up the stovepipe and pray the chimney worked. Someday they might even have another stove in the parlor or front room. He had installed the vents for one.

"All this, our dreams coming true." He held out his hand. Signe took it with a smile.

"We are indeed most blessed. During those months we were slaving for Onkel Einar and Tante Gerd, I was beginning to think life would be like that forever."

Rune nodded. "But he taught me so much about cutting down the big pines and the whole logging business. He was a worker."

Signe snorted. "He was a cruel taskmaster who could think of nothing but the trees, with no regard for anyone or anything else."

Rune stared at her. "You hated him. Signe, he can no longer hurt our boys or us, or Gerd. You need to forgive him."

Signe wagged her head slowly, as if it were heavy and unmanageable. "I-I don't think I can. How am I to forgive him for his cruelty to Leif, who is the most caring child I know, who prayed for him and tried so hard to be good to him? Who felt sorry for him? And Gerd—he nearly killed her."

"But he did bring us here so you could help her get well again."

"Ja, so she could resume doing all the farm chores so he could spend his days out in the woods."

Oh, my Signe. He dropped his voice. "But Jesus said to forgive, as we are forgiven." He reached out for her, but she backed up. "Please, my Signe, if you don't forgive, bitterness will eat you alive. You can't let it grow and take over your heart." This time when he reached for her, she came into his arms. He stroked the beautiful hair she had been brushing before going to bed. "Lord, help my Signe forgive Onkel Einar. He is beyond hurt, but she is not."

They got into bed, but Rune could not quiet his thoughts.

Mor is on American soil. Mor is here somewhere. Morning and the day's work would come early, but Rune couldn't sleep. He wandered out onto the porch and sat with his boys as they prepared for the vigil, since they'd missed a couple of nights. Knute would keep watch for the puma with Bjorn from up in the haymow.

"If it comes on your watch, just touch my shoulder," Bjorn said. "They have good hearing too, you know."

"I know, but remember Mr. Edmonds said to take your time to get the shot."

"I learned one thing—you can't get excited."

The two boys hopped off the porch and headed for the barn.

Finally Rune went upstairs. He tried to slip between the covers without disturbing Signe, but she was awake.

She said in the darkness, "You think they'll ever get it?" She laid a hand on his shoulder.

"They've got as good a chance as anyone. Bjorn is shooting more surely all the time. I think the night he missed, like he said, he got excited. He's mighty determined."

He found her hand and lifted it to his mouth. One kiss on the palm, and then he held it to cup his cheek. The darkness that surrounded them closed out the rest of the house, cocooning the two of them in their rope-strung bed. "Come. Let us pray together." He began, "Our Father who art in heaven . . ." With a sniff, she joined him, both of them saying the words carefully, as if to engrave them on their hearts.

He kissed her face. "And tomorrow will be a new day, a wonderful day."

"Ja, a new day."

The moon hung in the west, and when the pigs squealed, the dog flew down the stairs, and the rifle fired once.

Even from their bedroom, they could hear the boys whooping. Before Rune could get halfway down the stairs, he heard another shot.

"Bjorn! Are you all right?" he called as he slammed the back door.

"We're fine."

Rune breathed a prayer of thanks as he trotted up to the pen. Leaning against the fence, he saw that the boys had let the hogs out into the bigger pen and were standing over a tan form that lay inert on the ground. He pushed open the gate. "You sure he's dead?"

"I put the second bullet in his head for good measure." Bjorn stood with his rifle in the crook of his arm, pointing toward the ground. "He's kind of skinny. You can see his ribs. Look at those claws."

"I'll get a lantern." Knute passed his far at a run.

"No wonder those pigs were scratched up." Bjorn moved a front paw with the tip of the rifle barrel.

"Careful!" Rune stopped beside him. The cat lay stretched out on the ground, blood puddling just behind his front leg and his head, the odor rising like a miasma. "Good shooting, son."

Knute ran up with the lighted lantern and held it so they could really inspect the beast. Rune knelt by the puma's head and lifted a tawny lip. "See why he's skinny? He's old, and half his teeth are gone."

Bjorn squatted down beside his far. "He's still strong enough to lift a pig over that fence." He blew out a breath. "I'm glad it isn't a female, or Leif would have had us all out looking for her den."

"And if we found 'em, we'd have to shoot them too." Knute sounded relieved.

Rune stood back up. "Well, let's haul it out of here so the pigs will come in for morning feeding. Knute, get a rope, will you? We can tie his feet together and slide a pole between his legs to carry him out."

By the time they had shut the carcass in the machine shed, both boys were yawning.

They dipped water from the bucket on the porch and washed their hands before going in the house, where they took off their boots at the door.

"I'm proud of you two," Rune said.

"Thanks, Far. Morning's going to be here before we know it."

"Did they get it?" Signe asked as he sat on the edge of the bed a few minutes later.

"Ja." He slid back under the covers. "Whatever my dreams

118

were about coming to the new land, they did not include lions."
And he fell asleep.

The next morning at breakfast, Knute asked, "Can we take
the puma to Mr. Edmonds as soon as we get home from school?"

"Bestemor will most likely be here by then."

"Oh. But Mr. Edmonds might not want it if it has started
to spoil."

"Bjorn and I will take it over right away." Rune nodded to
Knute. "I'm sorry, but we will have to do it this way. And no,
you cannot miss school for such a thing as this."

Rune caught Signe's nod as the boys headed out the door.
The glare Knute shot his way made him wag his head.

Signe asked, "Can I get you anything else?"

Both he and Bjorn shook their heads. "We'll get this done
immediately. Bjorn, please go hitch up the wagon. I'll meet you
at the machine shed." But when Gerd raised the coffeepot, Rune
sat back down in his chair. "Takk."

"It sure seems strange here without Nilda and Ivar." Gerd
poured coffee refills and sat again. Nilda and Ivar had left early
that morning to go to Blackduck to pick up Gunlaug, Selma,
and Eric from the train station. "I'll finish up the bread if you
skim the cream pans, Signe. I can hardly believe this is the same
house you all came to."

She nodded at the new curtains in the kitchen window and
in the workroom, which had been her old bedroom. They had
assembled the loom and spinning wheel, and both now waited
to be used. Carded wool lay in a basket by the spinning wheel,
and the string for the warp coiled beside the loom. What they
needed was time, and that would be as soon as the garden was
emptied of winter fare.

"What's for supper?" Rune asked.

"Those two roosters I dressed last night are in the well house, ready to bake, and gingerbread is for dessert." Signe smiled at him. "A real welcome-home meal." A grin split her face. "I guess I'll believe they're really coming when they walk through that door."

"Me too. We won't be gone long." Rune set his coffee cup down and pushed back his chair. He chucked Kirstin under the chin, making her grin and reach for him. "You be good for your mor, little one. Today you will meet your bestemor, and if I know my mor, you and she will be inseparable."

"At least at first." Signe jiggled her daughter on her hip and nuzzled her cheek. "And as long as Bestemor can catch you."

When Rune and Bjorn carried the puma out of the machine shop, the horses went wide-eyed and jerked forward.

"Whoa, there." Rune dropped the pole and leaped for the horses' heads. "Easy now, you got nothing to worry about." Stupid—he should have thought of this. Of course they would panic. "Easy now." Both horses jigged in place but settled back down as he talked to them. They snorted, nostrils flared, ears flicking back and forth. He stroked their necks and waited patiently. "Go get your mor. We need another pair of hands."

Bjorn did as he was told, being careful not to spook the horses further.

When they returned, Rune had the team calmed and waiting.

"All right. I'm going to lead them ahead so they can't see you as well. I wish we had blinders on these bridles. You two slide the carcass in the rear of the wagon. They can smell it, I know."

"Rune, they might run right over you," Signe said.

"No, no, they've calmed a lot." He backed up, his hand on the reins under the snaffle bit of the nearest horse. "Come on, that thing can't hurt you now." He stopped but kept talking, working to keep their attention.

Bjorn and Signe loaded the dead puma, shielding the cat

from the horses as much as they could. The horses tossed their heads, jerking the wagon. Ignoring the jolt, Bjorn pulled the post and cat farther up in the wagon, and then he and Signe stepped back.

"Good. Takk. Easy now." He kept a hand on the nearest horse while Bjorn climbed up into the wagon and picked up the lines, pulling them snug enough that the team knew someone was now in control. After climbing up on the seat, Rune nodded to Signe. "Thank you. We'll be back soon."

Moving briskly seemed to calm the horses even more. Mr. Edmonds greeted them as they trotted into his yard. "What brings you here?"

"We brought you the puma."

"You got him?"

Bjorn nodded. "Scared him off one time but hit him this last time in the night. The moon made a big difference."

"It would. Though it's still hard to see in the shadows." He motioned toward his work shed. "Come on, let's get him out of there so your horses can calm down. They have an inborn fear of all prey animals, but especially this one that can drop down on a horse from a tree branch and kill him with one bite."

At the shop, Rune stood at the horses' heads as Bjorn and Mr. Edmonds pulled the carcass out of the wagon and hauled it into the gray building. Rune joined them as soon as the horses settled.

"I have to tell you, I didn't think you could do this," Edmonds said. "You're good with that rifle. I've gone to several other farms around here to take care of a wild animal preying on sheep or cattle, but no one had any pigs to speak of. This old critter found an easy way to fill his stomach." He pointed to the boxes on the wall. "Some of those marten hides are from chicken coops. I'm surprised you've not lost chickens to the varmints around here."

"I guess we should be grateful, eh?" Rune watched his son studying the hides and skins around the room.

"Right. You see or smell any skunks yet?"

"So far, no." Bjorn shook his head.

Rune smiled. "Sounds like we've been remarkably free of critters, so far."

"Well, I gotta thank you for bringing me this one."

Bjorn looked happy. And proud. "I could see it coming across the field. The pigs all got real restless too."

"They would. I owe you one, young man. Have you done anything about the rabbit skins?"

"Not so far. They're stiff on the wall."

"Take them down and soak them until they're softened. Once they're treated, you can make what you want. I saw a rabbit skin vest one time. Warm as can be. Best to keep the fur side in for warmth, but it looks good on the outside too."

"More good ideas." Rune nodded again as they eased toward the wagon. "We're still trying to finish our house. I figure that kind of thing can be for blizzard days or longer evenings. Say, do you ever dry fish?"

"I have at times, but ice fishing helps us get through the winter. It's hard to beat fresh fish any time of year. You tell that younger boy of yours that he can come fish anytime. Any of you can."

"What will you do with the puma hide?" Bjorn asked.

"Skin him out right away, keep some meat for the dogs, and throw the rest out for the scavengers. It's a shame to waste it, but we're not that desperate. I'll stretch the skin out to dry and then decide."

Rune stepped up to the wagon seat. "We better get back. My mor is coming in from Norway today."

"Good news."

"Mr. Edmonds, did I see snowshoes up on your wall?" Bjorn asked.

"That you did. I made them years ago and have had to restring them a couple of times, but they're the best mode of checking my trap lines."

"Far started making skis last year."

Mr. Edmonds nodded to him. "Skis are faster. How did yours do?"

"I'll finish the first pairs this fall. I'd never done it before, so I learned a lot."

"You Norwegians are famous for your skiing. What are you using for wood?"

"Ash. My far used to make them. I still wish I had brought mine with me, but they took up too much room."

"If you ever decide to do snowshoes, I'll show you." Mr. Edmonds smiled at Bjorn.

"Thank you." Bjorn climbed up next to his far.

Edmonds held out his hand, and Rune leaned over to shake it.

"You seen any bears?" Bjorn asked. "I want a bear rug."

"Watch for tracks. They hibernate pretty soon, so think about next year."

"Ah, sir, could Knute and me come with you sometime on your trap line?"

"You gotta have skis or snowshoes. I've got a couple extra pairs of snowshoes, though, so might be we can arrange that. It'll be December at least, more than likely January." He stepped away from the wagon. "Come on back anytime, and thanks for the puma."

Bjorn nodded. He clucked the horses into a trot once they were out on the road. "I think he really means for us to come back." Suddenly he moaned, "Oh no!"

Panic grabbed Rune. "What?"

"I forgot to ask him about hunting ducks and geese. I was thinking maybe a fine goose for Christmas."

Anger almost replaced the panic. Rune took a deep breath and shook his head. "Don't give me such a start!"

"Sorry. But I'd love to hunt ducks and geese."

Rufus greeted them halfway up the lane, yipping and dancing his welcome as they neared the house.

"They aren't here yet, so unharness and let the team out in the field," Rune said. "I'll see if they need any help up here. If not, we'll work in the shop so we're close by."

Bjorn nodded and flipped the reins.

Mor is in America.

The fragrance of yeast greeted Rune when he stepped up on the porch. He could hear Kirstin chattering, most likely at the cat. Rufus bounded up the steps and waited at the door, tail wagging, body wriggling. Kirstin crawled her way over to sit and wave her hands, jabbering at the dog. When she saw Rune, she squealed and bounced in place, her plea for him to pick her up.

"Well, looks like I'm even more important than the dog. How about that?" He scooped her up and stood at the door, looking around. "Smells wonderful in here."

"When do you think they'll be here?" Signe asked.

"I figured before dinner." He looked up at the clock. "We've got an hour to go. If you don't need anything, Bjorn and I will be in the shop."

Mor. Rune felt like dancing.

Chapter 12

It wasn't raining anymore, but the swirling mist almost felt like rain. Nilda stood underneath the train station overhang beside Ivar. Mor was here at last, but what a terrible price to pay: Far, dead too young, gone forever. Nilda was so full of emotions, she could not sort them out. She could not think clearly.

One thing she knew for sure. Today they would put sorrow aside. Today they would celebrate and be happy. Mor was here in America! And Nilda could not stop grinning. She was glad she could greet her mor with a big happy smile in spite of it all. And very shortly the train would arrive.

With Mor and Selma.

Ivar stepped out to look up at the station clock. "Almost time. I wonder why Rune didn't come."

"I asked him if he was sure, and he said, 'That's all right. You welcome them to this new land, but I will welcome them home.'" Nilda smiled at the thought.

In the distance, the train hooted. Mor was almost here. A gray cloud of coal smoke boiled up above the trees. Finally, here came the engine. It was shining wet and glistening, except for the hot boiler. It pulled into the station and ground to a hissing, steamy stop.

There they were! Mor and Selma stepped off the train onto the platform and immediately turned back toward the baggage car, walking quickly. Selma's little boy scurried along as best he could. He seemed so small. Ivar started toward them, so Nilda hurried along behind him.

"I'm glad we brought the wagon," Ivar commented. "I think most of that luggage is theirs."

The stationmaster was stacking up a pile of two trunks, several carpetbags, and a crate. Now he threw yet another carpetbag on the pile. Mor and Selma stopped beside the tower of luggage. Then Mor glanced toward Nilda and Ivar, and the most wonderful smile spread across her face.

Nilda broke into a run, greeting smile with smile. Her mother started jogging toward her, arms outstretched. Nilda's smile disappeared, dissolving in tears. She ran into her mother's open arms and clung to her, buried her face in her mor's shoulder, and wept with huge shuddering gulps. So many emotions, and they all poured out at once. "Oh, Mor! Mor!" She held on tighter.

"Nilda, Nilda! Ivar!" Mor pulled Ivar in against her.

Nilda straightened and stepped back, still sobbing. So much for cheerful intentions. Mor dug into her big pocketbook and pulled out a handkerchief.

Ivar was just unwrapping his arms from Selma. Nilda stepped in and hugged her warmly. "Welcome to America, Selma."

"Takk. I don't see any mountains on the horizon."

"They're all in Norway yet. So is the cod."

"There is no cod? Uff da!" But Selma was grinning.

Finally Nilda's smile made it to her face. They loaded the baggage into the wagon and almost had no room for themselves.

Selma sat on carpetbags, holding her son, Eric. Eric did not seem particularly happy to be in the New World, but he was only five.

"I feel I'm in shock." Gunlaug sat on the wagon seat next to Ivar.

"I felt the same way." Nilda turned on the bench behind the wagon seat so she could see her mor. "Everything can be overwhelming. So many differences, so much to see."

"But there's no rush. You don't have to remember the way back to Blackduck or anything." Ivar grinned at his mor. "You'll be living in Tante Gerd's house with us. She is living with Rune and Signe so she is not far from Kirstin. As far as she's concerned, the sun rises and sets on that baby. She says it's the closest she can be to having a grandchild, something she never dreamed she'd have, with no children of her own."

"It's a shame they never had children," Gunlaug said with a sad shake of her head. She turned to look at Nilda. "I pray that never happens to either of you."

"Give us time, Mor. We're not courting or being courted, even."

Ivar hastened to add, "Although there are a couple of young men with an eye for Nilda. I'm far too young to be thinking of courting, let alone marriage."

"I thought you were a bit sweet on Lisle Olson in Valders." Gunlaug nudged Ivar in the ribs.

Nilda snorted. "Look at his neck getting red."

"Ja, possibly, but that was Norway, and now I live in America, and I will become an American citizen as soon as I can." He pointed ahead. "This is Benson's Corner coming up. The school and the church are there, along with a store that sells everything, including feed and some machinery parts."

"And if they don't have it, Mrs. Benson will get an order to come out on the train. She—well, both she and her husband have been such good friends to Rune and Signe in spite of the way Einar threatened everyone off his land. She was a big help both before and after Kirstin was born." Nilda turned to Selma. Eric was firmly gripping her shawl, his eyes as big as fried eggs. "If all works well, your place will be about a mile or so straight north on this road and then to the right. He's a fine man and a real hard worker. It's hard to get by with two small children and no relatives around to help." Nilda patted Eric's knee. "And you will soon meet our baby Kirstin. She is too little to walk yet, but you might play with her anyway. She's pretty funny."

Eric moved closer to his mor, if that was possible, scrunching his eyes as if Nilda had struck him. Selma put her arm around the quivering little boy. "It's all right, Eric, we will be to Cousin Rune's farm soon. I heard they have a puppy and cats and horses and cows."

"I want to go home."

"I know you do, but this will be our new home." Selma lifted him onto her lap and wrapped both arms around him, rocking him gently with the sway of the wagon.

Nilda knew how he felt, like all the world he knew had been taken from him.

"H-have you met Mr. Kielund's children?" Selma asked.

"No, but we saw them in church. The little boy is about five, I think, and the little girl three or so. We did everything so fast, and with all that has gone on at our place to make it possible for you to come with Mor, a lot of things did not get done. We thought to let you settle in for a couple of days and then meet them at church on Sunday. Our Reverend Skarstead is the one who approached Mr. Kielund with this idea."

"B-but . . ." She looked down at her son. "We will talk later."

"That is best."

Nilda smiled as Ivar pointed out the other farms and told

Mor everything he had learned about the area. "And here is our lane." The team turned in without even a twitch of the lines and tried to pick up their trot. "The horses are always glad to get home. See, that is our house. I have to remember that Gerd said it is no longer hers. Mor, the Tante Gerd you will meet soon is not at all like the Tante Gerd Signe and Rune wrote home about. Not that they ever said how bad it really was, but we've learned more in bits and pieces, especially from Gerd herself. Right, Nilda?"

"Yes. Oh, and we are trying speak English more at home. Leif has learned the most, but he and Knute use it all the time in school. That makes a difference."

"I tried to learn some, but I didn't get very far." Gunlaug wagged her head. "It is not easy, let me tell you." She nodded to the woman behind her. "And Selma didn't have a chance at all."

"Well, Leif will teach you," Ivar said. "You won't recognize him. Knute either. They've grown so much."

"Partly because they eat so much better here. You will be amazed at all the food we canned, shelves and shelves of jars in the cellar," Nilda said. "And we smoked a lot of meat too."

Rune and Signe waved from the porch while the boys ran out to meet them, Rufus dashing ahead.

"Bestemor!" Leif danced beside the wagon. "We thought you'd never get here."

Eric peeked around his mor. "Big boys."

"Ja, they must seem that way to you. You knew them in Norway before they moved here." Selma kept a comforting arm around the quivering little boy.

When Ivar stopped the wagon by the back porch, Rune helped his mor down over the wheel and to the ground, where she wrapped both arms around him and laugh-cried into his chest. He held her close and let her cry.

"I never thought I would see you again either," he whispered. "But now you are here, and you can begin a new life."

She nodded and mopped her face. "I-I wanted Thor to come too."

"I know, but he couldn't. Some people come and go back because they miss Norway so much. Others like Far can't bear to leave in the first place. But he made his choice, and you honored that. See, God is good—you both got what you wanted."

She sniffed again. "Ja, but he left, and I never even got to say good-bye." The tears started anew.

Nilda hugged her mor too. "Remember, you will see him again, but I hope not for a long time. We all want you here with us for years to come. Now, come and meet your newest grand-daughter. She's a bit shy of strangers at first, but she warms up pretty fast." She tucked Gunlaug's arm in her own and led her up the steps.

Signe's smile could have lit the night sky. "Gunlaug, I-I . . ." She sniffed and swayed with Kirstin, who stared at the woman before her, one finger in her mouth. "I want you to meet our Kirstin. Baby, this is your bestemor, and she has come to live with us."

Kirstin's eyes widened as a frown tugged at her mouth. She turned her face into her mor's shoulder, peeking out but not moving yet.

"And this is Gerd. I think the two of you might have met years ago." Nilda drew Gerd into the circle. "See, you have a good family here too."

Leif stood beside Gunlaug and made one of his funny faces at Kirstin, who peeked between her fingers. She started to smile, then looked at Gunlaug again and hid her face.

"Come, let's not stand out here. Dinner is ready and waiting," Gerd said. She held out a hand to Selma, whose son clung to her skirt. "Welcome. You are brave to come on a moment's notice like this. I remember Nels as a young boy a little older than your Eric. How time goes by." She looked at Ivar and Rune. "Why don't you unload the wagon on the porch so the boys can put the horses away before we eat?"

"There are two rocking chairs in the crate to be put back together, along with my loom," Gunlaug said. "I would have brought more, but the shipping was too expensive. The chairs are wrapped in rugs and several fleeces."

Rune nodded. "We'll put them in the shop until we can get to it."

By the time they sat down to eat, they had put two leaves in the table to make it larger, and the boys were sitting on a bench brought in from the porch.

"Let's say grace." Rune bowed his head and began with the old words, "*I Jesu navn gär vi til bords . . .*" At the *amen*, the women wiped their eyes, and Rune and Ivar cleared their throats.

"Tante Gerd, have you ever had this many people at this table before?" Leif asked.

She shook her head. "No, never. That's why I almost forgot we had leaves to put in it. They came with the table, and I put them back in the closet so Einar wouldn't cut them up for kindling." She heaved a sigh and smiled around the circle. "I'm glad he didn't."

"Me too." Leif grinned at her. "Tante Gerd, do you know you are smiling a lot nowadays?"

Signe and Rune shared a look, but when Gerd actually nodded and chuckled, they both breathed a sigh of relief.

Nilda nearly choked. She twitched her eyebrows at her mor, and Gunlaug did the same back. Leave it to Leif.

Gerd and Nilda kept the bowls of noodles and baked chicken full as well as the rolls circulating until everyone complained of being too full. Then they poured the coffee, and the catching up continued. Kirstin went down for a nap, and at Signe's insistence, Gerd went with her. Eric fell asleep in his mor's lap, so Selma carried him into the parlor too.

"Mor," Rune said a bit later, "we had a discussion. Since Gerd lives with us, the women decided to turn her bedroom into the women's workroom. We can put a bed in there for you, but for now it is upstairs. Is that all right with you, managing the stairs?"

"What do you think I am, an old woman?" Gunlaug's mock horrified look made Nilda hide a chuckle.

"See, I told you," she said.

Rune shrugged. "I know, but—"

"We brought two feather beds too," Gunlaug continued, "one for you and Signe, and one for me, unless Gerd would rather have it."

"A real feather bed again?" Signe sighed. "I have saved the feathers from the geese Bjorn brought home, but I think I only have enough for a pillow."

Gunlaug looked at Bjorn. "Well, you better get that shotgun and go for more. They should still be flying south, aren't they?"

"Bestemor, we've been trying to make beds and such ready for you to come," Bjorn protested. "I'd much rather go hunting than cut down the big trees, even."

"And that means a lot from our young logger here." Rune laid a hand on Bjorn's shoulder. "He hopes to bring in a buck that shows up in the cornfield once in a while."

"The geese sometimes set down in that same cornfield. When I shot ducks over at the lake, I couldn't get to them all. Mr. Garborg lets me use his boat. It'd be good if Rufus learned to retrieve ducks in the water."

"They've gone fishing a couple of times too, but I still miss the northern cod and salmon, the ocean fish." Nilda shrugged. "But you can't have everything."

"Would you be surprised if I brought *lutefisk* and some dried cod in that crate?" Gunlaug asked.

"Really?" Rune's face lit up. "I shouldn't be surprised, but I am. And we even have potatoes to make *lefse*."

"I tried the lefse without potatoes, like some places do, but it just was not the same. I only did it once." Signe nodded. "I'll make it again, to serve with *real* fish."

Nilda patted Signe's shoulder. "Just think, lutefisk and lefse, like home."

They moved out to the porch and kept talking until it was time for chores. All the males left the conversation and went to help.

"Bestemor, maybe tomorrow you can come and see our animals and chickens," Leif said. "We have lots to show you."

Gerd and Kirstin joined them after their naps, and Eric climbed back on his mor's lap. Signe flipped a piece of an old sheet over her shoulder and settled Kirstin in to nurse.

"Is she feeding the baby?" Eric asked in a whisper loud enough to be heard in the garden.

Selma nodded. "Like you did when you were a baby."

"Where did the boys go?" he asked.

"It is chores time, just like at home. There are animals to take care of."

"Oh."

"Well, one of the little ones is warming up." Nilda stood and stretched. "I could heat up the coffee."

"And we probably should start supper." Gerd started to rise.

"No, you sit there," Nilda said. "Supper is easy tonight. Those carrots we pulled yesterday and rabbit and noodles. I brought up some pickles, and we'll throw squash in the oven too."

"And there is gingerbread in the pantry," Signe added.

Leif came charging out of the barn. "Guess what? Gra had her kittens. There are four. She brought them out for milk. They were behind the oat bin."

Eric leaned forward. "Kittens?"

Leif nodded. "Tomorrow you can come with me to see them."

Eric withdrew to the safety of his mor's chest.

"Perhaps Leif will show us all tomorrow," Selma said into her son's hair, receiving a bit of a nod in return.

Kirstin sat up and burped. Signe rolled her eyes as Leif laughed, making Kirstin giggle. "We can peel the carrots out here," Signe said. "I think there are enough of us to get that done."

"You could make more cookies too." Leif looked hopefully at Gerd.

"You go on and get the chores done." She made shooing motions with her hands, sending him off with a smile.

"I like your smiles, Tante Gerd," he called over his shoulder.

That night, after the others had left for the new house and Selma had taken Eric up to bed, Nilda, Ivar, and Gunlaug continued talking around the table.

"Have you heard any news about Dreng from the Nygaard house?" Nilda asked, careful not to sound too interested.

"Oh, his mor is raving proud of how well he is doing, working for his onkel in Minneapolis."

"Oh, really?" She exchanged a look with Ivar. "Anything else?"

"She said that his onkel is going to give him a promotion, but I'm not sure what his business does." Gunlaug tipped her head slightly. "Why do you ask? I thought you never wanted to hear of him again."

"I didn't and I don't." *Tell her. Don't tell her.* An argument started up in Nilda's head. She could feel her mor's stare even when she didn't look at her. *Come on, Ivar, change the subject.*

Ivar asked, "Johann and Solveig are getting on all right?"

"Johann and Solveig moved into our house, and they like it very much. They haven't mentioned emigrating. Oh, and they are expecting a baby this winter." Mor cleared her throat. "Are you planning on telling me what is so heavy on your mind?" she said softly but firmly.

"Dreng is in Blackduck, not Minneapolis. I have no idea what happened with his onkel, but he is looking for work." Nilda could hear the flatness of her response.

"Or a handout," Ivar threw in.

Nilda wished she'd never even brought up Dreng. Why couldn't she just let it alone? "And I have accepted a job with Mrs. Schoenleber for two days a week. I start next Monday morning, so someone will take me there, and her driver will bring me home. Perhaps eventually I will take the train, if we can work that out."

"I see." Gunlaug patted her daughter's hand. "My word, how I have missed you. But I'm glad you have found another job. Mrs. Schoenleber sounds like a delightful woman. You will be a maid there?"

"No, I will be her assistant, whatever that will mean."

Ivan grinned. "There is a certain young man who works at the lumberyard in Blackduck. We met him on the ship to Duluth and quickly became friends. I think I, or rather Nilda, wrote about him."

"Good thing you corrected that, as we did not receive one letter from you." Gunlaug tapped him on the arm, but her smile took any sting out of the words.

Ivar hung his head. "Sorry, but you know how much I dislike writing letters. And besides, Nilda is a good letter writer."

"Ja, she is, when she writes." Gunlaug studied her hands.

The moment stretched as far as Nilda could stand. The words clashing in her head broke loose. "I don't ever want to see him again, but I'm afraid that if I am in Blackduck, I will see him. He seems to have ingratiated himself with Mrs. Schoenleber."

"I see."

Nilda wished *she* could see, but just the thought of that man made her stomach knot. Was the position with Mrs. Schoenleber worth taking the chance?

Chapter 13

I think it's time we start having breakfast here in our house," Signe announced. She lifted her shawl off the wall hook and thought for a moment about how much their lives had progressed in a few short months—new house, more farming, and now, Gunlaug.

Rune looked at his wife. "Now that there are so many people over there, that is fine with me. We can try it and see how it works."

"I'm heading over to the other house," Gerd called up the stairs. "You want me to take anything?"

"We're about ready, so we'll go with you." Signe finished dressing Kirstin, who waved her arms and chattered back at her.

When they stepped out onto the porch, they saw that frost lit the tips of the grass, the sun not yet up enough to turn it into a carpet of jewels.

"Are the boys at chores?" Gerd asked as she smiled at Kirstin, who leaned toward her tante. "I sleep so well in this new house. I wonder if it's because there are no bad memories here."

"Could be," Rune answered with a nod.

The four of them set out on the now well-worn path.

"By winter I'm sure we'll wish the houses were closer together," Gerd said. "It's a long way to string a rope to the barn for a blizzard."

Rune tucked her hand into the crook of his arm and smiled down at her. "Somehow we will work it all out. I think today we will put together Gunlaug's loom and the rocking chairs. Then after church tomorrow, the boys can go fishing, and I can finish those up. Monday we'll start back in the woods."

Gerd nodded and stopped to catch her breath.

"Sorry, we got to walking too fast. The ideas got me going." Rune and Signe waited patiently. "What, no argument about getting out to the trees?"

Gerd shook her head. "You did as I asked. Of course there is always the fall field work. . . ."

"I know. I'll string a fence around the cornfield so the cows and horses can clean that up. Leif can take the sheep out to graze the oat field when he gets home."

Leave it to Rune to have a plan all ready, not like Einar yelling his orders for the day at the breakfast table. Signe nodded to herself. Life was so much more peaceful without him there. *What a horrible thought*, the demanding side of her mind intruded. What kind of Christian would think something like that? *How do I control these thoughts that sneak in? I don't want to be like that. Lord, thank you for forgiving me in spite of me.*

They entered the kitchen of the other house to find Nilda, Gunlaug, and Selma already there.

"So, Mor, you are really here. I was afraid I dreamed yesterday." Rune looked in the woodbox. "Uh-oh, better bring some in."

"I'm spoiled from the boys taking care of the woodbox. I was going to get a couple of armloads in a minute." Signe filled the coffeepot and set it on the hottest part of the stove.

"I'll help too." Selma followed Rune out the door, as did Nilda. After two loads each, with the woodbox about half full, Selma put on one of the aprons from the hook behind the stove.

"But you are a guest." Gerd tied on her own apron.

"I was yesterday, but today I am a cousin who is used to working with her family." She turned and almost tripped on her shadow. "Eric, why don't you go talk to the baby? Maybe you can make her laugh like Leif does. After all, he will be going to school, and she needs a brother more her size."

Nilda and Signe grinned at each other.

Signe nodded at Selma. "Good for you. Welcome to all of the family gathered here. Now this feels even more like home. Remember all the times we baked together, or shelled peas or snapped beans, anything that needed doing?"

Gunlaug joined in. "At whatever house the doing needed to be done."

"That is something I really missed." Signe tried to stop her sigh but couldn't quite contain it.

Gerd looked wistful. "I haven't had that since we left Norway. I think I began to believe it was a dream and let it go."

Signe hugged Gerd around her thin shoulders. "Well, we have it now, and perhaps others from the family will come here."

Gerd stopped stirring the oatmeal. "I wonder if that land either south or west of us might be for sale. Or any other land nearby."

All the others stopped and gaped at her.

She went back to stirring. "Well, it is something to think about. Don't look at me like that." She brushed a hand at them as if they were flies, which brought out several chuckles.

Signe wished Rune were there, but he had gone down to the barn to see how things were going. Wait until she told him Tante Gerd's new idea.

She watched Selma, with her mousy brown hair pulled straight back and tucked into a snood, and her capable hands doing whatever she saw needed doing, and a smile that, when it came out, made her square face almost beautiful. The gentle way she handled her small son was how she would treat Mr. Kielund's sad-faced children. Signe nodded. Surely this union was going to be a good thing. And even if it was sort of an arranged marriage, surely they would grow to love each other. She added a *please, God* to that thought and set about fixing breakfast for her family.

Later, after the house was cleaned and Gunlaug's loom was set up in the workroom, Signe sat in one of the reassembled rocking chairs and fed Kirstin her noon meal before the others came in to eat. She watched Gunlaug rethreading her loom.

"I will thread the other as soon as I am done with this one." Gunlaug finished with the plain off-white string that formed the warp and tied on a yarn of deep blue to start the weft. When she threw the shuttle and slammed the batten on the first thread, she smiled and inhaled a deep breath. "My first rug in the new land. This one is to go by Gerd's bed. She needs some color in that room. Perhaps we could buy the fabric for a quilt for her bed. After all, she refused the feather bed, saying her corn and hay mattress is just fine. Once we shear those sheep next spring, perhaps we can use some of the wool for her mattress. If only I had some money to buy more."

"Don't say that too loud, or she'll go find some and trade a hog for it."

"Who'll go find some what?" Nilda asked as she brought in a cup of coffee for each of them. "Since you are too busy to come out there, I brought it in here."

Selma carried in two of the kitchen chairs, and Nilda fetched another before she returned to grab the tray of gingerbread drizzled with hard sauce and the other three coffees. And two cookies and a glass of milk for Eric.

When everyone was seated, Signe announced, "It just dawned on me that Kirstin's birthday is less than two weeks away. With all that has happened, I nearly forgot."

"I didn't." Gerd rolled her eyes. "What a terrifying day that was."

Signe settled her daughter down on the floor and set her dress back to rights. "I thought I was going to die and my baby too, but Gerd saved us."

"You saved me first," Gerd said firmly. She leaned over and lifted Kirstin, who was standing at her knees, jabbering at her, onto her lap. "Uff da. Baby girl, you are getting so big."

"How close to walking is she?" Gunlaug asked as she slammed the batten again.

"She won't let go of anything to step out, just plops back down and crawls." Signe took a sip of her coffee and wrinkled her nose. "Anyone else need a warm-up?" She started to stand, but Selma beat her to it and returned with the coffeepot.

"This feels so like home," Nilda said. "I need to go get my knitting from upstairs."

Signe picked Kirstin up off Gerd's lap. "You go play in your pen, and maybe Eric will come talk with you." She looked at him seated on the floor beside his mor's chair and nibbling on his cookies. Poor little guy probably hadn't had many cookies, at least since his far died. His glass of milk was empty. Signe set a circle of tin measuring cups and a ball of cloth stuffed with bits of leftover cloth in the pen with Kirstin.

"It's about time she had a doll, isn't it?" Gunlaug asked. "I should have brought her one. I wonder what happened to

141

those rag dolls. I must have given them all away." Another slam of the batten.

"She'd probably chew it all up yet. Still teething." Signe watched Gunlaug. "I see you strung the other loom. Perhaps now I can find time to learn how to use it."

"Once it's strung, it's easy. What colors might you want? There are several to choose from over in that box." Gunlaug pointed to a wooden box by the sewing machine under the window. "The wool carders are in there too, so you could start that. We need to get those fleeces carded so we can spin it. I know I taught Nilda how to spin thicker thread for the rugs."

"You taught me what?" Nilda asked as she came through the door.

"To spin thicker thread for the rugs."

Nilda set her bag of knitting on the chair and went over to pick up the carders. "It's a shame we don't have another set. This is good for winter evenings. Why, I'm sure we could get Leif to card, and maybe even Knute."

"After their homework." Signe finished her coffee and stretched. Kirstin was sound asleep in her pen. "I'm going to the cellar to get apples for the pies for tomorrow. This was a nice break."

"I'll do the crusts." Nilda followed Signe.

"And I'll help peel." Selma gathered up the tray and carried it to the kitchen.

"Gerd, how about you keep me company?" Gunlaug asked. "You can knit in here."

"Or sew." Gerd pointed to the sewing machine in front of the window. "I want to finish the dress I started for Kirstin. Perhaps I will be ready to try it on her when she wakes up. I'm making it plenty big."

Signe looked at the clock when the pies went in a while later.

"Oh my goodness, dinnertime is almost here, and we've not even started."

"I'll get the soup from the well house," Nilda called over her shoulder as she was going out the door.

Working together, they had dinner ready in no time, and Signe thanked God for having her family around her again.

The wagon was full when they left for church the next morning. Gunlaug and Gerd sat up on the seat with Rune, and everyone else sat in back. As usual, Mrs. Benson greeted them at the door.

"I'm so glad you're here." She reached for Kirstin, who went willingly into her arms. "Finally, little one, you let me hold you."

"You bribed her with a cookie the last few times you've seen her, remember?" Signe said, laughing. "She never forgets where cookies come from."

"You are such a smart and beautiful little baby. Well, not really a baby anymore." Mrs. Benson had to untangle a questing fist from the veil on her hat. Once Signe had helped free the hat, Mrs. Benson handed Kirstin back. "And you must be Selma and Eric. We are so pleased to have you here."

"This is Mrs. Benson, the best neighbor anyone could have," Signe finished the introductions.

"Mr. Kielund and his children have already gone to sit down. We will introduce you after the service."

The gentle music from the organ shifted into announcing it was time to begin.

When they were seated, Nilda whispered to Selma, "He is sitting two rows behind us on the other side of the aisle."

They all stood for the opening hymn. As they sang "Holy, Holy, Holy," Signe, as usual, felt she was being lifted up to float above, rising like the music to praise her Lord. She wanted to sing it in Norwegian but made herself read the words in the hymnal to sing in English.

After the service, Mr. and Mrs. Benson brought Oskar Kielund and his children over to meet Selma.

"Good to see you again," Rune said, shaking Mr. Kielund's hand. "We want you to meet our cousin Selma Strand and her son, Eric." Signe stood right next to Selma, as if to give her courage.

"I am glad to meet you," Mr. Kielund said, looking as nervous as Selma did. "These are my children, Olaf, who is five and named after my grandfather, and Katie, who is three and named after her mother, Katrina." He stumbled a bit on his wife's name.

Signe translated for Selma, who then said, "I am glad to meet you too, and this is my son, Eric. He is five also." She stumbled over the words as she spoke the English Nilda and Signe had coached her on.

Neither of them looked the other in the face, Signe thought, but time would help. "Mrs. Strand is working on her English, but she came in such a hurry, she didn't have much time."

Rune introduced his mor, then said, "We'd like you to join us for dinner."

Mr. Kielund paused a moment. "We can do that." He included a nod and a half look at Selma.

Reverend Skarstead came to their group. "I see you've all met." He extended his hand to Gunlaug and used Norwegian. "And you must be the mother of these fine people. Welcome to America." He shook Gunlaug's hand, cupping it between both of his.

"And this is our cousin Selma Strand and her son, Eric." Rune turned to Selma and spoke in Norwegian. "This man has become not only our pastor but also a very good friend."

"Takk," Reverend Skarstead said. "Welcome. It is my pleasure to meet more of your families. I will continue to pray God's blessings on all of you and us." He shook hands with the rest of them and smiled reassuringly at Oskar. "All will be well." He turned to Rune. "How are you doing on the house?"

"All wintered in, but lots to finish on the inside. Winter and evening work."

"Can you use a couple of hands? Both Oskar and I are fair finish carpenters."

"I'd be glad to help too," Mr. Benson threw in. "How about next Saturday?"

"Ah, why—why, thank you. But you have already done so much."

"Don't worry, your turn will come to help someone else. Besides, swinging a hammer feels mighty good after all the reading and writing and office work I have to do. My wife helps as much as she can with that sort of thing, but now that the garden is put to bed, as I said, carpentry will feel real good." The reverend clapped Mr. Kielund on the shoulder. "I guarantee you'll have a fine meal at their house. All of you—enjoy."

As they were loading the wagons to head home, Leif went over to little Olaf. "I can take you down to our barn to see the new kittens. You could even hold one."

Olaf looked at him, eyes big, but he nodded and turned to his sister. "Can she come too?"

"Ja, and Eric too. Just think, you and he are both five. Do you have a dog? We do. His name is Rufus, and he likes to play, especially chasing sticks. You could throw a stick for him, if you like."

Olaf looked up at his father, who nodded.

"Good. See you at our farm." Leif ran back to the wagon

to jump in beside Knute, both of them dangling their legs over the back of the wagon bed.

Knute nudged his younger brother. "What did you say to them?"

"That I'd show them the kittens and that Rufus likes to chase sticks."

"Hmm. If only we could get him to bring them back."

"Maybe he'll get it today."

Signe nodded to herself. Maybe they'd all get it today. Leave it to Leif.

Chapter 14

Oh, for pity's sake, you could at least look at each other. Nilda bit her tongue. Thoughts were one thing, but saying something right now might only make it worse.

"We have plenty more," Signe announced. "Mr. Kielund, please help yourself." She passed the platter of baked rabbit around again. After he declined, Knute and Bjorn took more and Ivar, after a glance at Signe, cleared the platter.

This was almost as bad as having Einar back, only the feeling around the table was not anger. Just very quiet.

"Would you like to go see the kittens after dinner?" Leif tried again after catching Olaf's eye when he finally looked up from his empty plate.

The little boy shook his head—barely.

Katie climbed up in her pa's lap. They did not call him Far but Pa. Another difference, but surely not insurmountable.

Nilda rolled her eyes at Signe and stood. "I'll take your plates, then." When Selma started to join her, Nilda frowned at her.

"I will cut the pie." Selma motioned for Eric to stay seated.

"I want to see the kittens," Eric whispered to Leif.

Leif grinned back. "Ja, we will do that." He answered in

147

Norwegian, then switched to English. "Katie and Olaf, you can come too. After dessert. Mor and Tante Nilda make the best pies." He grinned at Gerd.

You two are the best. Nilda smiled at them both.

Selma dished up the apple pie and set a small plate in front of each person at the table.

Mr. Kielund softly said, "Thank you."

Ah, two words spoken. Uff da! Nilda picked up the coffeepot. "More coffee to go with your pie, Mr. Kielund?"

"Yes, thank you."

"You sure have a fine team, Mr. Kielund," Ivar said. "How I would like a team like that one day. They are so much bigger than Norwegian horses."

"I have not found Norwegian horses in this country. These are Belgians."

"And one is named Petunia." Knute grinned.

"And Daisy. My wife named them, and she loved flowers. They're the best team I've ever had. They can skid those big trees like none else I've seen, even when they get iced in."

When the pie was finished, Signe nodded to her boys. "You can be excused." She looked at Mr. Kielund's two children. "You can go along, and Eric too."

"Thank you, but I think we need to get on home." Oskar pushed back his chair. "What a fine meal. Best we've had in a long time. Come on, children. Say thank you."

Both of them mumbled a thank-you and took their pa's hands as if afraid he might leave them behind.

"Go say good-bye, at least." Nilda nudged Selma, who shook her head.

Rune and Signe followed them out to the porch. "Thanks for coming." Rune went to stand at the horses' heads. "See you in church next Sunday, if not before."

Kielund nodded. "Thank you again, Mrs. Carlson, for such a fine meal." He backed up his team, turned, and they trotted out the lane.

Nilda joined Signe and Rune on the porch. "Well, that was a disappointment."

"Don't give up yet," Rune cautioned as he wagged his head. "Not what I expected, though."

"I wanted to shake them both."

"Now, Nilda, patience is a good thing." He snorted. "Come on, boys, let's go on down to the barn. Knute, you bring Kirstin on your shoulders, and Leif, you bring Eric. Somebody is going to have a good time today." He turned to Signe, who was fussing over the baby. "I will make sure she is all right. You could come along if you want." He raised his voice. "In fact, you could all come if you want. We have mighty fine kittens."

Back at the house some time later, Gunlaug commented, "Since that cat had her kittens in the barn, she might train them to be good hunters. It would help with the mouse and rat horde there."

"I wonder if once she weans them, she will come back to the house. Having the two of them here was such a pleasure." Signe pulled the coffeepot forward.

"Kirstin sure thought so, but now she finds Rufus more entertaining." Nilda picked up Gul and petted her until she purred. "Hearing and feeling a cat purr is such a comfortable sound." She sat down on a chair and motioned Eric over. "See, you can pet her like this." When he did as she said and felt the cat purring, he looked up at her, almost smiled, and stroked the cat again. When he laid his ear against the cat and kept one hand on her back, even his sober little face relaxed, and he sighed. When the cat jumped down, Nilda held out her arms, and he let her lift him onto her lap.

"Now, that's better," she whispered against his head, which nestled into her chest. "Much better. I held you when you were just a baby and helped you learn to walk. I know you don't remember, but I sure do. You were so cute." She murmured her Norwegian words against his soft hair.

Nilda looked up and saw Selma smiling at them. If only she would smile like that at Mr. Kielund. He'd lose his heart for sure. Or at least be more interested.

"I keep thinking of those two little ones who were here today," Nilda said. "So horribly shy. They sure need a woman's touch again."

"Ja, but their mor left them, remember, and it wasn't that long ago. No wonder they hold on to their far so tightly. They're afraid he will leave too." She looked at Eric and then at Nilda. Her message was clear.

"Give them all time," Gunlaug said. "I know a little something about grief. Give them time."

"That's for sure," Gerd added. "Poor little kids, losing a parent like that. How can they be anything but afraid?" She had a faraway look in her eye. "Good thing time can indeed make things easier."

Gunlaug smiled sadly. "I certainly hope so."

Gerd looked at her. "You haven't had enough time yet, Gunlaug."

"Will there ever be enough time?"

Gerd studied her hands for a moment. "Perhaps not."

The next afternoon, when the boys rode in from school, Leif slid off Rosie with the dinner pails and waved a letter. "Tante Selma, you got a letter."

She wiped her hands on her apron and reached for it. "It's not from Norway."

"Mrs. Benson gave it to me." He dug in his lunch pail and pulled out a packet. "She made me promise not to look until we got home." With a wide grin, he opened the packet and displayed three peppermint sticks. "One for Eric too."

"Who is it from?" Nilda asked, her curiosity eating at her like a mouse on cheese.

The heat started in Selma's neck and climbed up her face. "Mr. Kielund. But it's in English. Leif, can you read this, please?"

Leif laid down his peppermint sticks and spread the letter out flat on the table, pointing to the words as he translated. "'I would like to invite you to come see my farm on Thursday. If you accept my invitation, I will come for you at one. Please reply by way of Mrs. Benson. Respectfully, Oskar Kielund.'"

"Oh." Selma looked perplexed. "Takk, Leif. Tusen takk."

"You're welcome." He scooped up his peppermint sticks and hustled off to the other room.

"And?" Nilda asked pointedly.

"What?"

"And you will go?" Nilda nearly stamped her foot at the hesitation on Selma's face. *Lord, help us.*

"I—I . . ."

Nilda and Signe both nodded. "Ja, you will go. Write to him now and invite him to come earlier for dinner."

"B-but what about Eric?"

Nilda stared at the ceiling. "He can stay here with us just fine. If he cries, he will stop. If Mr. Kielund asks for him to come too, he will go with you. This isn't a lifetime commitment yet. Just a ride to see his farm." She spoke slowly with extremely precise enunciation. The tightening of her jawline said more than the smile that was more of a grimace. When she rolled her eyes behind Selma's back, even Gerd had to bite back a laugh.

"I've got chores to do." Leif headed out the door. "Bye."

Kirstin gabbled at him, but when the door shut behind him, a frown replaced her smile, and thunder descended as she worked herself into a howl.

Gerd swooped her up and kissed her forehead. "Come on, little one, let's go find the cat."

"We need to make her some more toys," Gunlaug suggested with a nod. "Thor used to carve heads for dolls, and remember those trains he made for the boys?" Wistfulness sneaked over her face. "They're in a box for other grandchildren. I wish I had brought some along."

"As if you had any more space." Nilda headed for the workroom. "Since Selma said she'd make supper, the rest of us can get some work done in the other room."

"When we work in there, it's like the years and all that has happened in between kind of slip away and . . . and I don't know, I'm not saying it very well but . . ." Gunlaug wiped at the edge of her eye and sniffed. "Takk, tusen takk."

Another note rode home with the boys on Wednesday.

Thank you, that sounds like a good idea. I will be there at noon tomorrow, like you said. —Oskar Kielund

"Mrs. Benson must be getting a charge out of being the passer of notes." Nilda wiggled her eyebrows at Selma. "Where's Eric?"

"At the barn with Leif and Knute. Darkness seems to fall earlier with each day."

"That's only because it is. But at least we never have days of no sun like Norway and the lands up to the north in Canada."

Gerd tied Kirstin in the rocking chair. "To keep you out from under people's feet."

Kirstin babbled at her and slammed her hand against the spoons tied on a string to entertain her. Sometimes, like now, she used them as a statement of ire.

"Can we have chicken and dumplings tomorrow?" Selma asked. "You said there was an old hen ready for the stew pot."

"I know exactly which chicken." Nilda grinned. Supper was almost ready when she brought in two hens, all plucked and dressed. "We can start these tonight and let them simmer. Leif said one of these pecked him so hard she drew blood. I don't think she's laid an egg since." As she talked, she pumped water into a deep kettle and plopped the two birds in.

She wondered if Mr. Kielund even had chickens. Would Rune's family give the Kielunds any farm animals to help them forward? Probably. That was like Rune and Signe.

"*Gud dag*," Mr. Kielund said when he walked into the kitchen.

Selma nodded and replied, "Good day." Then the two of them actually smiled at each other. They had both learned the greeting for the other.

Nilda and Signe could have turned cartwheels.

"Come sit down before the food gets cold." Gerd ushered the others to the table. "Since Selma did the cooking, the rest of us will do the serving." She set a bowl of biscuits on the table. "Rune, grace, please."

This time the meal passed pleasantly, even if Mr. Kielund said very little.

Nilda turned to the others after Mr. Kielund helped Selma and Eric up onto the wagon seat after the meal. "At least they actually greeted each other, and both of them learned for the other." Her head kept nodding. "I think there is hope after all. On top of that, they looked at each other every once in a while at the table."

"There was indeed improvement," Signe agreed, her grin nearly matching Nilda's.

Rune rolled his eyes. "Go easy on the matchmaking, you two. After all—"

"After all, that's why he paid for her ticket, in case you had forgotten. We are just helping the situation along a little bit."

Nilda was sure she heard him mutter something about his sister as he left the house.

Signe caught her husband's mutter, which left her smiling even wider. "I think the children will be fine if they get a chance to play together without adults hovering nearby, even though they don't speak the same language. Children seem able to get around the language barrier far better than adults."

Some time later, Signe left off the spinning and headed for the kitchen. "I can't stand this waiting. I'm going to make cookies, lots of cookies. If any of you want to help, I won't turn down an offer."

"You mix 'em, and I'll roll and you can cut," Nilda said, following her.

They were on their third batch of cookies, sour cream with bits of raisins on top and applesauce with ginger. The applesauce ones they cut into diamonds and sprinkled with brown sugar.

"Bring the coffee and cookies in here, please," Gerd called at the stop of the *kathunk-kathunk* of the pedal that powered the sewing machine. That along with the slam of the loom and the whir of the spinning wheel made music that sent Kirstin to sleep every time.

The sun was already on its downward slide when the boys

trotted up the lane, and Leif bailed off Rosie to bring the dinner pails inside. "Another letter, this time from Norway, for Bestemor."

Gunlaug threw the shuttle across and slammed the batten before turning to smile at Leif. "You most certainly are the bearer of good tidings. Takk." She looked at the handwriting. "Ah, from Johann, what a nice surprise." She paused. "Or bad news."

"One for Nilda too." Leif handed her the envelope and snagged a cookie off the plate. One bite, and his eyes widened. "These are really good." He bit off another point of the applesauce diamond. "Where's Eric?"

"With his mor and Mr. Kielund."

"Oh. We had a spelling test today, and I got a hundred percent. Knute missed two." He headed for the pantry and poured himself a glass of milk. "Can Kirstin have a cookie?"

"Let her have a bite of yours. She crumbles everything when she tries to feed herself." Signe pointed at the rocking chair where Kirstin was tied in, reaching for Leif. "She is almost as good as Rufus at knowing when you will be home."

"Ef, Ef." Kirstin raised her voice a notch.

"She's trying to say my name. Listen to her." Leif's face split in a grin. "Leif, baby girl, Leif."

"Ef, Ef."

When he broke off a piece off his cookie and handed it to her, she used both hands to stuff it in her mouth, but crumbs still dusted her front.

Knute rushed through the door. "Tomorrow you take care of Rosie so I can get out in the woods for a little while at least." He grabbed a handful of cookies and headed for the door again.

"You know you do not have to go out there," Gerd said. "Not since Einar is gone."

"I know, but I want to. I'd much rather be out there than in school." The door slammed behind him.

Leif shrugged. "He didn't do real good on his history test either. Mr. Larsson said he needed to work harder on his homework."

Signe nodded. "Did he know the test was coming?"

"Ja, for the last three days."

"I see."

"Please don't tell him I said anything."

"Let me worry about that."

"You do the other chores and I'll come help you milk." Nilda sent Leif a smile over her shoulder. "Just come and get me."

The jangle of harnesses and clopping of hooves announced Selma's return.

"Takk," she called over her shoulder as she ushered Eric in ahead of her. She hung up her coat.

"Can I go down to the barn with Leif?" the little boy asked.

"Of course. Would you like a cookie first?"

He nodded and took one.

"What do you say?"

"Who baked them?" he asked.

"We all did." Nilda smiled down at him.

He nodded again. "Then takk to all of you." And out the door he went, leaving the women smiling and nodding at one another.

Nilda looked at Selma. "So?"

"So what?"

"So how did the visit go?" Nilda's tone said even more.

"He has a good, well-kept farm. But the house sure could use a cleaning."

"And?" Getting Selma to talk sometimes was as hard as cracking walnuts.

"And poor little Katie and Olaf. He has a hard time even braiding her hair. But he tries to be both mor and far. I told him we could come clean his house, if he wanted. Not speaking the same language . . ." She shook her head. "I have to learn English."

"We've been trying," Gunlaug soothed.

"I know, but I have to work harder at it. It will be good for all of us." Selma paused. "Won't it?" Her voice squeaked on the question. She looked at Nilda. "So much change."

Was that a tear she saw in Selma's eye?

Chapter 15

"I hate to leave right in the middle of this." Nilda checked the note again. Yes, Mrs. Schoenleber wanted her to come today. She had given Nilda the grace of an extra week since her family was arriving, but the job needed to start soon. Not that Nilda had any real idea what she was going to be doing at the huge formal house, but she'd said be ready at ten when George arrived to take her to Blackduck.

"She must want you to work for her mighty bad to go to all this trouble." Gunlaug looked at her daughter. "It doesn't make a lot of sense to me, but I am truly happy for you."

"Just so you don't go getting uppity on us." Signe stirred the diapers in the boiler on the stove.

"I'm really afraid of that." Nilda rolled her eyes and knelt in front of the pen where Kirstin was banging a wooden spoon on one of the pots. "Now, don't you forget your Tante Nilda, you hear me, little one?"

"As if anyone can hear anything with that going on." Gerd picked up the smocked dress she'd just tried on the squirming girl. "All I need to do now is hem it. You know, if you'd give up and walk, you could wear this," she said to Kirstin, "but crawling and dresses don't do well together."

"She'll probably take her first steps while I'm in Blackduck, and I'll miss it." Nilda stood at the sound of a trotting team coming up the lane. "See you all on Sunday."

Picking up her satchel, she blew kisses to Kirstin, hugged her mor, and, tucking the scarf Gerd had knitted for her around her neck, went out to meet her driver.

"Good to see you, miss. What a beautiful drive." George helped her up into the seat of an elegant open carriage and tucked a robe around her legs. "I debated on bringing the victoria, but with such a perfect fall day, here we are." He settled her satchel beneath his seat, mounted up to the driver's seat, and clucked the horses into a trot as soon as they straightened around.

I should have brought my knitting, Nilda thought. *I could be doing something.* "Mr. George?"

"I am not Mr. George. I'm just George."

"You must have a last name."

"Hemmelschmidt. Quite a mouthful, wouldn't you say? George is much easier."

"Do you mind if I ask you some questions? I need to practice my English."

"Well, then, you must make sure you understand what I say. If you're not sure, ask me. All right?" He smiled at her over his shoulder.

"Would it be easier if I were sitting up there with you?"

"Ah, yes, it might be. But that would not be proper, you see. Madam Schoenleber takes her position in Blackduck very seriously."

"Her position?"

"As a leader of society. Blackduck was a mighty rough town

when her father built that house and moved his family there. Social graces were few and far between. But he wanted his family to grow up with good manners and give back what the area had given him by supporting education, the library, and the building of churches and businesses. He grew up in Minneapolis, and his family there often made fun of the backwoods town of Blackduck."

"Oh dear. I lost track. Can you repeat it more slowly?"

He did so.

"My goodness. It looks like he was successful."

"When the timber companies started moving in, he foresaw the need for a railroad system, and while he had bought timberland, the railroads are what really made his fortune."

"Would you say that again, please?"

He smiled and repeated his sentence.

"One man did all that?"

"Oh, no. There were others, but he was the brains behind it all."

"What brains?"

"You know, his ideas and his ability to put his ideas into action." He tapped his head. "Brains inside the head."

"Oh, I see. *Hjerner.*" She tapped her head also.

By the time they arrived at the mansion, she felt that if she shook her head, some of the things she'd learned might fall out. "Thank you for your help in history and English."

"Mrs. Solvang, the cook, will be more than willing to help you too. In fact, she will be better, because she spoke both Norwegian and English growing up. You'll find Madam Schoenleber a wonderful person to work for."

I just hope I can meet her expectations. Nilda thought so loud, she was afraid she'd spoken. "Thank you, George." She let him help her down to the walk.

"I'll put your satchel in your room."

Charles opened the front door for her. "Welcome, Miss Carlson. Mrs. Schoenleber said for me to hang up your things and for you to meet her in her sitting room, which is also her office."

"Thank you." Nilda handed him her coat and scarf and unpinned her hat. "I can put them up. After all, I work here now. I'm not a guest."

"You take that up with Mrs. Schoenleber. I just do as I'm told." His smile removed any stiffness from his words. "You go through there." He pointed to the door of the sitting room.

Nilda tapped on the door before opening it. "Just me."

"Oh, my dear, it is so good to see you. And how is your mor? We'll have to make sure she comes with you sometime so I can meet her." She sat at the desk in front of the window. Laying down her pen, she straightened the paper she had been writing on.

Nilda nodded. "She would enjoy that very much, I think."

"I see you've been practicing your English."

"Yes, ma'am. Signe and I take classes with Mr. Larsson in Benson's Corner."

"Is he a good teacher?"

"Very good. Ah, excellent."

"I heard that you are an excellent student." Mrs. Schoenleber leaned back in her chair.

"I think he loves to teach."

"He *lives* to teach, but because he plays the organ on Sundays and teaches five days a week, I do not see him very often. I'm hoping he will come and play for our socials at times. I had thought to keep them on Saturday nights, but if I want him to attend, some will need to be on Fridays." She propped her chin on her index finger. "We have plenty to do to prepare for the next social. I hope your brother Ivar will come too." She stood and laid her palms on her desk. "I suspect you are curious as to what you will be doing here."

Nilda nodded. "Yes, indeed I am."

A bell rang.

"Ah, the dinner bell. We will talk over our meal, so bring a pad and pencil with you. You'll find an ample supply in that closet." She pointed to a closed door. "I believe keeping that stocked will be one of your responsibilities. Have you ever used a typewriter?"

"N-no, but I've heard of them."

"I'm thinking of purchasing one, so we will learn together." Mrs. Schoenleber moved toward the door. "I hope you are hungry. Cook appreciates folks with a good appetite." When they were seated at the table, she bowed her head. "How would you like to say the grace today? I would love to hear the Norwegian one." After the amen, in which Mrs. Schoenleber joined in, she laid her hand on top of Nilda's. "Thank you, my dear. Someday you must translate that for me."

Charles set a flat bowl of soup in front of each of them. "Cream of carrot soup. Cook said to tell you she is trying a new recipe, so you must tell her if you think it needs something else."

Nilda looked at her hostess. "Mrs. Solvang wants my opinion?"

"Yes, Verna loves to experiment with spices and foods. By the way, she goes by Cook or Verna, not Mrs. Solvang. She has been a widow since before she started working for me, which must have been over ten years ago." Mrs. Schoenleber thought a moment. "Hmm, eleven years by now. I found her in Minneapolis and convinced her that Blackduck was not the end of civilization." She dipped her spoon into the soup and savored her first taste, nodding.

Nilda copied her by picking up the round spoon, now knowing what that one was for. With all the utensils at the place setting, it was easy to be confused. She nodded too. "It is very good."

"You must tell her that."

By the time they finished the main dish of lamb stew and the dessert of custard with whipped cream, Nilda wondered if they would always eat like this. One could get spoiled quickly.

Back in the sitting room, Mrs. Schoenleber introduced Nilda to the leather-bound book she called her brain, as it contained her calendar and pages for notes. Another similar book held all the addresses of family, friends, and business associates.

"I still hold the position of head of the board of Schmitz Enterprises, our family business. Schmitz was my maiden name, you see. My brother Heinrik is the chief manager. He lives in Minneapolis, so I frequently take the train to the cities for meetings and such. As your English improves, I will expect you to help me with correspondence. I have Miss Walstead coming to help you with reading and writing in English also. She will be here for two hours each afternoon." She glanced at the walnut clock on her desk. "Then my dressmaker will be here at four. Don't be offended, but you need gowns for the social and business events we will attend. We'll start with several waists, skirts, a more formal outfit, and one for travel. Here in Blackduck, we will wear mostly skirts and waists. Oh, and a good wool coat for winter."

Nilda felt her mouth drop open. "I—ah—"

Mrs. Schoenleber patted her hand. "I consider this all business expenses. You will be representing me, and in spite of what some people say, clothes do make the woman as well as the man. Those who dress more stylishly are respected more."

"But—but . . ."

"I know it's a lot to take in. Miss Walstead has taught high school, and now she substitute teaches and assists me when I need her. The two of you will work in the library—which, by the way, is another area in which I want your assistance. Not long ago I received a shipment of books, and I have not had time to catalogue them and organize them on the shelves." She looked up at the sound of the knocker on the front door. "That must be her. Come along, and we'll get you started. Mrs. Jones is the seamstress. Oh, and one other thing—have you ever used a telephone?"

Nilda shook her head. "No. Mrs. Benson has one at the store."

"I'm sure it won't be long until everyone here has a telephone and electricity instead of gaslights."

Out in the hall, Mrs. Schoenleber greeted Miss Walstead, who was half as round as she was tall. Her silver-streaked hair was in a tidy bun, and pince nez glasses were perched on her straight nose. She carried a very pretty brocade satchel.

Nilda had a feeling this woman could be formidable, but right now her smile was gracious, and she and Mrs. Schoenleber acted like old friends, which perhaps they were. Oh, there was so much to learn.

Mrs. Schoenleber led them to the library and closed the door behind her on her way out. What an amazing room. One whole wall was nothing except shelves full of books, from the floor up to the high ceiling. So many books! About six or seven feet above the floor, a metal track ran horizontally along the front of a shelf. It was, Nilda realized, the track for the ladder leaning against it. Little wheels at the top of the ladder ran along the track. Larger wheels were attached to the bottom of the ladder. You could push the ladder from one end to the other so that you could reach the highest shelves easily. Nilda realized she was staring and quickly closed her mouth.

Charles had made a fire that snapped and crackled in the fireplace, warming the room and making it more welcoming than formal. Miss Walstead beckoned Nilda over to the leather chairs in front of the fire. Nilda waited until the lady had seated herself, then took the chair opposite her.

"Gertrude has told me much about you and how pleased she is that you will be helping her. So, since I am to teach you as quickly as possible, here is what we will do. We will speak only English. You will read aloud from grade school textbooks at first and move on to newspapers. Have you done any writing in English?"

"No, ma'am." Nilda shook her head.

Miss Walstead smiled. "I know this must be overwhelming at first, but you will learn quickly. By the way, Mr. Larsson was one of my students before he went on to college. I believe that the more capable one is, the more a teacher should expect from them. You can rest assured that I drilled him hard. Music was always his reward for hard work. He was and is an amazing young man. When he plays the organ or the piano, those instruments become extensions of him. He loses himself in the music."

Nilda swallowed. "My onkel played the fiddle, a Hardanger, like that."

"Now, let us begin." Miss Walstead reached into her satchel, opened a small book, and handed it to Nilda. "Start at the beginning here and read to me."

Nilda sucked in a deep breath. "'What shall we dough—'"

"That is pronounced 'do.'"

"'What shall we do?' sayed—said—Fanny to . . .'" Nilda struggled.

"John."

"'To John. I do'"—she knew that word now!—"'not like to sit . . . still. Shall we . . . hoo—hoont for eggs in the barn?'"

"Stop. Try this." Miss Walstead handed her another book, a thinner one. "Page twenty-six. First read the ten vocabulary words there."

Nilda turned to the page. Who would guess that this word was "night"? It looked nothing like it sounded. And "eyes" was just as mysterious. "'What bird is this? It is an owl. What big eyes it has. Yes, but it cannot see well by day. The owl can see best at night. Nat Pond has a pet owl.'"

"Excellent! Nilda, you are a very quick learner. Next page."

Thanks to Mr. Larsson, Nilda stumbled along, swallowing the fear that tried to choke her off.

"All right, good. Now I know where we need to start." Miss Walstead drew two books from her satchel and handed one to Nilda. "We will begin on page twenty. I will expect you to read the pages leading up to twenty when you get better at English. Don't worry about it now. Let us go down the lists, reading together."

Nilda was deeply thankful when Miss Walstead said, "I think we will stop for tea." She reached behind her and pulled the cord to call the kitchen. After ordering tea, she stood and stretched. "We must remember to move the body more too. When you do that, your mind works better also."

A knock sounded at the door, and Stella backed her way in with a tray. "Cook figured you would be ready about now." She set the tray on the low table between the chairs. "Mrs. Schoenleber said to remind you that the dressmaker will be here in an hour. And, Miss Walstead, she said to remind you that the invitation to dinner still stands."

"Tell Gertrude that I will be delighted to stay for dinner, if I may keep working with Nilda at the same time."

"Yes, ma'am."

Miss Walstead poured tea and handed Nilda a delicate cup. "What are you drinking, Nilda?"

"I am drinking tea."

"Would you like sugar?" Miss Walstead gestured with the sugar bowl.

"Yes, I would like sugar. Takk. I mean, thank you."

And so they went.

Some time later, Charles knocked at the door and announced, "Mrs. Jones is here."

"Fine, we will move to the sewing room." Miss Walstead set her book down. "Do you know where the sewing room is?"

Nilda shook her head. "I am confused." That was a word she knew well now.

"Come along."

The English lessons continued as Mrs. Jones measured Nilda and showed her and Mrs. Schoenleber fabric samples and pictures of garments. Everyone spoke English. *I am confused* became the cause of many grins.

"Are you sure?" Nilda gestured to all the paraphernalia. "I mean . . ." She sucked in a breath. "All this?"

Mrs. Jones smiled. "Be grateful she is not insisting you wear a corset."

Nilda motioned to the garment of torture laid over the back of a chair. "Corset?" She rolled her eyes.

"Yes, but I have not entirely decided against it. Just the overly tight lacing of it." Mrs. Schoenleber motioned pulling the strings.

"She is well muscled with not an ounce of fat," Mrs. Jones said. "But with a ball gown, it might be wise."

Nilda blinked, trying to follow the conversation.

"Speak slowly," Miss Walstead admonished the seamstress. "I think today has about overwhelmed her."

"You are probably right. If I were learning another language in a rush course like this, I would be overwhelmed."

"Overwhelmed." Nilda stumbled on the word. Miss Walstead explained it.

Supper was more of the same, so when Nilda went to bed and picked up her textbook to study some more, she fell asleep with the book on her chest. When it hit the floor during the night, she woke enough to pick it up and place it on the nightstand. So much for extra study time.

The next morning after breakfast, Mrs. Schoenleber had Nilda copy the invitation she had prepared for the social coming up in two weeks. She studied the copy when Nilda finished, nodding. "Good. Now, here is the list of names and addresses of those who attended last time and others recommended by those same people."

Nilda glanced down the list, her gaze stopping at the name most dreaded. Dreng Nygaard. She had hoped he'd left town. Should she tell Mrs. Schoenleber about his reputation in Norway or not?

Chapter 16

The temperature dropped, staying below freezing.

"We start butchering tomorrow," Rune announced at breakfast on Tuesday. "We'll sort the hogs and put four in a separate pen. That's about what we can do in one day."

"But we have to go to school." Knute stared at his far.

"There's plenty to do. We've sold three butchered hogs, so we'll do them first. It's cold enough to hang them in the machine shed. Good thing we got doors put on that so the meat is safe from wild animals." Rune looked at Signe. "How about sending a note to Mr. Benson to put on the board, that we have butchered hogs for sale? We should have done that earlier."

"I will."

"We have three and a half sold, right?" Knute asked. "So we keep half of one?"

"Yes."

"So we will brine the hindquarter, but what about the shoulder?"

Rune looked to Gerd and Signe. "We can do both and the bacon. It might be good to grind some for sausage and smoke that too."

"I'd rather make sausage patties and put them in a crock," Gerd suggested, then shrugged. "So many choices and all good. The pig for the Bensons will pay off our bill there, not that we've run up much lately." She heaved a sigh. "The cost of feed was most of what we owe."

"I've been thinking on another idea," Rune said. "We could increase the size of the smokehouse and besides our own, smoke for some of the people in town. I know Reverend Skarstead talked about buying half a hog, but he has no way to smoke it himself."

"What would you do for wood?" Signe asked.

"You'd have to find more hardwoods. Pine is not good." Gerd leaned forward. "Come on, Kirstin, walk over here." She patted her hands together and held them out. "You can make it."

Kirstin was standing at her mor's knees. She bobbed up and down, took one step, and bobbed some more. She waved her free hand at Gerd, took one more step, then plopped down on her rear and crawled the two feet to Gerd's knees.

"Now walk to me." Leif dropped to his knees and held his hands toward her.

The others all watched, almost holding their collective breath.

"Come on," Leif urged.

Keeping her eyes on him, Kirstin took one step, then let go of Gerd and took another before falling into his hands.

"You did it." He waved her hands in the air. "You took a real step!" He picked her up and swung her around, making her shriek with laughter. "Kirstin walked all by herself."

"We better get over to our house," Bjorn said when he came through the door. "I hitched Rosie to the cart." Rune had sent him over to stoke the stove so the house would be warm.

"Good thinking. Thank you, son." Rune held Signe's coat for her, and Bjorn held Gerd's. With Kirstin wrapped in a quilt, they all scrambled into the cart, and Rosie trotted them over to the new house. Then Bjorn drove her back to the barn.

After the boys went up to bed and Gerd had taken Kirstin to her room and shut the door, Rune banked the fire so he and Signe could climb the stairs to their room.

"I'm going to plant posts in a line from the barn to this house for when the blizzards come. We need to do it before the ground freezes solid." Rune hooked his shirt and pants over the pegs in the wall. "It would sure be handy if these houses were closer together. I've thought more than once about moving that one, like you said."

"But what about the cellar?" Signe snuggled closer to him, laying her arm across his chest.

"I know. We'll see how we do this winter. At least the posts will be in place, though that will take a lot of rope." He rolled over and kissed her. "I like having our own room."

She kissed his chin. "Me too."

While the boys did their chores the next morning, Rune, Ivar, and Bjorn set up the tank for scalding the hogs and started the fire underneath it. Hauling the water in cream cans from the pump took more time, but all was heating when they headed to the old house for breakfast.

"You two better leave a bit early to stop at Benson's," Rune told the younger boys. "Tell Joe his hog will be ready for him on Monday."

"It seems strange without Nilda here. Not that she's been gone long." Gerd set the platter of fried eggs on the table. "The thought of bacon again makes my mouth water."

"I want corn bread with cracklings in it." Signe flipped the pancakes on the griddle. She smiled at Leif and Knute. "Your dinner pails are ready. Make sure you take a blanket along for Rosie." Signe set more pancakes on the table and checked the batter. Gunlaug was busy feeding Kirstin, who liked pancakes with syrup. Since Signe was weaning her, nursing only once or twice a day, the baby had more interest in solid food. "Just think, Kirstin will be one year old next week."

"Will she have a birthday cake?" Leif asked as he shrugged into his coat.

"We might be able to work that out." Gerd turned over the eggs for the women. "She likes sweet things."

"Ja, like pancakes." Gunlaug wiped Kirstin's face and hands. "You're wearing almost as much as you ate."

"As soon as that water is hot enough, we can start."

"Should we make *brokrub*?" Gunlaug asked.

Rune rubbed his hands together. "You grate the potatoes, we'll save the blood."

Gunlaug looked wistful. "I haven't had that for far too long. Remember when we used to make big batches for all the families? Since Thor didn't want to raise hogs any more, we only had it when we butchered a steer. All the meat we have here . . ." She tied the baby into her rocking chair. "But no cod."

"We'll make big batches today," Signe assured her mother-in-law. "I'll get the grinder out. We'll need some of the side pork too."

"Ja, I know." Rune motioned the other two men ahead of him. "Bjorn, what about the rifle?"

"I took it to the barn already." Since they'd moved into the new house, the rifle and shotgun had gone along with them, both on hooks over the kitchen door.

Signe brought potatoes up from the cellar and scrubbed them in the sink while Gerd attached the grinder to the edge of the counter. She flinched when she heard the two rifle shots. At least

Leif was not here. The killings were hard for him. After quartering the potatoes the long way, she fed them into the grinder with one hand and turned the crank with the other. By the time Bjorn brought in the bowl of blood, the mound of salted potatoes was ready for flour and the blood. Once the ingredients were well combined, the women formed the mixture into cup-sized balls around a piece of side pork and lowered them with a wooden spoon into the pot of water simmering gently on the stove.

"We don't have any cheesecloth to cook them in?" Selma asked.

"Sorry, no, but this works fine too. Some fall apart, is all," Signe said.

By the time they finished setting two pots to simmering, Ivar arrived with the hearts and livers in a bucket. "Far said he already rinsed them well, so leave them in cold water."

"Will you ready for dinner at noon?"

"We'll be done with the first two by then. We sure could use Nilda to help scrape."

"I can come if you want." Signe reached for her coat. "Has it warmed up?"

"Not a lot. That wind bites down to the bone. Rune and Bjorn are scraping now. He said the sale hogs will not be scraped." He shook his head. "We can manage, unless you have nothing else to do." He ducked the dish cloth his mor threw at him. They could hear him laughing as the door closed.

"At least if we grind the sausage for patties, we don't have to clean out the intestines for casings." Signe never had appreciated that stinky task, but if they wanted smoked sausages, it had to be done. The grinder had an attachment for the casings.

The first pot of brokrub was ready for dinner when the men trooped in, this time with the leaves of fat that would become lard after being ground and rendered.

When Gerd took her first bite, she closed her eyes and sighed. "I thought I'd never taste this again. All of this brings back memories of when I was growing up in Norway."

Signe nodded. "It sounds like they were good memories."

"Ja, they were. My family is all gone now, or at least I think so, since I never hear from them anymore. Or maybe I just quit answering. There wasn't a lot of good news to share from here, other than how many trees were felled."

Gunlaug nodded. "I heard that your mor and far are gone, but I think one of your sisters is still alive. And a brother too, surely nieces and nephews. I can ask Johann to find out, if you want."

Gerd stared at her. "He might be able to. I never thought of that. Or perhaps I just gave up." She passed the bowl of brokrub around again. "I'll think about it."

When the men went back out, the women took turns grinding the slabs of fat and set it in low pans in the oven. They cooked the rest of the brokrub and watched over the pans in the oven, spooning out the melted lard and pouring it into one of the smaller crocks, where it cooled and turned as white as could be. Like the canning and the garden produce, they kept the crock in the cellar. They'd grind the leftover bits of pork into sausage, make patties, and pour lard over them to preserve the meat.

By the time the boys came home from school, three dressed carcasses were hanging in the machine shop to age for the next two or three days before they would start brining the haunches and cutting up the rest of the meat. Bjorn and Ivar were still scraping the bristles off the fourth.

"I'm hauling the innards out to dump in the woods. Do you want to come?" Rune asked the younger boys.

Knute slid to the ground. "I do. Should I hitch up the new team?"

"Ja. Rosie did her work today. Get something to eat first. We're not in a big hurry."

"I'll milk." Leif paused. "Get me a cookie too, would you, please?"

Knute laughed and ran to the house. He turned and hollered, "Maybe even two if you're nice."

"We'll be hearing the coyotes sing tonight," Rune announced as he sat down at the supper table that night. "They've got enough offal out there to feed a few of them."

"Just so they don't get the idea to come near the barn." Signe set the big bowl of brokrub in the middle of the table. "Heated in cream, just the way you like it."

"There will probably be more fighting than singing." Ivar inhaled the steam rising from the bowl. "This will be even better tomorrow. That's what Mor always says."

"Only because it is so." Gunlaug took her place beside Gerd at the table.

"Kirstin walked from Tante Gerd to me when I came in from school. You should have seen her, she was so excited." Leif spread his arms wide. "At least this far."

"Leif?" Eric tugged on his sleeve.

"What?"

"I went to see the kittens today. Mor took me. When they get older, can we take one to Olaf and Katie? They need a kitten."

"You sure can, but it will be a while. Probably a month."

"How long is that?"

"Thirty days."

"That's a long time."

Listening to their conversation, Signe smiled. Eric was stringing more words together every day. She'd almost been afraid that he'd be quiet for the rest of his life. Or at least the foreseeable future. And perhaps, by the end of a month, he and Selma would be living with the Kielunds. Perhaps they needed to start planning a wedding. After all, it was bound to happen, although she hoped sooner rather than later.

"Leif, do you have homework tonight?" she asked.

"Not much. I got it done at school." He looked at Selma on the other side of Eric. "Do you want an English lesson? Eric can learn too." His smile included Ivar. "We could have a party if someone brought cookies."

"I get the hint," Tante Gerd said. "Good thing we have some made. The oven is still busy rendering lard. You boys did a good job with those pigs. Maybe we should build a bigger pig house too."

Rune rolled his eyes. "Keep this up, and we'll spend all our time building instead of felling trees."

"Will the skis be ready for when it snows?" Gerd asked.

Rune nodded. "I just need to attach the bindings and finish the poles."

Signe caught his sigh. At least this winter, Onkel Einar would not be yelling at them to hurry up. The thought was not nice but so very true.

Chapter 17

I saw him," Nilda whispered when she slipped into the pew next to Signe in church on Sunday.

"Saw who?" Mouth open, Signe shook her head. "Not Dreng."

"Oh yes, Mr. Dreng Nygaard, big as life." And just as evil. He'd had the nerve to tip his hat to her and mouth *I'll get you* as George drove past him, taking Nilda out to the church in Benson's Corner. And there was a sneer in his smile. George did not seem to notice, but Dreng made sure to make eye contact with Nilda. His smile, even the tip of his hat, had sent a chill down her back.

The organ moved into the prelude, and she forced herself to sit back and concentrate on being here, in church, safe, where Dreng wasn't. All through the service, she had to keep jerking her mind back to the moment. *Pay attention*, she ordered herself repeatedly, but the vision kept popping back in. How could evil be so handsome? Wait. Didn't the Bible say Satan disguised himself as an angel of light? How apt.

Lord, help me. I can't stand this.

Just as the organ music had ushered them in, now it ushered

them out as the service ended. Mr. Larsson played so beautifully, Nilda thought, he really ought to be playing for some huge church or a cathedral, not this tiny rural church. The music ended.

"Miss Carlson! A moment of your time, please." Here came Mr. Larsson hustling out the door.

Nilda turned. "Good morning. I was just thinking about how beautiful our music is. Thank you for your gift to us, Mr. Larsson."

His whole face brightened. "Why, thank you, Miss Carlson. I'm flattered. As you know, music is my joy." He stepped in closer. "I'm eager to hear how your first few days in my aunt's house went. She has all sorts of wonderful things to say about it, but what do you say?"

Thank heavens he was using Norwegian so she could understand him easily. "Wonderful things, I assure you. I don't know the English word for *opulent*, but it pertains. Most of all, I love working for such a fine, considerate woman. I've had some very bad experiences with bad employers"—she did not mention Mrs. Nygaard out loud—"and this position is joy."

He smiled and switched to English, speaking slowly and carefully. "She says the same thing. And how is your English coming?"

"Overwhelming." She at least had learned that word! "I am learning so much so fast, my head might burst."

He laughed. "Good to hear. Not the bursting part. The learning part." He took her hand and squeezed it. "Good day, Miss Carlson."

"Good day, Mr. Larsson, and thank you for the music and the English lessons."

Once they were in the wagon going home, Signe told Mor, "Nilda saw Dreng in Blackduck. So he is still here."

"I wonder what kind of job he got in Blackduck."

Nilda added, "He dressed like he did in Norway, not like he lacked money."

"Anyone want to bet Mrs. Nygaard is sending him money somehow?" Gunlaug wagged her head. "He's not worth discussing. Forget about Dreng and tell us what you did."

"I was in school every hour until I went to bed, and then I dreamed about lists of words and how to pronounce them. Speaking English all the time wears me out. I'd rather be scrubbing walls or something."

"You can do that with me at Mr. Kielund's house," Selma said. "I offered to clean his house."

"And he agreed? He wasn't offended?"

Selma clapped her hand to her mouth. "Oh, I didn't think of that. I had a hard enough time getting him to understand what I was saying."

"Maybe you should come with me to Mrs. Schoenleber's. You learn quickly that way. I thought it was wonderful that he learned to greet you in Norwegian. In my mind that shows he is interested." *In living up to the bargain; after all, he paid for your ticket.*

"He is a very nice man." Selma's voice cracked. "But I still miss Nels so very much."

"Of course you do. Sometimes I turn around and think I will see Thor sitting at the table, waiting for a cup of coffee." Gunlaug dabbed at the corner of her eye and sniffed. "Sometimes the missing hurts so bad."

Nilda took one of her hands and Selma the other. "Keep this up, and we'll all be crying."

"I want Far to come back." Eric looked up from playing with Kirstin. She made even him giggle.

"We need to talk about something else," Gunlaug said firmly.

Nilda turned to Selma. "When are we going to clean? Mrs. Schoenleber asked if I would come a day earlier this week. What can I say, with all she is doing for me?"

"You say, 'Yes, thank you.'"

"I know, but I hate missing out on what is happening at home."

"We could have used you out scraping those four hogs we butchered." Ivar locked his arms around one knee and rocked with the wagon. He raised his voice. "We doing more this week, Rune?"

"Ja, at least two. We can start the smokehouse today."

"And we have more lard to render." Gerd turned to talk over her shoulder. "Today I am making corn bread with cracklings. I've been hungry for that for years. The last hog Einar butchered, I was too weak to even keep the stove going to render the lard. It made him so angry to not have plenty of lard, as if it were my fault."

"That's why you ran out of soap too?" Signe asked.

"Ja. I did not expect to live much longer, and then you came and bullied me into getting stronger again." She reached down from the seat and patted Signe's shoulder. "For which I am ever thankful."

Signe clasped her hand. "We all are. Did you invite Mr. Kielund for dinner?" she asked Selma.

"I offered, but he said he had some things he had to get done."

"Far, the Garborgs are waving at us." Knute pointed toward their lane.

Rune turned the team into their lane and brought them to a restless stop.

Mr. Garborg walked up beside them. "Rune, I hear you've got hogs for sale."

Rune nodded. "We do, either on the hoof or slaughtered."

"How about I buy two? But I have a favor. Could we butcher them at your place, since I am not set up for it? I would come help, and if you have more to do, I'd stay or return to help with those."

Rune nodded. "That would be a good thing. I need to butcher two tomorrow. Shall we make it four? Do you have a place to hang 'em?"

"Ja. I'll bring some burlap to wrap them in." He slapped the wheel. "See you in the morning."

Rune drove up to the house. "Can you beat that?"

"Then maybe we can get out in the woods tomorrow." Bjorn nudged Knute. "You want to put the team away?"

"I'll help you."

Nilda suggested, "Since Mr. Garborg is coming to help butcher, I think we should make soap. What's one more fire?"

"One more fire means some of us better split wood today, that's what." Ivar grinned at his sister. "It'll be good for you after lazing around at Mrs. Schoenleber's."

"I dare you to study as hard as I've been doing. At least I will be home for Kirstin's first birthday."

Later, Nilda took a bucket of ashes waiting to be scattered on the garden and dumped them into a leaky wooden bucket. She poured water over the ashes and set the bucket over a larger pail to collect the lye that dripped out. By morning she would have plenty.

Back in the house, she asked, "Gerd, what did you make soap in?"

"There's a big iron kettle that I used to use out in the machine shed. I think Einar kept nails and other metal in it." Gerd set a plate of leftover corn bread with cracklings on the table. "I figured this would make a fine coffee time. You know that fire ring out by the clothesline? I used the kettle for laundry until Einar came home one day with the washing machine. You could have knocked me over with a puff of wind, I was so shocked. But I still made the soap out there. Until I was too weak that last year."

Nilda glanced at Signe, who nodded. What had this woman been put through?

Knute and Leif each brought in an armload of wood and dumped it in the woodbox. "It smells good in here." Leif looked over at the table.

"Bring in one more load, and you'll get some." When they returned, Signe handed each of them a piece of corn bread with jam spread in the middle. "Eat outside, please."

"When you're finished, would you dump the stuff out of that big iron kettle down in the machine shop and bring it up?" Gerd asked.

"Sure. You want it scrubbed too?" Leif asked.

Nilda nodded. "I'll split wood while you do that."

But by the time she'd been splitting wood for an hour, her shoulders were complaining rather loudly. She planted the ax head in the chopping block and rotated her shoulders before taking an armload over to the fire pit. Now she needed kindling. She split some of the lumber pieces left over from building the new house and left that beside the pit also. Everything needed to be in order for when they started in the morning.

The next morning she was just pouring buckets of water into the kettle, which was set on rocks with a fire snapping under it, when she heard two rifle shots. When the water was boiling, she added the blocks of lard and set to stirring. This was the hardest part, stirring the mix long enough that the water and fat melded together. When she judged it was just right, she added the lye and made sure the bubbling didn't splash on her bare skin before calling Signe to come help her.

"There must have been some splashing. You've got holes in your apron," Signe said, pointing at the apron Nilda had wrapped around her.

"Uff da, and I was being so careful."

Together they tipped the kettle to pour the liquid soap into the molds Nilda had set up on the benches. The flat frames, once placed on the porch in the sun to cure, would hold the soap until it set hard enough to cut into squares.

"Next year we'll keep rose petals and mint leaves to add for fragrance," Signe said.

"Remember when we did this at home? It seems so very long ago." Nilda used a rake to scatter the ashes in the fire pit.

"That's because it was." Signe studied the molds. "You did a good job. And think, we didn't have to wash the drippings from the can on the stove. When that steer is butchered, we could make more using the tallow."

"I read you can make soap from cream, especially goat's milk," Nilda offered.

"That will be the day, when I have goats to milk." Signe made a face. "I didn't care for goats at the seter, and I don't now either."

"You have to admit they make good cheese."

"Next spring I'm going to start making cheese. With three cows, we should have enough cream. But we don't have space in the well house to cure cheese."

"Oh, I'm sure Rune could add that to his building list." Nilda rolled her eyes. "There goes Mr. Garborg, and here come the boys."

Later, the setting sun took all the warmth of the day with it as they carried the soap molds onto the porch.

"Mor, look!" Leif called, coming from chores with Knute.

"Your skis are finished!" Signe said, smiling.

"I sure hope they work." Knute showed her the bindings. "Far is working on the ski poles. He's using deer hide leather for the hand straps."

"They look good." Nilda ran a hand down the ski. "Good wax job."

"Takk, I did that." Knute copied her motion. "I didn't think I'd ever get enough on."

"Where you going to keep 'em?"

"Here on the porch. Far said he'd put up racks or long pegs." The boys leaned the skis against the wall.

"Rosie is going to get fat this winter if we don't ride her," Leif said.

"I'm glad she's not going to be standing in that shed all day, even though you did blanket her. She's getting kind of old for that." Nilda led the way into the house.

"We better take some of that soap with us," Signe said the next morning as they prepared to head to the Kielund house. "And plenty of cleaning rags. You're sure he said he would not be home today?"

Selma nodded. "He's taking the children to Blackduck with him. And yes, he knows we are coming, but he didn't seem particularly pleased."

"Probably not. Pride sometimes gets in the way when we need help." Gunlaug took Eric's hand. "Today you get to stay here and help us take care of Kirstin."

"Can I play with the kittens?" he asked.

"Ah, ja. We will bring one or two to the house."

"I'll get them." Nilda headed out the door.

The team already waited at the hitching post, their breath blowing huge clouds of steam in the frigid air. One stamped a foot and shook her head. "I'll hurry. Sorry." As if they understood.

Nilda trotted to the barn and scooped up two of the kittens playing in the square of sunlight at the open door. "It's okay, mama, we'll bring them back."

She paused for a moment and inhaled the crisp air. The glittering sun shot over the frosted world. Steam billowed from the trough of hot water for scraping the two butchered hogs. One of the men laughed at something. Mr. Garborg had returned like he said he would.

With both kittens tucked under her chin, she kicked against the screen door, now covered with tar paper to help keep out the icy winter wind. Inside, she tucked the kittens into a covered basket by the door. "You ready?"

"Ja." Selma used potholders to lift the kettle of soup they had started the day before using bones from one of the butchered hogs. They tied a dish towel over the lid to keep it from spilling. "Catch the door for me."

At the Kielund house, the fire in the stove revived with open drafts and small wood pieces, and the water in the reservoir was still hot enough to use for scrubbing. They set the soup to continue cooking and, wielding broom, mop, brushes, and rags, attacked the kitchen first.

"At least there are no mice," Signe muttered as she wiped out cupboards. "He must have a good cat."

They finished the kitchen, paused for a bowl of soup, and then swept and dusted the rest of the house, mopping the other floors.

"The windows need washing outside too, but that might have to wait until spring." Nilda gave the last one an extra polish. "We could come another day to do the wash."

Selma brought in another armload of wood and dumped it

in the woodbox. After banking the fire, they left the soup, now in one of Mr. Kielund's kettles, to simmer on the back of the stove. "Well, we made a difference, that's for sure."

Signe paused at the doorway. "This is a good house, and Oskar Kielund is a fine man. I believe you will be very happy here."

"I sometimes wonder if I will ever be happy again." Selma sniffed and cleared her throat. "But if he asks me, I will say yes."

"No *if*. He is a man of his word, like you are a woman of yours. Just *when*. When you are both ready to take the next step." Signe gave Selma a hug as she passed her on the way to the wagon. "Let's go home."

That night, when they were still seated at the table after supper, Gerd set a cake on the table in front of Kirstin, who sat on her mor's lap. She immediately reached for it, but paused when Gerd spoke. "You are now one year old, little one."

Kirstin reached for the plate with both hands, then looked to Gerd, who nodded. One baby finger touched the white frosting on top, then immediately popped into her mouth. Leif and Eric giggled from across the table, catching her attention. She grinned at them, then focused on the cake. This time she used a finger from each hand to scoop off some frosting. When the boys laughed, she grinned back and smacked the table, then sucked the remaining frosting from her fingers.

That night when Nilda finally made her way upstairs and collapsed in her bed, she was almost asleep when the vision of Dreng came again. Both the memory from Norway when he was attacking her and the most recent one in Blackduck. *How do I drive that—that filth out of my mind?* She managed during the day, but this was the fragile time. She flopped over on her other side, setting the ropes in her bed to creaking.

"What is it?" Gunlaug spoke softly so as not to wake the others.

"Dreng!" Nilda spit out the word, wishing she could do the same with the memories.

"Only prayer and Bible verses work, as far as I know."

"I wish." *Oh, how I wish.*

Chapter 18

Whatever is true, whatever is honest, whatever is just, whatever is pure . . . The words she'd gone to sleep remembering still floated in her mind. *Thank you, Mor.*

Nilda lay without moving, knowing that her squeaky bed would rouse the others. She smiled at the faint sound of cat feet coming up the stairs, barely disturbing the hush of the early morning. The cat jumped up on Nilda's side of the bed and walked up the length of her body to sniff her hair and curl up around the back of her head. It was a shame Mrs. Schoenleber did not have a cat or two. They were such a comfort.

"Are you going to start the fire, or am I?" Gunlaug asked.

"I was trying not to wake you." Their whispers sounded loud in the stillness. "You stay here and sleep a few more minutes."

"Nei, I am awake, so I get up."

Nilda ignored the squeaking of the ropes and heaved herself out of bed. She grabbed her robe from the post and, shoving her feet into slippers her mor had knit—wonderful slippers with soft leather soles stitched on—made her way down the stairs, the cat padding beside her.

The flare of the match when she lit the lamp made her blink.

The cat chirped her request for a dish of milk. "You must wait until I get the fire started."

Nilda lifted the stove lids as quietly as possible. The stove was still warm but nowhere near hot. Stirring the ashes set bits to glowing red, plenty to start a fire. Sprinkling curls of wood from the workshop on the coals and blowing a couple of puffs started the smoke tendrils that, with another puff, burst into flame. She added kindling and a couple small chunks, then set the draft in the chimney and the lids back in place. There was something about lighting the fire in the morning that welcomed the new day. Wrapping her arms around her middle, she shrugged and shivered.

Getting the coffee going was always the next step in the morning routine.

"All right," she answered the cat who wound herself around Nilda's feet, her request moving into demand. "I hear you." She was pouring milk into the cat dish by the side of the stove when Gunlaug and Ivar yawned their way into the kitchen.

"What time did you say George would be here?" Gunlaug asked.

"He said early, but he wouldn't start out before daylight. Are you butchering again today?" Nilda fetched the cups from the cupboard and added larger pieces of wood to the now blazing fire.

Ivar nodded. "Need anything from the well house?"

"Eggs and buttermilk. I'll make pancakes." Nilda paused. "When I am there . . ." She shook her head. "It's such a different life with all the staff doing the cooking, cleaning, serving, whatever needs to be done. I asked Cook one day if I could help her, and she looked at me like I'd insulted her. But then she laughed, and I felt better. I didn't mean to hurt her feelings."

"Don't worry, you can cook here anytime." Ivar sat down and pulled his boots on.

Gunlaug glanced at the calendar on the wall, then crossed over to flip to the new month. "I wonder if they've had snow yet at home."

"This is home now, Mor," Nilda said with a smile.

Gunlaug nodded. "Ja, it will become so."

I can cook and do these things when I come home. Now that Mor was here, this house did indeed seem more like home—except, of course, for the lack of good cod. Or would she become so spoiled that she didn't want to do the usual things? Like pouring coffee. She handed the full cups around.

Later, while everyone else was doing the chores of the day, she heard the jingle of harness above the noise of the washing machine.

"Sorry to leave in the middle," she told the others.

Today George climbed down from the seat of a closed carriage and opened the door for her.

"I decided it was cold enough to switch to this one," he added after his greeting. "Cook sent wrapped hot rocks along, so your feet will be warm."

Nilda blew kisses to her mor and Signe at the washing machine on the porch. Gerd was already hanging the first of the diapers on the line and waved too.

"Looks like the men are butchering?" George inquired.

"Yes, we have hogs for sale, on the hoof or hanging. We smoke hams and bacon and other meat too."

"Hmm. We need to mention this to Mrs. S."

Nilda shrugged. "Of course, if you think it wise."

As he closed the door, she looked around the inside of the carriage. Curtains were tied back from the windows, and the seats were well-cushioned in velvet, with the same fabric upholstered on the roof and walls. A window in the back gave even more light. She settled back for the ride, since this way she could not talk much with George. But when her mind switched to Dreng, she clamped her eyes shut in frustration. This could not be tolerated! Instead she leaned over and pulled the lists of English words out of her satchel. She repeated them all softly, including the Norwegian definitions, making sure she enunciated carefully to help correct her accent. After pages of word lists, she began on the phrases and finally moved on to reading the paragraphs. Amazing that the coach was so well sprung that she could read in spite of bumps in the road.

The ride passed so swiftly that she was surprised when George slowed the team to drive the streets of Blackduck. She tucked her pages back into her bag and heaved a sigh. She'd not spent as much time on the pages as she'd hoped to at home, but the words were sticking in her mind, so she wouldn't be embarrassed when Miss Walstead began her coaching.

When they reached the house, she thanked George and hurried inside.

"Just in time for tea." Mrs. Schoenleber put down her pen and closed the ink bottle. "Pull the cord, please." After gathering the papers scattered across her desk, she turned and held out her hands. "I am so glad to see you looking so fresh and—and just lovely. Are you ready for more?" At Nilda's nod, Mrs. Schoenleber's smile widened, and she stood. "Let's have tea in front of the fire. I always hate to waste a fire." She glanced at the carved wooden clock on the mantel. "Miss Walstead should be here any minute. She can join us."

"George says I should mention that the men are butchering hogs at home."

"I see. Hmm. Let me think about this. Do they smoke the hams and bacon too?"

"You can order that." Nilda waited until her employer sat down before taking the other chair.

Just as Charles entered with the tea tray, the knocker on the front door announced company. He set the tray on the low table and headed for the front door.

"So tell me the news. Has Mr. Kielund proposed yet?" Mrs. Schoenleber tsked when Nilda shook her head. "Men can be so slow. You tell Selma that I know of a family here in town who are looking for household help, and they have no problem with having her son come too."

Miss Walstead was unwrapping her scarf as she came into the room. "Thank you, Charles." She let him help her with her coat and handed him her scarf and gloves. "It's brisk out there."

"I told you George would pick you up."

"I know, but I needed the walk." Miss Walstead held her hands out to the fire. "The better to appreciate the fire and the company."

"Milk with your tea?"

"Please." She turned so her back could be warmed. "And how has your week gone, Nilda? By the way, I met a friend of yours the other day. A Mr. Dreng Nygaard. He said the two of you come from the same town in Norway."

Nilda's jaw clamped before she could stop it. Her teacup rattled in the saucer. Setting it down very carefully gave her time to school her face. She inhaled and smiled.

"Oh, did I say something wrong?" Miss Walstead asked.

"Not at all." *Liar.* Her interior voice reprimanded her rather succinctly. "Yes, but he's more my older brother's age, so I would not say we were ever friends." *Not that he ever had friends that I know of.* She could feel both women studying her.

"I think there is more to this story, but we will let it go for now." Mrs. Schoenleber passed the plate of sugar-dusted scones.

192

"One of Cook's favorite recipes. She grates orange peel into the batter. And, yes, one of my favorites too."

Nilda forced herself to take a bite, quickly followed by a swallow of tea to keep it from sticking in her throat. How could that—that vermin claim to be her friend? He was doing what he did best, ingratiating himself with the women of the town.

Why could no one see beyond his slimy smile? But she knew the answer to that. Dreng could be charm personified when he desired. Or when he wanted something.

"Nilda, come back."

She swallowed and reminded herself to drink tea, nibble her scone, and take part in the conversation. "I'm sorry, my mind wandered." She looked up from the scone that was now a pile of crumbles in the napkin on her lap.

"We can talk of this now, if you would prefer." Mrs. Schoenleber's voice fell gently on the silence Nilda had not realized existed. The fire snapped and popped, sparking against the screen.

"Dreng Nygaard's name is on the guest list for the next social," Mrs. Schoenleber continued. "He replied that he is looking forward to attending, as he and Petter might be out in the lumber camp before the next event."

Can someone drop a tree on him? Nilda's hand jerked, and the scone crumbs scattered over her lap and the beautiful Persian rug at her feet. "Oh, I'm so sorry! I mean, I . . ." She tried to gather the crumbs as heat raced up her neck and to her face. *Do not cry!* The words echoed around and around her head.

"I see. We will discuss this later. In the meantime, the maid will take care of the crumbs. The two of you adjourn to the library for your morning work, and Mrs. Jones will be here for a fitting right after dinner. And Miss Walstead, I do hope you are planning to spend the rest of the day and the evening here.

We have much to accomplish." Settling her teacup on the tray, Mrs. Schoenleber rose. "Any questions?"

Nilda shook her head. How could she make such a fool of herself? Surely she needn't dread seeing Dreng again that much? After all . . .

She couldn't come up with an end to that thought.

By the time Charles announced that dinner was served, Nilda felt like running out of the library and around the house. She chose to step outside just long enough for the crisp air to clear her head and make her shiver.

"Feel better?" Mrs. Schoenleber asked when Nilda entered the dining room, her smile warm and caring.

"Yes. The cobwebs were taking over my head." Nilda inhaled and sat down as Charles held her chair.

"I think I worked her into quite a tizzy." Miss Walstead took the chair on the other side of the table, with Mrs. Schoenleber at the end. "Now." She laid her napkin in her lap. "Let's have a discussion about the meal and how Cook prepared it. Perhaps compare it to another meal you have had."

"After grace," Mrs. Schoenleber interjected.

"Of course, after grace."

"We will have three courses today," Charles announced. "First we will have fish chowder." He set a flat bowl of soup on a plate in front of each of them, with grated cheese and dried parsley sprinkled on top.

"What kind of fish, if you please?" Miss Walstead asked.

"Walleye, fresh from Duluth."

Nilda dipped her first spoonful and savored the flavor. "Fish, potatoes, and cream or milk."

"Good. Besides salt and pepper, there is another flavor."

"Dill?" Nilda closed her eyes, the better to concentrate on the food in her mouth.

"Butter, I am sure."

"Cook always has a secret ingredient that sets her dishes apart." Mrs. Schoenleber looked up at Charles.

"I am wiser than to give away her secrets, so I will never do so." He raised his hands palm out and backed out of the room.

Nilda sat back. "Delicious. I like that word. It even sounds good."

"You are doing well with your English. You have come a long way." Mrs. Schoenleber nodded.

"I thank both of you."

"I was talking with Fritz, and he said he missed you in his class," her employer said. "I told him we are working you to death here, and he laughed. I do hope he can come to one of our socials. I told him I would move it to Friday just for him."

"When he plays the organ, I think he gets lost in the music." Nilda spoke slowly so she could think ahead to the right words.

They had just finished the meal, with the promise of apple *formkake* with tea later, when Charles announced the dressmaker and her helper were waiting in the drawing room.

"No rest for the wicked," Miss Walstead said as she pushed her chair back.

Nilda gave her a puzzled look. "We are bad?"

"No, no, that is a saying that means, uh . . . we are keeping very busy." She shook her head. "That's the problem with sayings like that, they are hard to translate. I'll be careful not to throw something like that at you."

"I should catch what you throw?"

"Sorry, Nilda. You go on for your fitting. We can talk about those things later."

As Nilda left the room, she heard Mrs. Schoenleber laughing and making a comment. Again, something that did not quite make sense. Perhaps with time she would understand.

Standing for the fitting of a black silk jacket made Nilda restless. Mrs. Jones could not speak with pins in her mouth, and her assistant spoke German so softly that Nilda couldn't really pick up the words that sounded much like Norwegian. She had spoken with emigrants from Germany on the ship, and they managed to understand one another, so she knew it was possible.

"I will return with the two serge skirts and the off-white waist tomorrow. The day gown is almost ready for a fitting, as is the watered silk skirt to match the jacket with the jet beads." Mrs. Jones folded the bodice of the jacket and tucked it back in her bag. "I think I found a hat and purse to go with the black jacket." She glanced down at Nilda's shoes. "You will need new shoes too. I will tell Mrs. Schoenleber." She paused and nodded. "Yes, and underthings. You really should wear a corset with that outfit. And the gown."

Nilda rolled her eyes. Not if she could help it. Corsets made breathing difficult.

That afternoon, she and Miss Walstead made their way through the house room by room, with Miss Walstead identifying the furniture, the paintings, the decorations, and each item's purpose. At the end of the tour, she gave Nilda more sheets of paper with columns of words and phrases to study. "We will do the upper floors next week," she promised.

Shaking her head, Nilda made sure she greeted the announcement with at least a half smile.

At supper, Mrs. Schoenleber asked Miss Walstead, "Do you think she will be ready to assist with the tea on Saturday?"

"Oh, yes. Probably not to take part in the conversation a great deal, but Nilda will do fine."

"I will do what fine?" Nilda asked.

"I'm having two ladies in for tea on Saturday afternoon because I want you to meet them. They are my closest friends here in Blackduck, and they have been wanting to meet you."

Nilda bit back her "why." Why would anyone want to meet her?

Saturday she dressed in her new waist and navy serge skirt on instructions from Mrs. Schoenleber and pinned the brooch lying on her dressing table at the center of the standup collar trimmed in lace. Narrow lace was stitched into the pin tucks down the front and along the wide cuffs of the leg of mutton sleeves. Nilda stared into the mirror. Never had she had so fine a waist. She looked over her shoulder at the three kick pleats in the back of the skirt.

Mrs. Schoenleber nodded when Nilda came downstairs, her smile crinkling her faded blue eyes. "Very nice. As soon as we've eaten, we'll set up the tea table in the parlor so you learn where linens and things are stored. Charles will set up the table for us." She dished up her usual breakfast at the sideboard: two poached eggs, two strips of bacon, and a sweet roll.

Nilda tried something new each day. Today she chose the eggs scrambled with bacon and cheese on top, one of Cook's sweet rolls because they were irresistible, and fresh applesauce. As they sat down, Nilda asked, "What will be served at the tea?"

"Finger sandwiches, deviled eggs, and tea cakes. I wanted more of the fish chowder, but the fishermen didn't have any fresh walleye this morning, I guess. Cook is rather particular. By the way, I have called an order in to Mrs. Benson that she is passing along to your brother—Rune, is it?" At Nilda's nod, she continued. "George will bring back half a hog fresh, and then the other half will be smoked, but for the chops, and picked up when finished."

"Why, that is good of you. Takk—er, thank you."

"And before I forget, I would like you here four days a week, but if you can only do three, I will have to be content. Next Saturday is the social." She checked off her list. "Oh, and Petter would like to call on you this evening, if that is acceptable?"

"I, uh, of course."

What in the world will we do? The thought of Petter visiting pleased her more than she expected. And a thousand questions popped into her head. Would they sit in the ornate parlor? Would they sit back in the kitchen, where Nilda felt so much more at home? Would refreshments be served? Should Nilda make up the refreshments beforehand, since this would be a personal event and not one of Mrs. Schoenleber's invitational events? Should she arrange the refreshments or just see what came? And the heaviest question of all:

"Will we have to speak all English?"

Chapter 19

That afternoon, when they had finished setting up for the tea, Nilda admired the round table draped in a white brocade tablecloth embroidered with gold ivy leaves. Matching brocade cushions on the five chairs and napkins with gold rings made Nilda's jaw drop when she stepped back to view it. At home, if they put on a tablecloth, they were being really fancy.

"Is this usual," she stuttered, trying to remember the correct English word, "for a tea?"

Mrs. Schoenleber and Miss Walstead both nodded. "If the group were larger, we would probably serve in the dining room. But this is more intimate, and these ladies are good friends of ours."

Miss Walstead stroked her chin. "We are missing something. What is it?"

Mrs. Schoenleber smiled. "Of course. Some flowers in a bud vase. Nilda, have you been out to the hothouse yet?"

Nilda shook her head. "Hothouse?" She must have looked bewildered, since the other two exchanged smiles. What in the world was a hothouse? It was plenty warm in here already.

"I will take her out there and do another lesson at the same time." Miss Walstead smiled at Nilda. "Come. Oh, are there cutters out there?"

"They should be hanging in the bag to the right of the door."

"Grab a shawl," Miss Walstead instructed as they went out the back door.

A glass building took up part of the kitchen garden space to the right, at the end of the brick walk. *How did I not notice this?* Nilda wondered, but then she realized she'd not had a tour of any of the buildings other than the house itself, and she had not even seen all of that.

Using a key, Miss Walstead unlocked and pushed open the door. A gust of warm, floral-scented air made Nilda automatically inhale.

"Oh, I remember reading about a place like this in a book, but the name for it was different."

"Do you like working in the garden at home?" Miss Walstead asked.

"I love to watch things grow, but I've never seen this many flowers in one place. And in the winter?"

"It is not winter in other parts of the world, and within a building like this, we can duplicate other climates."

"Duplicate?"

"Copy." Miss Walstead pointed with the clippers. "See those golden flowers over there? We'll take a few for the tea table. Gertrude loves to have fresh flowers on the table by the front door. Learning to arrange flowers is another skill you might learn."

"Does the snow make it too cold for this in real winter?"

"If the heat goes out, yes, but George takes care of that, along with the horses. He does have a helper, a groom, out in the stable." While she talked, Miss Walstead clipped gold- and rust-colored flowers from a row of plants, keeping the stems as long as possible.

How will I ever remember all this? Such thoughts stormed rampant through Nilda's mind as she tried to repeat what Miss Walstead was telling and showing her. Choosing the appropriate vase made her shake her head. Life on the farm might seem complicated, but it was far more simple than all this.

On their walk back to the house, Nilda thought about her reaction to Dreng's name. That was terribly embarrassing. She must control her reactions and treat him like any other person, at least when his name was mentioned.

The two guests arrived promptly at two that afternoon. Charles took their hats and wraps and showed them into the parlor, where a fire welcomed them. Once Nilda was introduced, they turned their backs to the fire and sighed at the warmth.

"It looked so nice outside, I thought the walk would be pleasant," Mrs. Grant, the taller of the two and dressed in navy, said. "What is your excuse, Annabelle?"

"I thought the same, but when we met at the corner where that wind blew through like a tunnel, I wished I had told my driver to bring around the hansom. But it seemed a waste for such a short distance, harnessing two horses for a quarter-mile trip." She took a lace handkerchief from her burgundy reticule and wiped her nose. "Goodness me."

"Nilda, call for the tea, please. That will help warm them up." Mrs. Schoenleber rolled her eyes just a bit.

"Of course. Shall I throw another log on the fire also?" Nilda asked.

"George will do that while you take care of the tea."

Nilda returned from the kitchen in time to overhear Mrs. Grant's comment about a young man who was such a fine addition to the society of Blackduck. "Have you met Dreng Nygaard yet? He has the most charming accent and, well, if I had a daughter, I would make sure she met him."

Nilda grabbed the back of the nearest chair.

"How did you happen to meet him?" Miss Walstead asked.

"Hmm, it was at church last Sunday. Reverend Holtschmidt introduced him to several of us at the same time. He said he'd received a letter of introduction from a friend in Minneapolis that the son of a relative of his had immigrated to America and was looking for work and to establish a home here."

"How did the reverend get the letter?" Nilda asked.

"Why, I believe Mr. Nygaard gave it to him."

He probably wrote it himself. What person who actually knew Dreng would ever give him a letter like that? "If you ladies would like to be seated, Charles is bringing in the tea."

"Oh, that will be perfect." Annabelle Parsons rubbed her hands together. "Thanks to such a fine fire, I feel much warmer. Thank you, Gertrude, for seeing to our comfort so perfectly."

"George will take you home so you will not get so cold again. I know it is easy to think it's warm outside when the sun shines like this, but remember, you are in northern Minnesota, and fall has finally arrived in full force."

Following one conversation was hard for Nilda, but keeping track of four women talking seemed next to impossible. She refrained from rubbing her forehead by pure determination. The discussion moved from the weather, to the socials Mrs. Schoenleber was hosting, to someone in town who needed help that two of them could provide, to the fundraiser for the library. Mrs. Schoenleber was in charge of that. Miss Walstead announced she would be teaching an English class at the church on the street behind the saddlery.

"The Catholics and Lutherans are gathering food and warm bedding to give away at Thanksgiving," Miss Walstead said, "but we need all the churches to be involved in this. Yes, the preparations should have begun earlier. However, since we all go to different churches, we can mention this to our pastors and the women's groups."

They all nodded in agreement.

"Where are people to bring their donations, then?"

Miss Walstead took a sip of tea. "They said directly to the Catholic church the weekend before. The Lutherans will bring their donations there also. Warm coats, especially for children, are greatly needed too, as we have had more immigrants than we expected. While the men go work in the camps, the families need help."

Nilda made sure the teapot was refilled and the ladies' cups could be too. When they stood to leave, she smiled and nodded at their comments and fetched their coats and hats.

After the good-byes were said and reminders given, and Charles had closed the door behind their guests, all Nilda could think of was the quiet of her room and the bed that would welcome her.

"And now you have been through your first tea and introduction to how most of the social events happen in Blackduck." Mrs. Schoenleber sank into one of the wingback chairs in front of the fire that Charles had just stoked again. "This is the kind of thing I want you to accompany me to. You will find it much easier as you understand English better."

"You did well," Miss Walstead said with a smile. "There is something that concerns me, however. I think I saw you flinch during the discussion of that new young man, Mr. Nygaard. It's not the first time you've reacted to mention of him. Do you know him?"

"It is a long story." Nilda swallowed. "Can we talk about this another time?"

"Is he from a good family?" Mrs. Schoenleber asked.

"The wealthiest in Valders. His far—I mean, his father is

highly respected as a businessman." Nilda took a sip of cold tea to moisten her dry throat. "Everyone seems to hold Dreng in high esteem."

Yes, he threatened me, but perhaps he can change. Is it my place to tarnish his reputation? After all, everyone deserves a second chance, don't they?

"I can see you are reluctant to say anything. Either it is very bad or only errors that can be ignored." Mrs. Schoenleber nodded slowly. "If I see or hear of slight problems, I will not be dissuaded. I know he and Petter are good friends, and Petter has proven himself to be a young man with integrity. He will be here later. I will think and pray on this before I say anything, and I want you to do the same." She paused. "Do you have anything more to say?"

Maybe Ivar can tell them what went on. But no, she had been the one accosted; he had been on the disciplinary end. Was there any chance that Dreng had changed or ever planned to change?

After supper, the doorknocker announced a guest. When Nilda put her knitting aside and started to stand, Mrs. Schoenleber shook her head. "Charles will show him in." They were sitting in the parlor while the fire provided entertainment as they discussed the upcoming social.

"Mr. Petter Thorvaldson." Charles had hung Petter's coat and hat on the hall tree and showed him into the room.

Mrs. Schoenleber rose to greet him. "Thank you for coming, Mr. Thorvaldson."

He took the hand she extended and kissed her knuckles. "Thank you for having me, Mrs. Schoenleber. And thank you again for hosting that delightful get-together."

"You are welcome." Mrs. Schoenleber sat down. "Please be seated."

Petter sat in the chair indicated. "I'm glad we have this chance to visit. We have a lot to catch up with since I saw you last. At the social, wasn't it?"

Nilda nodded. "Ivar said to greet you if I saw you. He wonders if you are still planning on going out to one of the logging camps."

"It's getting colder out there. I asked when logging will start, and the boss said most likely in December. The ground has to be frozen first and the camps set up."

"And your uncle does not mind your leaving?"

"Not as long as I promise to return in the spring." He smiled at her. "How are things out on the farm?"

"Our big news is our mor, er, mother—I am supposed to speak only English." She shot Mrs. Schoenleber a partial smile. "Anyway, my father passed away suddenly, and so Mother and a cousin came with her little boy a couple of weeks ago."

"I'm sorry to hear about your far, but I'm glad you've been reunited with your mor." He settled back in his chair. "I suppose that means there's even less of a chance that Ivar will come with me to a logging camp?"

Nilda nodded. "We have too much to do at home. Rune, Ivar, and Bjorn will be back out in the woods as soon as the butchering is done."

"I tried to talk my brother into coming over and logging, but he said if he comes, he'd rather farm. But Dreng is ready to go out with me. He said to greet you for him."

Nilda could feel Mrs. Schoenleber's gaze on her, and Nilda's head was saying, *Be polite, at all costs, be polite.*

"Tell him you did. Would you like some coffee? Dessert?" A glance at her employer earned her a nod. "Cook makes the best pies. Tonight we had chocolate pie with something else in it. She always has a secret ingredient." She walked over to pull the cord. "What have you heard from home?" She felt sure she had passed the test, even though she could feel herself shaking.

Petter described his job and temporary living arrangement in a boardinghouse. "Only until I get enough money saved to build a small house. Lumber here is much less expensive than it is in Norway."

Verna, the cook herself, entered with a tray of dishes, each with a generous wedge of chocolate pie with a mountain of whipped cream on top.

"How do you like living in Blackduck?" Mrs. Schoenleber asked after the pie was passed around and the coffee poured. "Mr. Goddard says you learn very quickly, and he's pleased to have you working at the lumberyard."

"I like it here. I still miss my family and hope some of them will immigrate too, but I have a good job and the people here . . ." He nodded. "It would be different if I were living in a house or someplace by myself."

She asked, "So why are you going out in the woods?"

"Two reasons, ma'am. I want to learn all I can about the lumber industry. Mr. Goddard knows so much, and he is a good teacher." He smiled and shrugged. "But there's something about those giant trees."

Nilda nodded. "I know. When I walk out in our woods and look up, it is quiet until you hear the wind in the tops of the trees, like they are singing. Like being in a huge church. I visited the Stavanger Cathedral one time, and going out in the woods feels much the same." She shrugged and shook her head just a bit at the same time. "It's hard to explain. But I went out in the summer, not the winter. I'm looking forward to going out with my brothers after the snow falls."

Petter smiled at her. "Ja, I—I think you described it very well. Mr. Goddard said when one of those trees goes down, there is a hush as if . . ." He stopped. "I guess I will find out."

Nilda smiled back. What a pleasant friend Petter was becoming. She thought of his helping at Rune's house-raising. And he wasn't afraid of work—not like someone else she knew.

Why did that miserable Dreng have to keep showing up in her mind, let alone in her town?

Chapter 20

"I f we can fell three trees today—get them on the ground, that is, not limbed—I will be pleased." Rune rubbed his left eye.

Signe frowned slightly. His eyes seemed to be bothering him more lately.

"Three down and one limbed." Bjorn elbowed his far. "That's a better goal."

Rune looked at their two youngest. "Come out and load the wagon as soon as you get home. We need more wood up here."

Knute heaved a sigh. "I could stay home and help."

"You will go to school first." Signe laid a hand on his shoulder. "Your dinner pails are ready, and Rosie is impatient to get under shelter. Oh, and on your way home, stop and see if there are any messages at Benson's."

"When is Nilda coming home?"

"We'll meet her in church on Sunday like we did last week." Signe turned to Selma. "Mr. Kielund is hauling the hog sides into Benson's Corner today, right?"

"That's what he said." Selma reached for the breakfast plates and bowls on either side of her. "I invited him to dinner like you said."

"That's right, I forgot he was coming. That means we have

to come in early to help load his wagon." Rune puffed out his cheeks. "So many things to be done."

"So much for three trees." Bjorn huffed a breath. "Ivar and I can stay out there and keep working."

"There is always tomorrow."

"If Onkel Einar heard you say that, he—"

"He would have been so furious, he'd have broken the glass in the door going out," Gerd finished for him. "But he didn't butcher and sell fifteen pigs either, nor dress and hang a spike deer."

"Or keep the smokehouse going twenty-four hours a day for weeks," Signe added.

"Dinner will be ready for you—a hot meal, not cold food out in the woods." Gerd leaned over and helped Kirstin climb up onto her lap. "Won't it, baby girl?"

Kirstin wiggled around until she was facing the table and slapped her hands on the surface. Looking straight at Bjorn, she said, "B-Born," clear as could be.

The boys all laughed, and Knute and Leif grabbed their coats and hats along with their dinner pails.

"Now, Rufus, you stay here," Leif ordered, but Knute laughed.

"You know he will go with us to the road and stand there watching us ride away, so why confuse him?"

Signe shook her head. Rufus would indeed do what Rufus decided to do. While Rune had built him a shelter on the back porch at the new house, he still slept on a rug by the stove, unless he climbed the stairs to sleep with Leif.

"We have a good dog in that one." Gerd patted the backs of Kirstin's hands on the table. "Kirstin thinks so too."

"M-m-mo." She grinned up at Signe. "M-m-mo."

Selma filled the boiler and set it on the stove. "I will wash the baby things."

"I'll crank the wringer." Signe grinned back at her little daughter. "We should be teaching her English."

"She will mimic whatever she hears the most." Gunlaug took over at the dishpan on the stove. "She learns faster than I do, that's for certain."

"Learning a new language is easier when you are young." Rune pulled his hat down on his head and tucked a scarf around his neck. The three of them waved goodbye to Kirstin as they left. She waved and jabbered something at them, "B-Born" again being the clearest word in her speech.

Gerd kissed the top of her downy hair, only one shade darker than white. "Come on, you and Tante Gerd will go finish your new dress. Now that you are a year old, you can help more."

Signe smiled as she watched them go into the workroom, a baby fist clasped around Gerd's index finger, the little one chattering away. "That little girl is going to be some talker. You can go in there too, Eric, if you want. Perhaps Tante Gerd will tell more of the story I heard the other day."

"Come on, Eric," Gerd called. "We can work on your numbers and the alphabet again. Signe, remind me to ask Rune to make a slate for the little ones. There's no reason Eric can't learn to recognize the basics now."

"Can you tell 'Three Billy Goats Gruff' again?" he asked.

"We'll see. Numbers first. Hold up two fingers. No, no, use one hand."

Signe heard the jangle of harness just as she was slicing the bread. She looked out the window and saw that Rune and the boys had a load of pine in the wagon. They tossed the lengths into a pile, and Bjorn took the team back to the barn just as another team trotted up the lane.

"We'll eat before you load," she called out the door.

With the kettle of venison stew on the hot pad at the table, she set the bread in the middle and the plates next to the kettle.

"Mr. Kielund is here," Selma said as she came in from hanging the last load of wash on the clothesline. She rubbed her hands in the heat of the stove. "He's blanketing his horse."

Selma held the door as the gentleman entered with his children. Signe caught the smile he and Selma exchanged and chuckled inside. Things were indeed progressing.

When they were nearly done with the meal, Mr. Kielund looked to Signe. "Do you mind if the children stay here while we deliver the hogs?"

"Not at all." Gerd answered before Signe could. "I have a favor to ask. Would you please ask Mrs. Benson if she has a couple of slates, like they have at school? And chalk. The children and I are practicing."

His eyes widened. "Of course."

"We need to get you loaded." Rune pushed back his chair. "I hate to hurry things along. . . ."

"But dark is coming too fast these days." Ivar and Bjorn swapped looks.

"I will help." Selma snatched up her heavy coat.

"Did you bag that deer?" Mr. Kielund asked Bjorn as they filed out the door.

"Yes, sir. A spike, so the meat is tender." Bjorn smiled. "You just ate some of it."

"When do you plan to butcher the steer?"

Selma answered him, but Signe could not hear what she said.

Eric and Olaf stood before her. "Can we go get one of the kittens?"

"I'll go with you and bring up the churn." Signe smiled down at the two little boys. "Perhaps you can catch two of them, but be careful—the mama might scratch you."

Eric shook his head. "She likes me."

Hours later, Signe was just taking a gingerbread cake out of the oven when she heard trotting hooves coming up the lane. Sounds carried farther in the cold air. She'd discovered that when she waited without breathing outside the house, she could hear the ax blades on the trees out in the woods. She set the cake to cool on the table and fetched a pitcher of cream from the pantry, making sure she kicked the rolled-up rug back at the bottom of the door.

"Pa is here." The two Kielund children leaped to their feet and ran to the door, leaving the kittens for Eric.

Selma entered first, her face aglow. She sent Signe a slight nod as she removed her coat with Mr. Kielund's assistance.

Signe kept a knowing grin from her face, but she wanted to throw her arms around Selma and dance her around the room.

"Oh, it smells so good in here." Mr. Kielund hung Selma's coat and his own on the clothes rack by the door.

"Ja—yes, it just came out of the oven. The coffee is hot too," Signe said in English as she beckoned them to the table.

Mr. Kielund handed her a paper-wrapped package. "This is from Mrs. Benson. She was delighted to send those here with us."

Signe cut the pan of gingerbread into good-sized pieces. Perhaps she'd better bake another one for after supper.

"What smells so good?" Leif burst through the door. "We got to hurry."

"Surely you have time for . . ." Signe slid one of the pieces onto a plate.

"Mor, that's not fair." Leif set the dinner pails on the counter. "Knute is harnessing Rosie to the cart."

Signe tied two pieces of gingerbread in a napkin. "Here you go."

"Thanks!" He spun out the door and leaped down the steps.

"They take their work seriously." Mr. Kielund shook his head. "What fine sons you have."

"Thank you." Signe passed the plates of gingerbread to Selma, who poured cream over them and handed the dessert around the table.

"Pa, Tante Gerd told us the story of the Three Billy Goats Gruff. Do you know that story?" Olaf looked up at his father, who sat beside him.

Mr. Kielund smiled at his son. "Yes, I do. My ma used to tell it to us. I've not heard that story for a long time. Thank you, Mrs. Strand."

Gerd nodded. "You are welcome. We will have to remember another story for next time you come." She smiled at Mr. Kielund. "Your children enjoy the kittens so much. Perhaps you would like to take them home with you when they get a bit older."

Signe was having trouble following the English, but she thought she got most of the conversation.

"Oh, Pa, can we?" Olaf's eyes grew wide.

Mr. Kielund looked to Selma before answering. "That's possible." He cleared his throat. "I wasn't going to say anything yet, but . . ." Again he looked at Selma, who was studying her now-empty plate. "Selma?"

He'd called her by her first name! Signe nearly jumped up from the table. It was a shame Nilda wasn't here. She would be so delighted.

The drop of a piece of wood in the stove sounded loud in the waiting silence.

"I-ah . . ." He cleared his throat again. "I—I asked Mrs. Strand to marry me, and she agreed."

A communal *whoosh* circled the table.

Gunlaug nodded, beamed, and finally said, "That is wonderful. I pray God blesses you both as you build a new life together as a family."

"I am so happy for you." Signe picked up Kirstin, who had been pulling at her skirt. "Have you set a date yet?"

"I'm thinking we will talk with Reverend Skarstead this Sunday, and if he agrees, we will be married after church the next Sunday." His smile at Selma said more than his words. He rested his hands flat on the table. "And now we better head home so we can be there before dark. Thank you for—for helping this all be possible and for making us all feel at home here."

"You are so welcome," Signe said slowly, searching for the right words.

"Remember, you are part of the family now." Gerd smiled and nodded. "Such a good thing to celebrate here in our kitchen. Thank you for telling us."

"I planned to wait until I spoke with Rune, but today just happened." Mr. Kielund stood. "Come along, Katie and Olaf. Tell them thank you for letting you stay."

Selma, with Eric at her side, waved them off from the back porch. When she shivered her way back into the kitchen, she looked around at the others, shaking her head. "Now, that was some surprise."

"A good surprise?"

"Ja, we were on our way back, trying to talk and understand each other, when all of a sudden he said he had something to ask me, and he did, and I understood what he meant, and I nodded and said yes and nearly fell off the wagon seat."

"Remember, Reverend Skarstead said this was a fine plan, and he prayed the two of you would let God bless you this way. He will be so very pleased when you talk with him." Signe puffed out a breath. "And now I better get to baking another gingerbread for supper. We need to celebrate!"

Sunday on the way to church, Signe could barely sit still. Wait until Nilda heard the news! Selma wore a secret smile most of the time. Except when she let panic creep in.

"What if we find we just don't get along?" Selma asked in one of her panicked moments.

"All couples go through periods like that." Gunlaug shook her head. "Did you and Nels get along all the time?"

Selma shook her head. "I tried to keep him from going out on the boat again, but he would not listen. And look what happened. Then I felt so terrible because we were still upset with each other when he left—and never came back." Tears drowned her voice. She looked up to see Eric studying her, tears running down his cheeks too. She gathered him close and stifled her weeping. "It will be all right. Your Mor just let memories run away with her."

"But Far . . ."

"I know, but now we have our new life in America, and you will have cousins and a new brother and sister very soon."

"I want to live with Bestemor and Tante Gerd, like now."

"Eric, look at that big dog." Signe pointed off to the side, where a pony-sized brown dog patrolled land that had been cleared years earlier. "Isn't he handsome?"

"Too big." Awe softened the words. "Rufus could run faster."

Signe nodded. "Possibly. At first I thought it was a small horse or a donkey, but he doesn't have big ears. You could ride him."

Eric shook his head and scooted closer to his mor's side. "I don't like that dog."

Nilda was just being helped down from a carriage when they

turned into the churchyard. She spoke to the driver and stepped back, waving to him as he left.

Signe felt like leaping out of the wagon and screaming Selma's news, but forced herself to wait until Rune stopped the wagon at the hitching rail.

"Throw the blankets over the horses," he instructed the boys.

Steam billowed from the team until Bjorn and Ivar threw the blankets over their backs. At least they were tied in the sunshine so they wouldn't be so cold. One of the horses in the team next to them snorted and stamped a foot.

"Isn't that Mr. Kielund's team?" Knute asked.

"I think you're right." Rune helped his mor down from the wagon seat and then his wife, who had moved to the tailgate with the others. His hands at her waist, he swung her to the ground, leaning close enough to whisper in her ear. "Isn't this Selma's news?"

Signe huffed a sigh and gave her husband a hint of a dirty look. His eyebrows arched as he held out one arm for Gunlaug and the other for Signe.

"I was afraid I would be late again, so I asked George to hurry." Nilda met them at the bottom of the steps. "What is going on? I know something has happened."

Signe rolled her eyes toward Rune.

"And you are under orders not to say anything?"

Signe nodded, rolling her lips together, but she tipped her head slightly toward Selma.

Nilda dropped her voice. "Selma's news?" Her eyes widened to match her growing smile. "Really?"

Signe nodded, grinning wider by the moment.

"You two are impossible!" Rune failed at sounding stern, though he tried.

Selma and Eric were slightly ahead of the others as they

216

walked in the door. Her face gave her away. They could have blown out the lamps in the narthex, her face shone so bright.

When Mr. Kielund drew her hand through his arm, anyone with eyes could have figured out that there had been a change in his life. His gentle smile at Eric and the way he ushered all of them into a pew made an announcement more clearly than any words.

Mrs. Benson stopped Signe with a hand on her arm. She nodded toward the new couple just sitting down. "Does that mean what I think it means?"

Signe nodded and grinned back at her.

"Have they talked with Reverend Skarstead yet?"

"After the service." She could feel Rune's frown as he motioned his mor to go in the pew before him and waited in the aisle for his wife and daughter, who for a change were not the sole focus of Mrs. Benson's attention. When Signe sat, she just caught Rune's slight headshake. And thanks to Gunlaug sitting between them, she and Nilda would not be able to discuss anything. Not that they would, but . . .

"But you can't get married next Sunday!" Nilda wailed after Mr. Kielund and his children left after dinner. "Mrs. Schoenleber wants me to spend the entire next week at her house. Well, actually all the next weeks, but that is beside the point."

"You mean she wants you to work there full-time?" Selma stared at her cousin.

"Yes, that she does."

"But I thought . . ."

"Me too, but she has changed her mind. She promised that I could come home for special events and I will have two days off every other week. George will provide the transportation, but she doesn't want him and the team out in bitter cold or stormy weather any more than necessary."

Signe sighed and shook her head. "On one hand, I am so pleased for you, and on the other . . ."

"Me too." Selma looked over her shoulder. "Coming, Tante Gerd." She patted Nilda's arm. "We will talk more later."

"This is a disappointment. A big disappointment." Nilda hung her head. "But she did say I could invite my family to visit, just preferably not all at once. Ivar will come into town for the socials when the weather permits."

Signe dropped her voice. "Have you heard any more about Dreng?"

"Oh yes. He is the darling of the fashionable ladies. Two of Mrs. Schoenleber's good friends were raving about him. I nearly choked."

"Did you tell them about the real Dreng Nygaard?"

Nilda shook her head. "No, but Mrs. Schoenleber picked up on my feelings and said we would talk about it when I get back to her house."

"How long will you be home?"

"Until Tuesday. But I will be at the church next Sunday. I told Selma that I would stand up for her, and I will." She paused. "Who do you suppose will stand up for Mr. Kielund?"

"I have no idea."

Chapter 21

"Oskar, I would be delighted to stand up for you. And honored."

"Thank you. I have no family in this area, and in these past weeks, you all have made me feel like part of your family."

Rune reminded himself to answer. This had caught him by surprise. A good kind of surprise. Surely in the years Oskar had lived here, he had made friends at church, but what did that matter? Signe would be as pleased to hear this as he was. Family. They were indeed growing a family here in Minnesota.

"Will it be good with you if we have a celebration dinner here at our house after the ceremony? We could invite others if you want."

"That sounds like a lot of extra work for the women. I mean, I am grateful and all, but . . ."

"Oh, I have a feeling plans are already underway, we men just haven't heard about them yet." Rune clapped Oskar on the back. "Are you sure you want to take the time to help us fell those trees?"

"Well, it's a trade, and good trades are good for both people. I only have a few trees left. I'm going to leave a couple standing, and right now is a slow season for me, so it just makes good sense."

How Rune appreciated the words *makes good sense*. "See you after breakfast, then."

"And the children won't be a bother? Or we could wait until after the wedding."

"Just more time for them to feel like part of the family. If you haven't noticed, they already have grandparents and aunts and uncles here." They settled the last of the sides of hogs in the wagon for Oskar and Rune to deliver to the meat market in Blackduck.

"Looks like it might snow finally." Oskar climbed up onto the wagon seat while Rune slung the horse blankets over the load. "I'll be switching to the sledge real soon."

At the house they picked up a basket with hot rocks and a jug of hot coffee and headed out. They planned to return with lumber for the addition to the workshop. The machinery was now under a shed roof while the machine shop was being fully enclosed and floored so they could work on more skis and furniture.

"I told the boys to work in the shop, but they insisted on the woods. We have three trees on the ground that need to be limbed and pulled over to the stack."

"They are hard workers, those two."

Rune smiled. "Ja. They're happy out in the woods. I never thought I would say that about Ivar. Bjorn took to it like a pro right from the beginning. But Ivar is too."

"In spite of Einar Strand?"

"Shame, that. He sure knew his woods and trees and taught us well."

Oskar stared at the road ahead. "I offered to haul logs for

him, and he threatened me with his shotgun if I set foot on his place again."

"You and everyone else. But we are grateful he brought us here and then Ivar and Nilda too. New lives for all of us."

"And Mrs. Strand too?"

"Gerd Strand most of all. It's strange how a sour attitude sinks right into a person, but happy seems to bounce off. She was a grumpy hermit when we came. I give the victory to Signe. Her patience and love won Gerd over. Then, when Einar died, Gerd"—Rune sought the right word—"blossomed. That's it. Blossomed."

Rune thought happy thoughts all the way into Blackduck. The snow started just as they reached the meat market in town.

"You got any more at your place?" the butcher asked.

"No," Rune replied, "this is the last for this year."

"Put me at the top of your list for next year. These are of fine quality. Firm but not tough and nicely marbled. How many sows you got?"

"Four, and we're raising two more gilts."

"You ever thought of putting heat in your barn and raising market hogs year-round?"

"Not really. We need someplace to store the feed. We can't raise enough corn for many more hogs. But thanks."

The man handed him a white cloth bag. "Here, try our sausage. We're getting orders from stores in Minneapolis, even. We just need more hogs and casings. Did you keep yours?"

"Only enough for what sausage we made."

The butcher nodded. "Well, save me your casings too, if you would. I'll pay well if they're clean."

"Thank you." Rune and Oskar climbed back up on the wagon seat.

They loaded quickly at the lumberyard and headed out of

town. The ground was now white, and the snow was falling harder. By the time they made it to Benson's Corner, the snow on the road was a couple of inches deep.

Oskar drove his horses into Rune's yard, and Rune climbed down. "It will take some time to unload. How about leaving your wagon here and hitching up to ours so you can get home faster?"

Oskar nodded. "Sounds like a good idea. Thank you." They hitched the horses to the other wagon, Signe hustled the Kielund children out to him, insisting he take quilts to put around them, and down the lane they trotted, disappearing into the snow curtain before they reached the curve.

"I hope they let school out early," Signe said, glancing at the clock. "Two o'clock, and it is already getting dark. Are you sure it was a good idea to let Mr. Kielund head home?"

"He has animals to take care of. But those boys better be getting in from the woods."

Rufus leaped off the porch and barked his way toward the road.

"Ah, good. That's got to be Rosie and the boys." Signe stared out the window in the door. "You can't see much beyond the porch."

"I'm going to the barn to help with chores. Good thing we got those ropes strung." Out on the porch, Rune waited for Rosie and her riders to appear through the snow curtain. "You two get in the house and get warmed up. I'll let the cattle and horses in." He took Rosie's reins and let her lead him to the barn. The cattle were bellowing, and the resting team nickered. "I know, that's what I'm here for," he told them.

All he had to do was open the doors, and the cows and heifers filed in, then the horses, all going directly to their stalls and stanchions. At the opening of their gate, the sheep filed over to the hayrack attached to the wall and began pulling out hay, munching as if they did this every day.

A thought grabbed Rune. "What will we do when the flock grows? We hardly have winter room for everyone as it is. Talk about a full barn!" He climbed the ladder to the haymow and forked down enough hay for the horses and cattle.

"Far?"

"Up here." The welcome sound of Bjorn's voice made Rune smile. All would be well; all the flock was home. Kielund would be home before long, and Nilda was safe at Mrs. Schoenleber's. "Thank you, Lord." The prayer floated on wings of gratitude. He could not begin to count all the things he was thankful for.

"You coming down or taking a nap up there?" Leave it to Ivar.

"I learned a long time ago that a haymow is a good place for thinking."

"Really? Is it the smell of hay or because you are high up or . . . ?"

"Perhaps because it is one of the few places I get to be alone." Rune swung around the ladder post and backed down. The *ping* of milk into a pail told him someone was milking, and he could hear Leif talking to one of the cows. His son carried on conversations with all the animals as well as the people around him. Rune would swear the animals answered as much as the humans.

There was something immensely satisfying and calming about a barn in the winter, like a world apart. The cat wound herself around his ankles and chirped up at him.

"You ready to move back to the house and leave your children out here to deal with the rats and the mice? You've done a fine job, yourself."

"Who are you talking to?" Bjorn paused from carrying buckets of water to the horses.

Rune shrugged. "Just the cat."

Bjorn gave him the same look he gave Leif. "Like father, like son?"

Rune cuffed him on the shoulder. "Thanks for watering the horses."

"We're supposed to be talking English." Bjorn snorted and lifted a bucket in for Rosie. "Not much for you yet, girl." He lifted his voice. "Hey, Ivar, bring a brush and a gunnysack over here. We need to dry her off."

Once all the animals were taken care of, Rune waited at the door. "We'll stop by the shop and unload that lumber before we head for the house. Ivar, bring that broom so we can sweep off the snow."

With all of them working, unloading didn't take long, even when they swept the boards again as they stacked them off to the side, getting them as close to dry as they could.

"Are we coming out here after supper, Far?" Leif asked.

"Why?"

"So I can put another layer of wax on my skis. It looks like we might need them by morning."

"If it keeps up all night, maybe you'll have no school," Rune said.

"Ha! Dreamer. They never close school here." Knute pulled his gloves back on. "I'm taking some of those rabbit skins to the house. I wish Tante Nilda was here to help me make more mittens."

"Bestemor can help you. She taught Nilda and me."

The idea of skiing to school delighted both boys the next morning. With their dinner pails in bags over their shoulders, they strapped their boots to the skis and pushed off from the edge of the porch.

"Takk, Far," they yelled back. "When we get there, everyone is going to want skis."

Rune watched them until they turned at the road. He nodded. The skis worked. This first ski journey seemed a bit shaky at the start, but both boys dug their poles in and had the rhythm right off.

"You can be proud of both the boys and the skis." Signe stood beside him until they turned back to the door.

"They were afraid they might have forgotten how to ski, but it comes back quick."

"Like Knute said, you'd better get down to the shop and get more skis into production. You're going to have customers." Gerd jiggled the chatterbox on her hip. "This one will be ready to ski before you know it."

"Is Mr. Kielund coming to help with the trees?" Signe asked.

"Probably not today. He has to get the wagon box on the sledge just like we do, and that will be first on the list." Rune nodded as he talked. "Nilda would have loved to see those two start out."

"Nilda loves to ski more than anyone else in the family, I think," Gunlaug said. "All winter long, she skied to work, first to the Nygaards—"

"Good thing that did not last long," Ivar commented. "The thought that he is in Blackduck makes my skin crawl. I know it is far harder for Nilda. If that man touches her, I swear I will kill him."

Rune stared at his brother. *Please, God, don't let him mean that, or . . . let me rephrase that. Lord, help us.*

"Rune, what is it?" Gunlaug was peering at him.

He shook his head. "Sorry, what?"

"You had a strange look on your face."

"I'm concerned about that . . . that . . ." Rune stopped, having no idea how to finish the sentence.

Ivar scowled. "There are no words bad enough, so don't

bother trying. The ones that fit . . ." He shook his head and looked at his mor. "You don't like us using words like that when women are around."

"I don't like you using words like that at all." Gunlaug's eyes narrowed. "But sometimes . . ."

"Sometimes actions speak louder than words. Remember when we talked about praying for our enemies and those who spitefully use us? That verse, I can't remember where it is. I think Jesus said it." Ivar drummed his fingers on the table. "Matthew, beatitudes?"

Gunlaug nodded. "That was some time ago, back home. I don't remember what brought it up. And then the minister preached on that same thing. Maybe that is why you remember."

"No, but what I want to happen to Dreng is not the result of prayer but all action." He stood up. "Let's get out to the woods, Bjorn."

"I'm coming too," Rune said. "Swinging an ax is good for working off bad feelings. Many kinds of work are. If Oskar shows up, send him back. We'll return to the house for dinner. We've got to get the wagon bed on the sledge first."

With three of them working together, it wasn't long before the horses were throwing the powdery snow up with their hooves as they jogged toward the towering trees. Their crystallized breaths were making ice on their whiskers, so Rune slowed them to a walk.

"They sure want to go, don't they?" Bjorn sat next to Rune on the seat, with Ivar on the outside. "Does the glare off the snow bother their eyes as much as it does ours?"

"I have no idea." Rune wished he could see more than blurs where he knew the horses' rumps to be. His glasses steamed up and his eyes watered. What a miserable combination.

They tied the team to a tree off where they were safe and threw the blankets over them.

"Did you bring some oats for them?" Rune asked.

"Always." Bjorn pointed to the sack in the wagon. "Feed them now or later?"

"Now. I'm not sure how long we're going to stay out here."

"It's not as bad as I thought it would be, since there is no wind." Ivar pulled the saws and axes out of the wagon. "Let's get at it." He tucked his scarf into his coat and pulled his knit hat down over his ears. "We don't need any frostbite."

Before long they were all shedding their coats, and then their sweaters, leaving their wool long johns to soak up the sweat. Rune notched the next tree, and he and Ivar picked up the rhythm of their axes, one on each side of the cut. They were nearing the tipping point when Rune ordered Bjorn back away from where he was sawing limbs off the last tree. "Just being careful!" He wiped his forehead with the back of his gloved hand.

"You all right?" Ivar asked.

"Ja, er, not really." Was it time to confess how bad his eyes were? Or ignore it, like he had been? Was this putting the boys or the horses or anyone else in danger?

"Your eyes?"

"The sun's too bright."

"Let's end this one and then talk."

"Ja."

They picked up their axes, and chunks of pine flew again. The tree trembled. They both backed away and leaned on their ax handles. With a growing roar, the tree gave up and hit the ground, taking one much smaller tree with it.

"We should have taken that one out first," Ivar grumbled. "We lost part of it now."

227

"Ja, we should have. Look, both of you—if you see something that needs doing, you tell me, you hear?"

"Sorry, Far." Bjorn hung his head. "I—I almost said something, but . . ."

"But you didn't. Son, you and Ivar are both men, and you are men who know what we are doing. I have to be able to depend on you."

"But . . ."

"No buts. We work as a team." Rune grabbed his sweater and pulled it over his head. "Let's get this one done. When Oskar comes, we'll have his team to help skid trees too." He chose the bucksaw. "Have either of you counted how many trees we have in that stack already?"

"Not enough."

Bjorn's rejoinder made Rune snort. "There never will be, son, not ever."

Chapter 22

"Have you considered coming along to my church so you can hear Mr. Larsson play for the service? The wedding will be right after the service, since Reverend Skarstead has a second parish." Nilda placed Mrs. Schoenleber's address book back on her desk.

Mrs. Schoenleber cocked her head and nodded slightly. "Why, that sounds like a marvelous idea." She paused to think more. "Then we will return here after the wedding."

Nilda licked her lips. Dare she ask? Yes, she dared. "We can, or perhaps we can go out to the farm for the celebration dinner they are preparing."

"So much depends on the weather. I know you agreed to stand up for Selma, but if the weather is stormy . . ."

"I know."

"All right." Mrs. Schoenleber combined a nod and a smile, then glanced down at her list. "You remember that Petter is coming for supper, yes?" Her eyebrows arched as she leaned forward. "I think he is sweet on you."

Nilda's smile made her feel warm inside. "I enjoy being with him. The three of us had a good time on the boat. But, you know, I really thought he was more Ivar's friend than mine."

"Well, we shall see. His supervisor says he's not happy that Petter wants to work out in the woods this winter, but he'll let him get it out of his system. Young men dream of being lumberjacks or cowboys, or so it seems." Mrs. Schoenleber paused at the sound of the door knocker. "Miss Walstead is here. Are you ready?"

"As I'll ever be."

"If she can stay for supper and the evening, we'll have a fourth for whist."

Nilda groaned inside. Whist was one of the things Miss Walstead insisted she learn. It was not an easy accomplishment, but she was improving. However, it was not her favorite way to spend an evening. A book to read in front of the fire, along with a cup of tea or hot spiced cider—that was pure pleasure. Or knitting and visiting, or knitting and being quizzed by Miss Walstead. Lately she had been teaching Nilda both American and Minnesotan history. She had progressed from first readers into third, the same with history. Reading them all aloud and answering questions both written and verbal, along with studying English grammar, was a challenge—but a good one. Nilda had always enjoyed school, and she could tell she was learning fast this way. Every time they worked on English words now, she had to put them in a sentence. Even when she was at home, using the English came easier.

"Are you ready for another day?" Miss Walstead greeted her. "I thought today we would make a trip to the mercantile and perhaps stop by the millinery shop. You need a hat to go with that black outfit."

"And shoes. Leather gloves would be nice. Oh, and a bag." Mrs. Schoenleber nodded as she spoke. "I know—the three of us should make a trip to St. Paul and do some real shopping."

Miss Walstead grinned brightly. "When would you like to go?"

"The social is next Saturday, so let's plan to catch the train on Monday and return, say, Thursday? We could go to my brother's house, but staying downtown would allow us to be right in the middle of the good stores. We can have supper with him and Belle one evening." She nodded more vigorously. "Yes, this is a fine idea, thank you."

Nilda looked from one woman to the other. Delight lit their faces. A trip to St. Paul, as if they did that kind of thing every other week. Nilda had never done something like this in her entire life. When it came to clothes, you made it yourself, or if you couldn't, such as shoes and boots, you might order it from the store, or you did without. She and her family passed clothes and such around all the time. Her stomach shook. She set her coffee cup very carefully back on the saucer so they would not hear it rattle.

"You are awfully quiet." Miss Walstead smiled gently. "A bit much to take in?"

Nilda nodded. And blinked. *Nilda Carlson, for pity's sake, you are a grown woman who is just experiencing new things. This is not worth crying over. Now, stop!*

If only it were that easy.

She inhaled and blew out a heavy breath, looking Mrs. Schoenleber in the eyes. "Are you sure you want to spend all this on me? After all, I . . ." Nilda lifted both shoulders and her palms. "I mean, I . . ."

Mrs. Schoenleber reached over and patted Nilda's hand. "You would deny an old woman this privilege of taking you shopping for the first time? I do not see it as spending, but investing. You are a young woman of rare beauty and character, and the wonderful thing is that you have no idea. To help you grow

231

and become all that you can be, I see that as a gift to me. Such a privilege, is it not, Jane?"

"I absolutely agree, for that is what I see too. Teaching you and watching you grow is such a privilege. I look forward to every day and lie awake at night planning what to do next." Miss Walstead leaned back in her chair, and the two women exchanged grins of both conspiracy and delight.

"But I am a farmer's daughter," Nilda said.

"Yes, so you will have the best of both worlds. Gertrude, I believe it is time Nilda starts music lessons too. That piano of yours is not used enough." She looked at Nilda. "Did you ever dream of learning a musical instrument?"

"My onkel played the fiddle, but he never really had time to teach me, nor I to learn."

"I imagine we could find a fiddle player to teach you, but I was thinking Mrs. Potts to start you on piano, and lessons sometimes with Fritz."

"Ahh." Mrs. Schoenleber nodded slowly, her smile growing. "A fine idea."

Nilda spent the day in a haze of too-muchness. *Overwhelmed* was a word she not only knew but felt. All the way from the top of her hair to the tips of her toes. Toes that were now encased in soft house shoes rather than her normal winter boots.

How she longed to be home to share all of this with Signe, although it might be too much for Gunlaug. Things like this just did not happen in the Carlson family—or any others, as far as she knew. A fairy tale, that was what this was.

"Well, then let us begin." Mrs. Schoenleber nodded briskly. "While you two go about your explorations, I will write to my brother and ask him to make the hotel arrangements."

"You could telephone him," Miss Walstead said.

"I know, but sometimes it is hard to understand people on

that newfangled machine. I much prefer letters. Then he can't insist that I come for the board meeting too."

"Which you will do anyway, because you know how important that is, and you don't want him to get the idea that a woman should not be the head of the board."

"True." Mrs. Schoenleber smiled at Nilda. "And that will be good training for you too, Nilda. You have a good head on your shoulders for business."

Disagreeing would be impolite, so Nilda kept from it with extreme self-control. As she'd thought—a fairy tale, and she was in it.

By suppertime that evening, Nilda was looking forward to Petter coming so she could sit and enjoy a casual conversation. Or so she thought.

After all the greetings, he had just been seated in the parlor when it became obvious he could scarcely sit still.

"Something surely has you excited, Mr. Thorvaldson," Miss Walstead commented with a smile.

Petter nodded and leaned forward so far, he could have fallen off his chair. "They have posted that the logging camps will open in two weeks. I think Dreng and I were the first to sign up. The foreman, Mr. Nicholson, said that returning loggers are hired first, but that there is always room for new men."

Nilda nodded and smiled. He was excited, all right. But her mind leaped at the idea that Dreng was soon to be heading into the woods. *Ideally never to return.* Even thinking such a thing made her heart stop. How could she? Earlier Mrs. Schoenleber had given her such high praise, and now she was wishing death or injury on another human being. No matter how horrible the man was, he was still human. How could she pray? *Oh, Lord, get him out of here and yet keep him safe from—from* . . . The argument raged in her head.

She glanced up to see Mrs. Schoenleber watching her. Sucking in a deep breath, Nilda forced a smile onto her face. At least she hoped it was some semblance of a smile. *Think of something good, something lovely.* A verse fought its way to the front of her mind.

She smiled at Petter. "I am glad you are getting your wish." There, that was good and true. "I know Ivar had thought about going, but he is already out in the woods felling our own trees."

"Supper is served, madam," Charles announced from the doorway in his most sonorous voice, something he did when they had company. Nilda made sure she did not catch his eye, because it might make her laugh, and that was truly impolite.

Petter offered her his arm, another thing that tickled her funny bone. "You should offer to Mrs. Schoenleber first," she whispered.

"Oh well." He held out his other arm, and Miss Walstead took it with a chuckle.

Mrs. Schoenleber rolled her eyes and walked beside Charles into the dining room. "You better enjoy and appreciate the meals here. They say they have good food in the logging camps, but I know it cannot compare to what Cook prepares for us."

"And the company here is far more engaging." Miss Walstead smiled up at Charles, who pulled out her chair after seating Mrs. Schoenleber. "I so enjoy dining here. Matilda is not nearly as good company, and I am not nearly as fine a cook."

"Matilda?" Petter gave her a questioning look.

"My cat. She is large, fluffy, and queen of our house. She makes sure no one forgets her position."

"Is she a good mouser?" Nilda asked, thinking of their two cats at home.

Miss Walstead laughed. "No, that is far too plebian for Her Highness."

"Plebian?" Nilda repeated.

"Of lower class."

"I see. Queenly and plebian are at opposite ends of the social strata."

Petter stared at her. "Would you like to explain to me what you just said? How have you learned so much English so fast?"

Miss Walstead said, "I work her nearly to death, or at least exhaustion. She is in school all her waking hours here and most likely dreams about what she is studying too."

Petter looked from one of the older women to the other. "Truly?"

Later at the card table, he asked, "Is whist part of your training too?"

"Yes," Mrs. Schoenleber answered for her. "It is part of entertaining guests."

"I like checkers and backgammon better, but this game is for four people, and those aren't. Did you play cards of any kind at your house when you were growing up?" Nilda asked.

"I don't remember much play time. We were always working at something. Far taught me both woodworking and leatherwork, even how to make boots. He used to make boots for all of us. His brother would tan the hides of cattle, hogs—their hide was used for the soles—and caribou. He lived farther north than we did."

"He patched boots too, then?" Nilda asked.

Petter nodded. "Over and over. After a while the boots were more patches than original leather, but we'd grease them and keep on wearing them, or when we were young, pass boots on to the smaller ones." He laid his cards down. "I won."

"That you did. Congratulations," Mrs. Schoenleber said.

"This just isn't my game," Nilda groaned. "One more round?"

"You have to keep track of the cards," Miss Walstead pointed out. "You can't let your mind wander."

"I see that, but seeing and doing are not necessarily the same thing."

Petter nodded. "How well I know that. Not just in cards."

"What do you plan to do with the rest of your life, when you come back from the woods?" Mrs. Schoenleber asked when they were nearing the end of the next round.

"I promised I would return to work in the lumberyard. It is a good job, and I have a lot to learn. The manager, Mr. Goddard, says he is willing to teach me everything I need to know. I would like to buy a house here in Blackduck and settle down." He looked directly at Nilda, who was shaking her head at the hand she'd been dealt.

She looked up and was startled by the look she caught in Petter's eye. "Is everyone ready to continue?"

"Yes," Miss Walstead said. "I believe it is my turn first."

When they finished, Nilda excused herself to the necessary, and when she returned, she had the feeling she'd missed out on something.

"Why don't you see Petter to the door?" Mrs. Schoenleber suggested. "Jane, I want to show you something in my office."

Petter already had his coat on and stood twisting his hat in both hands. "I, uh, I talked with Mrs. Schoenleber, and she said to mention this to you."

"All right." Nilda waited. But when his hat was starting to look rather misshapen, she asked softly, "Petter, what is it?"

"I—I asked if when I return from the woods, I might, uh, court you."

"Oh." She blinked at him. "I . . ."

"Is that a possibility, even?"

"I-I never thought about it, but I, well, yes. Of course." *Why not?*

Relief stopped the destruction of the hat. "Good. Oh, if, or rather when I write to you, will you write back?"

"Yes, I will do that."

"Good. Good." He nodded, his grin growing. "See you soon." He opened the door. "Good. Takk." He held out his hand, so she shook it.

"Good night." Closing the door behind him, she thought she heard a whoop from outside. Had she really agreed to a possible courtship? Wait until she told Signe.

"Nilda, dear, oh my." Mrs. Schoenleber and Miss Walstead returned to the parlor. "He asked you?"

"Ja, he did." Nilda looked over her shoulder with a slightly puzzled look.

"I told you he was sweet on you," Mrs. Schoenleber said.

"I don't know. Somehow I feel he is more like my brother." Nilda shrugged. "But perhaps that will change."

"Who knows?" Miss Walstead smiled. "Well, I will see you again tomorrow. Her Highness awaits my return."

Nilda smiled. A royal cat. Of course.

Mrs. Schoenleber said, "George will have the carriage around in a minute."

Miss Walstead frowned. "I hate to have him go to all that trouble."

"You are not walking home this late at night, so don't bother fussing. You know you are always welcome to stay here."

"And pay the penalty at home. Surely you jest." But Miss Walstead looked a bit relieved. A harness jingled outside, and she went out the door. A blast of cold blew in.

After Miss Walstead left, Mrs. Schoenleber laid a hand on

Nilda's arm. "I know you are tired, but I think we need to have a talk."

Good or bad? Can't it wait until another time? Nilda blew out a puff of air. *Perhaps a later time when my English is better.*

"Come, let's go back in the parlor in front of the fire. I will have Charles bring in tea."

Tea. Oh dear. *I will need fortifying?* Nilda chewed the inside of her bottom lip as she followed Mrs. Schoenleber back into the parlor, where two of the wingback chairs were now closer to the restoked blaze.

"I ordered tea," Mrs. Schoenleber said as they sat down, "but would you prefer something else?"

"No, tea is fine." Nilda stared into the flames, which dipped and danced, sending shadow patterns out onto the rug.

"I know you would rather go up to bed, but I think this needs to be dealt with, and the sooner the better."

Nilda took the offered tea and held the saucer with one hand while she held the china cup in the other. Blowing on the steaming surface, she waited.

"I believe there is more to the Dreng story than you have let on. Every time his name is mentioned, you go rigid."

"I really do not want to talk about this."

"I know."

Nilda sipped her tea, still hot enough to make her lips tingle. "He has—that is, he *had* a bad reputation in Norway."

"I see. Was this a personal experience or . . . ?"

"Yes, personal. My experience and that of other young women too."

"He is a very good-looking young man."

"Yes, and he believes—believed—that he could . . . have his way with any young woman, especially those who worked for his very wealthy family. Do what he wished with them." Was she explaining clearly enough in English? "And his mother believed her baby boy could do no wrong."

"You said his mother. Did his father not agree with that?"

"No, he knew his youngest son was, uh—" *Ah! That's the word.* "Spoiled. Spoiled beyond measure."

"But he did nothing about it?"

"He did when Dreng's actions were finally brought into the light. Uh, to his attention."

"And did Dreng attack you?"

"Attack. I think I remember what that word means. He would not stop his advances when I told him to. So I spilled water out of the scrub bucket and soaked his clothes. The next time he tried to drag me in his room. His mother came upon us and I ran away. My . . ." She searched her mind for the English word and found nothing. "My friend Addy warned me not to work there, but I needed the money for my ticket to America."

"I see."

The tea was much cooler. "I heard rumors about him. I mean, I *had* heard rumors about him. And we all heard of one young woman who suddenly went to live with an aunt somewhere else. But I thought that . . . that . . ." Her English totally betrayed her. She started over. "I thought that saying 'no' would stop him from doing anything bad." She snorted. "It did not." *Can we stop talking about him now? Please?*

Mrs. Schoenleber nodded slowly. "What happened when his mother found out?"

She yearned to speak Norwegian, but she could not. "His mother did not know why the girls she hired always quit suddenly. She fired me when I ran away, of course, as if I would continue working there. When she saw me later, she called me names. Dreng had told her it was my fault. I told my older brother and his fiancée what had happened, and the boys, my brothers and some others, took care of him. They would not tell me what they did, but Mr. Nygaard found out and sent his son to America. I hear that he told his wife she could not have contact with him. Dreng believes I ruined his good life by telling the truth."

"But you think his mother does have contact with him?"

"Yes, ma'am. A young man with no money or job, and he dresses in fine clothes and walks about being so nice to everyone."

Mrs. Schoenleber nodded. "This explains much. I too hear rumors. I know angry brothers, and I am fairly sure they would have killed him if they didn't thoroughly respect the reprise."

Nilda tried to sort out that sentence. The meaning came clear. "I see what you are saying. And I am not the only girl he, uh, he tried to . . ."

"Take liberties with?"

"Yes. . . . There were many. Perhaps that is why his father banished him to America, to keep him alive." Not that that was a great gift to the world.

The snapping of the fire broke the silence.

"I heard from someone I respect that Dreng admitted he'd been banished and that he has learned his lesson. He wants to start a new life in America and leave that former Dreng behind. He sincerely regrets his actions and hopes that anyone who learns his story or knows him from before will be willing to forgive him and start anew."

"I have a hard time believing that." Nilda knew *impossible* was a more appropriate word but left it where she'd laid it. "He wrote me a letter that said, 'I will get you for this.'"

"I see. And you say he held you responsible."

"Yes. Ivar said that perhaps he has changed. After all, most people learn from punishment, and he knew what kind of punishment Dreng had been dealt."

"Does Ivar believe Dreng has changed?"

"I don't know. He knows I don't ever want to see him and that when I did, it . . ." What word? "It distressed me very much."

"I can let him know he is not welcome here."

"You would do that for me?"

"Yes, of course."

Nilda tried to read this woman. "But you are not sure that is the best way, right?"

Mrs. Schoenleber smiled. "Right. I believe there is evil in this world, but I also believe God's Word that says to forgive. Especially those who ask to be forgiven."

"'Forgive as you have been forgiven.' It sounds so simple. I only wish it were." There. She had just used the subjunctive. Her English was indeed getting better.

"I agree, Nilda. What about this? We believe his change of heart until proven otherwise. Can you live with that?"

Can I pray for God to drop a tree on him? Nilda kept that to herself and nodded. "I will try." *But if he attacks someone else, I swear I will kill him myself.*

Chapter 23

"Aunt Gertrude! What a nice surprise!" Fritz Larsson wrapped Mrs. Schoenleber in a bear hug as Nilda watched from beside her.

"My dear Nilda here suggested I come to hear you play on a Sunday like this."

Nilda smiled and nodded. Why would a comment like that make the heat come up her neck and face? This felt too much like when he paid attention to her in class.

"And she was right," Mrs. Schoenleber continued. "Hearing you on the organ in church like this is far different from playing on the piano at my house. Which, by the way, I hope you will do soon."

"I hope so." Fritz turned to Nilda. "Thank you for bringing her out here. You'd think it was fifty miles instead of five."

"If it were fifty, I would take the train," Mrs. Schoenleber countered. "But you are right, I have not come out here very often."

"Once or twice?" His eyebrows arched into the hair drooping over his forehead.

Pastor Skarstead stepped in beside Mr. Larsson. "Good to see you, Mrs. Schoenleber. Welcome to our congregation. Thank you for joining us for this wedding." He glanced at his pocket watch. "Which we need to start right now. Fritz will play for Mrs. Strand as she walks down the aisle, if she would like." He looked to Selma, who shook her head after a glance at Mr. Kielund.

"We can just come up together, can't we?" Mr. Kielund asked.

"Of course. Now, if the guests will take their seats in the front pews, Fritz will play music to make us feel joyful at the union of these two fine people. And yes, children, you can stand here by your respective parents." The reverend nodded and smiled at the children, actually bringing shy grins to their faces.

The organ burst into "Joyful, Joyful, We Adore Thee," with Mr. Larsson smiling and nodding as the small group took their places.

Nilda fought the tears that always came when she heard that hymn. *Joyful, joyful* was right. *Lord, make this marriage joyful. These two have been through so much, and their children too.* She stood by Selma with one hand on Eric's shoulder.

When Mr. Larsson had played the closing notes, Reverend Skarstead held up his Bible. "We are gathered today in the presence of God and this company to bring this man and this woman into union as one. These will all become a family. Let us pray. Father God who ordained the sacrament of marriage, we thank thee for all thou hast done to make this day happen for these people. Give us pure hearts to hear thy word and live by what thou hast taught us. Let us hear what the scriptures have to say concerning marriage."

He read a few marked places in his Bible, then looked from Mr. Kielund to Selma. "You, Oskar, take her hands in yours. . . ."

Nilda chuckled along with him and the others. She rejoiced with her friends as they repeated the ancient vows, promising to remain together until death parted them, to love, honor, and care for each other. *Someday, Lord, I pray I will stand up in a church and declare these same vows with a man who will love me as I will love him.* She wished she had tucked a handkerchief in her sleeve. She glanced down when Eric leaned against her and returned his angelic smile.

"I now declare you husband and wife. Oskar, you may kiss your bride."

When he did, all three of the children giggled. They tickled Nilda so much, she had to fight to keep the giggles down herself. It was such a happy occasion. *Thank you, Lord, that I could come.*

Amid all the hugging and chuckles, Reverend Skarstead got the right people to sign the papers on the right lines. He folded the marriage certificate and handed one copy to his wife and the other to Oskar Kielund.

"I hate to do this, but I have to leave right now. This was such a privilege. Blessings on you all." The reverend waved as he turned to leave.

"Don't forget to remove your stole," his wife called after him.

"Thanks for the reminder."

Nilda hugged Selma again. "You make a beautiful bride," she whispered. "I am so happy for you."

Oskar shook hands with everyone and then thanked Fritz for his playing. "That was an added gift, thank you."

"My privilege. I have not gotten to play for many weddings, so thank you for allowing me to."

Mr. Kielund turned to Rune. "Thank you, my friend, for making me and my children part of your family before this began." He leaned closer to whisper, "And thank you for even thinking of this preposterous plan that has now been accomplished."

"I would like to meet these dear people," Mrs. Schoenleber whispered in Nilda's ear, distracting her from eavesdropping.

"Oh my. I am so sorry." Nilda turned to Selma and Oskar. "I am honored to introduce Mrs. Schoenleber, Mr. Larsson's aunt and my employer in Blackduck."

Mrs. Schoenleber smiled elegantly. "I've not crashed a wedding before, so thank you for the privilege."

Rune stepped forward. "We would all be happy if you could come out to the farm for dinner."

"I wish, but those dark clouds on the horizon make George, my driver, very concerned about another storm coming in." She nodded to the back of the church where George stood waiting.

"Ja, we better be heading out too. Mr. Larsson?" Rune asked.

"I think the same thing, so I will come another time. Thank you." He reached out and actually took Nilda's hand, saying in English, "Thank you so very much for bringing my aunt. Or at least being the cause of her coming."

Now Nilda's neck really did get hot. "You're welcome."

Signe wrapped her arms around Nilda. "I miss you so and thought we could have some time today, but the weather is the dictator here." She nodded to Mrs. Schoenleber. "I'm so glad to meet you after hearing wonderful things. Thank you for taking in my family when they needed help."

"You must come sometime too and spend a few days. We will give you a vacation."

Signe nodded to the sleepy girl on her hip. "Someday, perhaps."

"How I would love to have a little one in my house again. It's been too many years. You come and bring her, please."

"Why, thank you." Signe reached for Mrs. Schoenleber's hand. "How we would love for you to come visit us one day too, perhaps in the spring or summer."

"Yes, yes, George, I am coming." Mrs. Schoenleber squeezed Signe's hand. "Yes, I will do that."

Reluctantly, even a little bit sadly, Nilda joined her employer in the carriage, and they rattled away toward Blackduck. Halfway there, the snowflakes caught up with them.

"Good thing I listened to George instead of my heart," Mrs. Schoenleber said with a sigh.

"You really wanted to go out to the farm for the party?"

"Oh yes, I really did. I lived on a farm until I was ten, when my father decided he could make more money with the trees than farming. He sold our place and bought timberland north of Minneapolis. He never looked back, and then he became interested in the railroads and met my husband-to-be."

"I figured you grew up in a wealthy family."

"Oh, we were wealthy, but our wealth was not based on money, but on hard work and my father's willingness to follow his dreams. He taught his sons and daughters the same. When he died fifteen years ago, he finally put my brothers in charge of all his businesses. I have three brothers and one sister. I am the eldest."

"Do they ever come to Blackduck to visit you?"

"Not often. They say it is too far and keep suggesting I move back to Minneapolis. I tell them the distance is the same for me as for them, and the train runs both ways."

Nilda chuckled. "Why do you stay here? Since you have a choice, I mean."

"Simple. This is my home. I have work to do here."

Nilda stared out the window at the snow that, while heavier than when they had left the church, was still not obscuring the view. Had it been snowing harder, George might have insisted they close the drapes on the windows. She felt sorry for him up there in the driver's box.

"Does George have a quilt or any protection?" she asked.

"He has a heavy wool greatcoat with a wide collar out over the shoulders, and good gloves. If I suggested he needed more, he would be offended. He is more concerned about us in here. Besides, we're almost home. When you pass that farmhouse, you know you are in the outskirts of Blackduck." She pointed off to the right, where they could see lights in the windows of a two-story house.

Mrs. Schoenleber looked thoughtful. Suddenly she said, "You know, I've been thinking about our talk regarding Dreng Nygaard."

"I wish he never existed."

"Not surprising, but God does provide help for those who ask, and perhaps he really has had a major change in his life. I am sure that would please his father no end."

"I don't think he has ever worked a day in his life. Mrs. Nygaard was afraid he might get hurt. I remember Mor and others in the family talking about that. I know, gossip is not a good thing, but . . ." Again English failed her. "But the gossip said that she spoiled him so much that he thought he owned the world. And he did nothing to earn it. Do you really think something like that can be turned around?"

"I know that people can change if the pain of staying the same is greater than that of change. I also believe that God still works miracles. I have seen them happen."

The carriage turned to the left, so they had only two more blocks to go.

Nilda watched the familiar buildings pass. "Thank you for having George take me to church for the wedding today and for coming along. Mr. Larsson was certainly surprised and pleased to have you there."

"True. He has always called me his favorite aunt. I'm the one who encouraged him in his music dreams, as well as teaching. His mother and father were not happy with me, but I am a strong believer in the value of dreams."

George pulled up at the front door and hopped down to open the carriage door for them. "Here you go. Be careful on that walk. Charles swept it, I see, but it could still be slippery. You hang on to her, Miss Nilda." He helped them both down and waited until they were at the door, which opened before they got there. Charles ushered them inside, tsking at their being out in the snow.

"What could we do? After all, the snow wasn't terribly bad." Mrs. Schoenleber dusted the snowflakes off Nilda's shoulders. "Shake your hat and scarf. Charles, I do hope you have the fire going in the day room."

"Of course, I expected you about now. Cook has hot mulled cider to warm you. A young man who was here at the first social dropped off an envelope for you. I put it on your desk."

They both stood in front of the fire for a bit and turned to warm their backs also. When Charles brought in the tray of cider, they sat down in the chairs and accepted the mugs from him.

"Cook said you probably did not eat out there, so she fixed you a light repast to hold you until supper."

"Cook was right. We headed back immediately since it looked like snow was on the way. I expect Mrs. Benson called too, didn't she?"

"Someone did. That is how we knew for sure you were on your way. The telephone is a rather remarkable improvement."

After sipping the cider and doing away with one of the fancy sandwiches, Mrs. Schoenleber slit the envelope open and removed the page, nodding as she read it. "As I suspected, this is from Dreng Nygaard."

As if there were any other Drengs that they knew of. Nilda stared at the fire as she swallowed and sipped, enjoying the heat both inside and out. Was it really possible for him to change into a decent man? Everything within her screamed, *No, no, never.*

"He is asking for a meeting with you." She focused back on the letter. "To try to make things right, is what he says."

Nilda closed her eyes and rested her head against the chair back. The silence grew. "Do I have to?"

"No, you do not have to." She emphasized the *have*.

"But?"

Mrs. Schoenleber humphed. "But I think that if he has left the old man behind and become a new man, you will be free of the hate you carry. I believe he is asking for forgiveness, and if you hang on to the bitterness, it will destroy you. Not him. *You.*"

"And if this is all a lie?"

"Forgiveness is freedom for the one who forgives, whether the other has changed at all. If he asks, or if he doesn't, you need to forgive for your own sake."

Nilda swallowed the tears for as long as she could, but when they brimmed over, she let them run. Her sigh when the well dried up was one of either freedom or defeat, but she finally said, "I will see him. I will forgive him. Only because I trust you will be right outside the door."

"Yes, both Jane and I will be waiting." Mrs. Schoenleber paused and grinned mischievously. "With raised cleavers."

The picture in her mind made Nilda shake her head and snort.

Later, Mrs. Schoenleber wrote a response for Charles to deliver the next morning, as it was already getting dark; the address had been on the envelope. "I told him tomorrow afternoon."

"Fine. Better to get it over with. And no matter what, he will be heading to the logging camp next Monday." Nilda didn't say *good riddance to bad rubbish*, but she thought it.

That night she dreamed she was being chased by someone in a black hat with a hatchet raised to strike. When she woke, she was panting like she'd been running all night.

The gray of dawn was lighting the snow-covered world. Tree branches hung low, and the iron spikes of the fence wore white toppers. But the snow had stopped, and someone had already been outside and shoveled and swept off the walkways.

Grateful for the furnace that heated the entire house, Nilda dressed in a wool skirt and knitted wool vest over a waist. With her hair brushed and bundled in a snood, she made her way downstairs to breakfast. Out at the farm, chores would be nearly done, and the boys would soon be on their way to school on their new skis.

"I sure hope my brother is making me some skis out in that shop of his," she said as she entered the breakfast room.

"We have skis in the carriage house." Mrs. Schoenleber looked up from reading the paper. "I haven't skied in years, but you are welcome to use them if you like."

"Really?"

"Of course. How easy it is to please you, my dear." She reached for the bell to the kitchen. "Cook has outdone herself with cheese blintzes this morning." Pausing, she asked, "Have you ever had them?"

"For special times, but not often. Mor—I mean, Mother used the soft cheese when it was fresh."

"She made cheese?"

"Most farm families make cheese when the milk is plentiful because that is the best way to keep it. We did up at the seter. Seter is when we'd take the cows, goats, and sheep up to the mountain summer farm. We used the milk there for cured cheese."

The day passed swiftly as always, and soon the clock was announcing two and her stomach was announcing upsets. When the knocker clanged, she stood beside the chair in the office while the two older women went into the kitchen.

"Thank you for seeing me," Dreng said as Charles showed him into the room after taking his coat.

"You are welcome. Please, be seated." She made sure her English was impeccable as she motioned him to a chair. She knew she looked her best, as she had very carefully seen to that.

"I would like to tell you how lovely you look, but I will get directly to why I asked to see you," Dreng started.

Smooth talker, as always. No change there. She nodded.

"I-I have come to beg your forgiveness for the way I acted toward you at home in Norway. My behavior was unconscionable." He was speaking Norwegian, not English. She stared right at him without moving. "I deserved everything that has happened. And more. But, Nilda, I beg you, please say you forgive my behavior."

His behavior? It was his attitude, his way of living that was wrong. "Your behavior?"

"Why, yes, the way I treated you. Surely you remember?" He blinked and turned his head slightly to the side.

"Oh yes, I remember."

"I-I need you to forgive me so that I can start over and have a new life." He sounded like he'd memorized his speech. "Can you find it in your heart?" He paused. "Please?" He dropped his gaze to his hands. "I don't know what else to say, other than I'm sorry. So very sorry." He started to rise. "I guess I'd best go and let you think about this. I know it must be a shock."

She forced her words out in a rush. "Only because of what the Bible says will I forgive you, not to make you feel better. As

I remember, there are others you treated the same way. Are you going to ask their forgiveness also?"

"I would if I could talk with them." His gaze left hers and shifted to his clasped hands. "Thank you."

"For your sake, I hope you mean this."

"You can count on it." He stood. "I will see you at the social. Thank you again."

"I hear you are going to become a logger."

"Ja, my onkel said that would make a man out of me if anything can."

"Well, I hope he is right." Nilda stood. She did not take the hand he offered her. "I will see you out."

But when she opened the door to the hall, Charles was waiting there. He bowed slightly. "I will see him out for you, miss."

"Thank you. Good-bye, Dreng."

"I will see you soon." He left.

She realized she was shaking when the two older women came through the door.

"Are you all right?" Miss Walstead came to her and clasped her upper arms.

"I don't think so." Nilda collapsed into the chair, melting into a puddle of tears.

Mrs. Schoenleber knelt beside her. "Dear Nilda, you did what God told you to do, and now you can cry all you need. Let the tears wash you into freedom."

"I said 'I forgive you.' I hope I meant it." *Because I am pretty sure he did not.*

Chapter 24

The nightmare woke her up again.

Nilda sat up in bed, trying to calm her breathing. Who was the man in the black hat, and why was he chasing her? She never saw his face, but light glinted off his raised weapon, be it cleaver or ax. Whatever it was, the whole thing screamed danger.

She reached for the glass of water she kept on the nightstand, almost knocking it over in the darkness. The cold water made her shiver. She knew if she pulled the bell, someone would come, would bring tea if she asked. Somehow, just the thought was comforting. In all her life, she'd never had a room or a bed to herself. There had always been someone right by to comfort her. Or, as was more often the case, she had comforted someone else.

She'd heard someone say once that dreams could tell a story. They did in the Bible. Jacob saw a ladder with people or angels going up and down on it. But did nightmares especially carry a message? One thing was for sure, the dream felt evil.

The only evil she could think of in her entire life was Dreng Nygaard.

And yesterday, he had asked for her forgiveness for his behavior. Why did that bother her? *Lord, I told him I forgave him. Wasn't that enough? Is there more? You said when you forgive, the sin is gone, as far as the east is from the west. Mrs. Schoenleber said I did what was required of me and now I am free. I want it all to be gone, especially the memories. Can you clean those out too?*

Are you going to trust me? The words seemed all around and through her, but gentle. A question. She felt like lighting the candle to see if someone else was indeed in the room, but she knew where the voice came from.

Trust. Forgiveness. She blew out a breath and laid back against her pillow, pulling the quilt up around her neck, tucking it under her chin. Easy words to say, but what did they really mean? She heard the curtain rustle in the warm air rising from the furnace that lived in the cellar. She couldn't see the air, but she could feel the warmth. Surely if she could trust the furnace would bring warmth, she could trust that God would live up to His word and teach her, protect her from the man in the black hat.

He said, *I am the light.* He said it over and over. She fell asleep again, trust and light filling her mind.

In the morning, she reached for the Bible in English that Mrs. Schoenleber insisted she keep in her room. She'd never had a Bible of her own before either. Her wise employer had said this one was hers. Propped against the pillows, Nilda held the Bible against her knees and turned to the New Testament where Jesus had said, "I am the light of the world." Surely it was in Matthew.

A knock at the door, and Gilda, the upstairs maid, peeked around. "I brought you some tea if you would like."

"Thank you, but you didn't need to do that."

"Cook thought you needed something warm this morning." She set the tray on the foot of the bed and poured a cup. "She says breakfast will be ready when you come down. Would you like help with dressing or with your hair?"

Nilda held the cup in both hands and inhaled the fragrance. "This is such a kind thing for you to do." *And especially this morning, for that horrible dream was lingering.*

"Miss Walstead will be here in about an hour."

"Is it that late already?" Nilda drank the tea, set the cup back on the tray, and flipped back the covers.

"What waist will you be wearing today?" Gilda stood at the door of the chiffarobe, holding up the light blue one. "With the navy skirt?"

"Yes, that will be fine."

"We could braid a dark ribbon in your hair."

"Gilda, you realize you are spoiling me."

"Oh no, miss, I am just doing my job." But her smile helped Nilda let go of the night and rejoice in the new day. "See, the sun is back out."

"I see, and if I can fit it in today, I would like to go skiing." Nilda let Gilda help her dress, then sat on the bench in front of the dressing table. "There is nothing like skiing on new snow, even though it is not deep enough yet for real drifts, and the land here is pretty flat."

"I will ask Charles to get the skis out and make sure they are well waxed."

"Do you ski?"

"I used to."

"Perhaps you could ski with me sometime."

"Perhaps." Gilda finished off the braid and pinned it in a coil on the back of Nilda's head. Handing Nilda the small mirror, she nodded. "This is all right?"

"Better than all right. Thank you."

"You might want a sweater along, just in case."

Down in the breakfast room, the sun slanted through the tall windows, giving the whole room a golden glow.

Mrs. Schoenleber looked up from reading one of the newspapers. "I was getting concerned about you."

"And so you and Cook sent Gilda up to make sure I had not run away?"

"Was that a thought?"

"No, but . . ." Nilda looked up at Charles. "Please tell Cook that whatever she has ready is perfect."

He nodded. "I hear you would like to go skiing."

"Do the very walls have ears here?"

He smiled and shook his head. "No, but Madam asked that I get down the skis and wax them."

"I told him." Mrs. Schoenleber rattled the paper as she folded it closed again. "We have several pairs of skis. I would much prefer you did not go alone, at least not this first time."

"But—" Nilda swallowed the words, but Mrs. Schoenleber obviously interpreted the look Nilda gave her and chuckled.

"I know, I have a tendency to be overly careful, but bear with me and my active imagination. Charles will go with you this first time."

"But I hate to impose . . ."

Charles rolled his eyes. "You would deprive me of a chance to go skiing on a day like today? I surely hope not."

"If you put it that way . . ." Nilda shook her head. "I'm surprised Miss Walstead isn't going too so she can quiz me as we ski."

"That too could be arranged." Mrs. Schoenleber was smiling broadly now.

After three hours of language, grammar, history, and social graces, Nilda was more than ready to ski, possibly even to throw herself into a snowbank, if they had any big enough yet.

"I'd like you to explain to Charles how to ski," Miss Walstead announced just after she closed her book and dismissed Nilda from the library.

"He said he knows how to ski." Nilda knew she looked confused, but how could she not?

"I know you could give good instructions in Norwegian, but . . ."

Nilda huffed a sigh and rolled her eyes. "Yes, ma'am." The first thing she had to do was learn the English terms for the equipment and the skiing terminology. "I think Charles better teach this first time."

Miss Walstead nodded, her shiny apple cheeks stretching with her knowing smile.

Nilda donned another woolen petticoat and wool socks that reached above her knees. Outside, she allowed Charles to buckle the bindings over her boots, repeating after him the terms. When they both stood, skis sliding properly and poles placed, he pushed off first, and she followed.

They skied on powder snow without a track, other than those left by rabbits and birds. She raised her face to the sun and sucked in the frigid air. Cold but not too cold. At least the snow would not melt right away.

Charles suggested, "We'll go out to the river and follow it south for a while, then come back around Blackduck. This will give you a good idea of the terrain."

"Terrain?"

"The land. How the land lies. The way of the land."

"Ah."

She realized the Schoenleber house was near the northern outskirts of the town, so they were quickly into farmland and young trees in wooded areas. The loggers had left some of the younger white pines to grow. Charles told her who the places belonged to, since this was an area of many larger homes.

They stopped at the riverbank. Ice extended out about a third of the width of the river on either side.

Charles waved an arm. "Before long it will be frozen solid, plenty thick enough to use as a road to haul goods up and down from Bemidji and farther south. People will drill holes for ice fishing and set tip-ups to tell them when a fish is on the line. Some make shacks they drag out here to protect them from the weather. They build fires in metal barrels."

"Would you please repeat all that?"

The second repetition helped, and she got it all. Ski poles, bindings, camber, and now shack, barrel, tip-up, drill . . . so many new words. At least she knew the word *fishing* and therefore *ice fishing*.

"Mr. Garborg, who lives on a lake near our farm, mentioned ice fishing. Knute was all excited; he loves to fish. Hunt too."

"My family does too. I never was one to like working out in the winter weather, let alone fishing or hunting."

"But you like to ski?"

"Of course, on a day like today. We better hurry back." He grinned at Nilda.

"So we ski faster." That suited her just fine. They arrived back at the house just in time for dinner.

"This came for you." Mrs. Schoenleber handed Nilda an envelope when she sat down at the table. "You look like you had a good time."

"We did, thank you." She looked at the envelope. "Should I leave this until later?"

When both of the older women shrugged, Nilda slit the missive open and read the few written words. "Dreng is thanking me for yesterday."

258

"That's polite."

Nilda put the paper back in the envelope and heaved a sigh as she laid it on the table. "He said he is looking forward to the social."

"I can still uninvite him."

"Thank you, but you need not. He will be out in the woods next week." *A good place for him.*

Miss Walstead mused, "It will be interesting to see how long he lasts out there. Logging is a hard life. And yes, they pay well, so I hear, but those men earn their money."

Nilda ate her soup, dipping the spoon into the far edge of the bowl as she'd been shown. Not that it made much sense, but she was learning that many of the polite or proper ways of doing things did not always make sense.

Presently Mrs. Schoenleber announced, "Petter is coming for supper tonight and looking forward to another evening of whist."

"By himself?" Nilda asked.

"Of course. I really don't think he would like to share the little time he has left with a male friend."

Miss Walstead snickered. "She means time with you."

"Oh." Nilda picked up the basket of crackers.

That evening Petter arrived with two packages, one for Nilda and one for Mrs. Schoenleber. "It's no wonder Mr. Goddard is the manager of the lumberyard. He knows so much about wood and woodworking. He has taught me how to make several things with wood. I started with spoons for cooking."

"One can never have too many good wooden spoons," Mrs. Schoenleber said, "or so Cook tells me."

"Good, I will bring her several different sizes. I thought to send some out to the farm with you, Nilda, next time you go."

Nilda nodded and smiled. "That will please the cooks there." But her package was too small for wooden spoons.

"Go ahead, open them."

Nilda watched as Mrs. Schoenleber opened her package. "Ah, a box within a box." From the wrappings she lifted a square wooden box made out of several kinds of wood and finished to a high shine. Its corners were joined with perfect dovetails. "This is beautiful work, Petter. What a lovely thing to do." She set the box on the wooden mantle and stepped back to admire it. "Thank you, Petter."

"And what a lovely skill to have," Miss Walstead added. "I know Mr. Goddard is good with wood, for I've used his services, but I have a feeling you might surpass your teacher."

Nilda opened hers to find a pin of tiny fitted wooden pieces that formed a delicate cross in the middle. "Oh. Petter, this is beautiful." She held it in the palm of one hand and traced the design with a tentative finger. *Oh, Petter, I hope this does not mean more than a gift. How can I accept something like this, and yet how can I not?*

"Mr. Goddard said he thinks I could sell things like this to one of the stores here in Blackduck," Petter said.

"Young man, you are an artist, not just a wood-carver." Miss Walstead looked closely at the pin. "From the utilitarian to the sublime."

Nilda grinned at Petter. "I think she just gave you a compliment."

"Could you say it in Norwegian so I know what she is talking about?" he asked.

"Uh, I-I . . . give me a minute to figure it out." She nodded and rephrased it.

Petter stared at Miss Walstead. "Tusen takk—er, thank you very much."

"You are welcome, and your English is improving too."

"Not as much as Nilda's."

"She has two teachers who apply pressure." Mrs. Schoenleber nodded to Charles, who announced that supper was being served. "Thank you. Oh, and Petter, I've heard that loggers at the camps speak several different languages. The more you speak English, the better off you will be."

"Thank you for the advice. Mr. Nicholson said the same thing. I know plenty of wood and lumber terms, what I need at work."

After supper, when they adjourned to the parlor where the card table was set up in front of the fire, the competition grew in intensity as both Petter and Nilda gained more skill at the game.

"I wonder if they play whist at the logging camp?" Petter leaned back in his chair. "You know, I really would rather win than lose like this."

Mrs. Schoenleber smiled. "But you almost won, and remember, Jane and I have been playing this game for years. You both played well tonight. When you come back in the spring, we'll play again."

"Thank you. And we'll be playing this at the social?"

"Yes, I thought a table of whist and one of backgammon. Perhaps we could play charades for a while first."

"In English?"

"Yes, Petter, in English."

The night of Mrs. Schoenleber's social arrived. Nilda greeted it with an odd mix of extreme enthusiasm and dread—both Petter and Dreng would be there.

Along with her studies, she was starting to perform some tasks. From Mrs. Schoenleber's notes, she wrote out the report of a library committee meeting. In English. She addressed and stamped a dozen envelopes. She cut and numbered fifty squares of paper, twice; one copy would be given to each person who came to the social, and the other placed in a jar. At the end of the evening, a number would be drawn from the jar, and that person would receive a frosted chocolate cake. Originally, the prize was going to be *stollen*, but Cook insisted that was too ordinary. A stollen? Ordinary? Because she worked in the household, Nilda would not be taking a number.

As young people arrived, they soon had enough for two teams for charades, numbering off so that hopefully the teams would be about even, rather than the ladies against the men, as someone suggested.

Nilda tried to make sure she was not on the same team as Dreng, but he changed places with someone else at the last minute. She turned away to give herself a moment to regain a pleasant demeanor so the other team members would not see her reaction. According to Miss Walstead, real ladies never revealed their feelings in a situation like this or any others. Not that Nilda ever believed she wanted to be a real lady.

She turned at a touch on her shoulder. Dreng. She knew it before she turned; she could feel his presence. She paused to give herself enough time to become that lady.

He smiled at her. "I hope I did not upset you. I just wanted to be on the same team as you. We'd have a good chance of winning then."

"And you always like to be on the winning team." At least she did not sound as sarcastic as she felt. At least, she hoped not.

"Yes, I do like to win."

"What a surprise." She wished she had a fan to flutter before her face. *I am a lady, a gracious lady. A very gracious lady.*

"And I know that you do too, so we'll all have a good time."

Why did what he said make her feel so uncomfortable? Instead of backing up like she wanted to, she held her ground and smiled back. If he had really changed, this would be a good night to prove it. It wasn't as if he were doing anything wrong. In fact, he was being the perfect guest, making several of the other young women giddy.

If only I dared warn them that they are flirting with danger. But he says he is changed, remember? And so far it looks like he has. If I didn't know better . . . but that is not fair. Shouldn't I give him a chance to prove himself?

The argument in her head almost drowned out the laughter at his antics to get their team to guess the right answers. She had to admit, Dreng was very good, so good that their team was ahead by quite a margin, in spite of the language barrier, which he turned into more to laugh about.

They never got around to playing cards. After the food was served and enjoyed, the guests gathered to thank their hostess and commiserate that Dreng and Petter would not be at the next social.

"Now, you be careful out in those woods. I've heard logging is a dangerous way to make a living," one of the girls said to Dreng. "We want you back in one piece."

He bowed with a flourish. "I promise to do my best. Petter too." He raised his voice. "If anyone happens to send letters to encourage two novice lumberjacks, I can guarantee they will be much appreciated." He deepened his Norwegian accent to bring on even more laughter.

Nilda did not roll her eyes but almost laughed with the others. She had agreed to answer Petter's letters, but Dreng was on his own.

As the guests were leaving, Charles—amazing Charles— knew exactly which coat and hat belonged to which guest. He handed each the appropriate wrap. When he handed Dreng his coat and hat, Nilda's blood ran cold.

A black hat.

Dreng's hat was exactly like the hat in her nightmare. Exactly! She had built a slight level of comfort in his presence over the course of the evening. That comfort was shattered now.

How could she ever learn to accept him, or should she even try?

Chapter 25

"Nilda's here!" Signe threw open the kitchen door and called from the porch. "Come in, come in. We're putting the coffeepot on, Mr. George, so you can get warmed up too."

"Thank you, I will do that." He helped Nilda out from the blankets in the sleigh.

"Tie your horses up here, or they could go to the barn." Signe reached back through the door and grabbed a shawl off the rack.

"I'll throw blankets over them here. I can't stay long."

Signe reached for Nilda's bag. "Get yourself in here. That wind—uff da." She held the door for the driver. "Come in, come in."

He stamped the snow off his boots and smiled at Signe. "If that coffee tastes anywhere near as good as it smells . . ." Once in the door, he swung his greatcoat off and started to hang it up on the peg by the door, but Signe took it from him before he could blink.

"I'll hang it nearer the stove so it will be warm when you go out," she said. "Thank you for bringing Nilda out here in spite of the wind and blowing snow."

George smiled and nodded in spite of her mixed English and Norwegian.

Nilda stood beside him. "I want you to meet my family; the men are all out in the woods." She pointed and gave names, and they all greeted one another.

Signe nodded as she poured a cup of coffee for him. "Cream? Sugar?"

"No, thanks. Black is best."

"Good to see you again," she said, handing him the cup.

Gerd pulled out a chair. "Surely you can take a minute to sit down and have some cookies."

"If you insist." His smile brought out one of her rare ones. "Now, you are Tante Gerd to the others, but to me you are Mrs. Carlson?"

"Actually, Mrs. Strand." She made sure she spoke English.

"And this is the little girl Miss Nilda brags about all the time? Kirstin?"

"Yes. Have another cookie. These are especially good for dunking in coffee."

He waved back at Kirstin, who was talking to him as if she'd known him forever. "I wish I knew what she is saying."

"So do we all. Oh, Mor, I forgot your letter." Nilda fetched her coat off the rack and dug in the pocket. "Here. We stopped to see if Mrs. Benson had something to deliver."

"A letter from Norway. It must be Johann. Tusen takk."

George drained his coffee and held up his hand to say no more. "I need to be on my way. Is there anything you need to send to Mrs. Schoenleber?"

"Yes, the ham I promised is ready." Signe grabbed her coat and scarf. "I'll be right back."

Once the ham was tucked in the sleigh, they waved George off and hurried back into the kitchen.

"I'm surprised you are here," Signe said.

"When an agreement is made, it will be honored unless it's utterly impossible. That's just the way Mrs. Schoenleber operates." Nilda reached for Kirstin. "Come to Tante Nilda, you sweet baby. You certainly charmed that nice gentleman who was here." Kirstin grinned at her and jabbered back. "When she learns to talk, we all better watch out. She'll just take over."

"She knows how, just not our language." Gerd finished pouring them all coffee and refilled the cookie plate. "This deserves a celebration."

Signe smiled as she sat down. "You think everything deserves a celebration nowadays."

"I know. I have to make up for all those years of no celebrating, not even smiling." Gerd put a cookie into a reaching baby hand. "What do you say?"

"Ta-ta." Kirstin's head bobbed. "Ta-ta."

Nilda raised an eyebrow. "You're supposed to teach her English, remember?"

"Takk is far easier than thank you."

Nilda asked Gunlaug, "So are you going to read the letter or, I know, wait until the men come in?"

"We'll wait like always."

"How are the newlyweds doing?"

"Sometimes Selma and the children come with him on the days Oskar is out in the woods here," Gunlaug said. "They both seem happy, and the children know how to play together. Kirstin is so excited when they come."

"Olaf has decided we are all Grandma here, or Aunty and Uncle. That way he doesn't have to worry about names." Signe got up to refill the coffee cups. "This is such a treat. Oh, and Rune has something to show you down in the shop."

"I hope it is another pair of skis," Nilda said. "I've been using the skis at the house in Blackduck. Mrs. Schoenleber said she would like to buy several pairs as soon as he has them ready. I think she wants to give them as Christmas gifts."

"You'll have to talk with your brother about that. I know he spends every minute he can in the shop."

"I told him to let the boys do the trees, especially when Oskar is here, but he won't listen to me." Gerd shook her head. "Men."

Nilda sniffed. "What smells so good?"

"We're baking the two rabbits Knute brought in. You should see their lovely white pelts. He said he wants to make a vest out of them. They're tanning hides in the shop now too; he learned from Mr. Edmonds."

"So many changes going on." Nilda lifted dishes out of the cupboard and started setting the table.

"Tell us what is happening with you in Blackduck." Gunlaug picked up her knitting, as did Gerd. "It's easier to hear in here. It's noisy in there when we get the machines all running."

Nilda entertained them until they heard boots on the porch, and then she and Signe set the food on the table.

"I see you made it back," Ivar greeted her. "I was beginning to think you forgot us."

"Hardly, but they keep me really busy there, insisting I learn English without an accent, history, grammar, manners, and social games. The latest is piano lessons. I started the other day, and I feel like I have all thumbs." She flexed her fingers.

"That is what you call work?" Rune hugged her as he moved around the table to sit down. "Welcome home, where we can give you real work to keep you in shape."

Nilda snorted.

"When do you go back?" Signe asked, hoping the stay would be more than a day or two.

"Sunday after church. George will pick me up there. Remember, Ivar, you are coming to the social next Friday. That's so Mr. Larsson can come. I figured you could ride back and forth with him. I believe he has a horse and sleigh."

"We could probably ski just as fast."

Signe looked at her family gathered around the table, laughing and teasing each other, enjoying the food. This was the way she'd dreamed her family would be, but that first year had almost made her give up hope. She didn't think a harsh word had been spoken since Einar died.

"Don't forget your letter," she reminded Gunlaug. "We've hardly had news from home since you came here."

"Hurry, Mor, we've got to get back out there." Ivar looked at the clock. "It's going to be dark before we know it."

"You're as bad as Onkel Einar was," Bjorn jabbed at him.

"That's not even a bad joke, let alone a good one."

Gunlaug was staring at the open envelope. She pulled out both another envelope and a folded piece of paper. Her eyes widened and then filled with tears faster than she could sniff.

"Mor, what is it?" Rune leaned forward to reach toward her.

"The envelope is a letter from Blessing. From Ingeborg, I am sure." Her hands shook so badly that she could hardly hold the letter. She unfolded the piece of paper.

"From Solveig." She mopped her face on her apron.

"'Dear Gunlaug,

"'This came the other day, so I hurried to get it back to you. To think the letter traveled both ways over the ocean when Blessing and Blackduck are only a couple of days apart by train. All is well here—well, as well as it can be without you and Thor. We lost you both at almost the same time. Nilda, Johann apologizes for not writing you back any sooner. He said he has not heard a thing about that Dreng. But then, we rarely see the Nygaards. I think she spends most of her time now at their house in Oslo, since her baby is no longer home.'"

Gunlaug rolled her eyes at that, as did the others.

"'Our big news is that I am expecting! We are so glad to be living here at home rather than in that house we had rented. Johann would rather be farming for us than working for someone else, as you well know. Good-bye for now. We all send you our love.

"'Solveig.'"

Gunlaug folded it and carefully slid it back into the envelope, all the while eyeing the one on the table.

"Open it," Rune said.

"I'm almost afraid to. What if it is bad news? I mean, if someone wrote to say Ingeborg has died? My hope will be all gone."

Signe reached over to pat Gunlaug's hand. "Do you want me to open it for you?"

"If you will."

Signe used her table knife to open the envelope, her heart thumping as Gunlaug's must be. She swallowed and pulled out the thin paper. When she unfolded it, she blew out a sigh. "It is Ingeborg's signature." She smiled as she handed it back to Gunlaug. "Here, you read it."

Gunlaug blew her nose and blew out a breath.

"'My dear Gunlaug,

"'We are all well here. I do not remember if I told you that Haakan passed away over a year ago. His heart gave out when he tried to chase the cows back through a hole they tore in the fence. I still feel so alone, even though all my family is nearby. I hope you have grandchildren too, and that your family is all well.

"'I so often wished when we sent pleas for workers that some would come from your family. Really I wished that you and Thor would come, but it never happened. Now that so many of our generation are gone, we do not get much family news from Norway. I do hope you will write back.

"'With love from your cousin,

"'Ingeborg Bjorklund'"

Gunlaug could no more stop the tears than she could stop a snowstorm.

Rune pushed back his chair. "We better get out of here before we are all weeping." He motioned to Bjorn and Ivar. "Tell Knute to hurry out there. I want him to load up the sledge with firewood for the houses and the shop. We sure do burn a lot of wood." He patted his mor's shoulder. "Such good news. I am grateful too. Somehow we will manage to get you to see Ingeborg."

When that made her cry even harder, Signe caught his look of confusion and nodded. "All will be well," she whispered as he passed her on his way out the door with his two helpers.

The next morning after the men had left, Nilda rubbed her forehead while she sipped her coffee.

"Are you all right?" Signe asked as she poured more coffee. Nilda looked like she'd been to a battle.

"She will be," Gunlaug answered.

"I had a horrible dream—again. Same dream. Well, a nightmare is what it is."

"How about a piece of toast? Eating something might help." Signe gave the scrambled eggs another stir. "This will be ready in a minute. You want to talk about it?"

"I'm always being chased by a man wearing a black hat and brandishing a hatchet or a cleaver, something horrible. And he is laughing and swinging his weapon. At least I wake up before he strikes. I never recognize the face, just the black hat. And the other night after the social—I told you Dreng was there."

Signe nodded. Yesterday afternoon they'd heard the entire story, including Dreng's plea for forgiveness, which Signe did not believe was even a minute possibility. She'd not said that, but after all, there was no need to add fuel to the fire. Yes, she believed miracles still happened. God said He did not change, so she believed Him. But this question—could a man as self-centered and evil as Dreng Nygaard really leave off that kind of behavior and become a changed man? Did he really believe in forgiveness? She doubted it.

Nilda had said Mrs. Schoenleber was willing to give him the benefit of the doubt, so she was too. She had told him she forgave him but admitted she did not trust him. He would have to prove himself.

"I was being the hostess and saying good night to everyone, when Charles, the butler, handed Dreng his hat and coat. A black hat, the same style as the one in my dream." Nilda wagged her head slowly, as if it were far too heavy to lift. "Surely it isn't a coincidence."

"She was crying and thrashing around and woke me, panting like she'd been running for a long way, running for her life." Gunlaug leaned over and gathered her daughter into her arms, shushing her like she would a baby. "Nilda, it was only a dream. A horrible dream, but still a dream. And dreams are not real."

"Sure feels like it is. Why does it keep coming back, the same dream?"

"Perhaps . . . in the Bible, dreams are a form of sending a message, aren't they? You know where it says an angel came to Joseph in a dream to warn him to take Jesus out of Bethlehem, and the wise men too." Signe finished dishing up the eggs and sank down in her chair. "I mean . . . well, I don't know what I mean."

Gerd's face hardened. "I'd say it means stay away from Dreng Nygaard. Do not trust him one bit."

"He already left for the lumber camp with the others, so I needn't give him any thought until spring. At the social, he asked for letters for the two novice lumberjacks, meaning him and Petter. I told Petter earlier I would write him back if he sent letters, but Petter is a real friend of both mine and Ivar's." Nilda gave them a small smile. "I think he would like to become more than a friend, but time will tell."

"Oh, really? I like him a lot. He sure worked hard on our new house, he and Mr. Larsson, along with all the others." Signe smiled at the memories. "I think he was sweet on you even then, but Mrs. Benson said Mr. Larsson was too. The women were all chuckling about it." She took a bite of egg and toast. "Now look, you're getting very pink there, my friend. Just like you did at the house-raising."

"Petter's been over for supper and whist several times," Nilda admitted. "Mrs. Schoenleber invites him."

"And you don't say no?"

"Of course not, that's not my place." Nilda huffed a sigh. "Thank you, I do feel better. Maybe this will be the end of the dream. I sure hope so."

The next afternoon, which was much more pleasant with no wind, Knute and Leif skied home, and Mr. Larsson, also on skis, was with them.

"I'm getting something to eat and then going out to the woods. Would you like to come with me?" Knute asked Mr. Larsson as they entered the kitchen.

"Thank you for the offer, but I better not." He greeted the others.

"If you want to, I'll come along, and you can see the barn on your way back." Leif smiled up at his teacher.

Nilda added, "And since we are nearing a full moon, you could stay for supper and then ski home. I know Ivar would go with you partway, if you want."

Both boys nodded as their teacher thought about it. "We could come too," Knute added.

"So you are saying we're going to have a ski party?" Mr. Larsson asked.

"You could call it that. It sure will be beautiful when the moon rises." Knute grinned at his mor, encouraging her to agree.

"How many pairs of skis are ready in the shop?" Signe asked.

"Two more waxed, plus the ones we use."

Signe nodded. "Then Ivar and Nilda can accompany you for a ways, at least."

"Why do I feel like I'm being ganged up on?" the teacher asked, laughing.

"Only because you are." Leif handed him two cookies. "Okay?"

"Okay." Mr. Larsson grinned at his students. "You talked me into it." He looked at Signe. "You realize this is actually my regular teacher's home visit."

"Of course." She smiled and motioned to Nilda. "Please join us. I want to use English, but I may need some help."

"Certainly." Nilda sat down at Mr. Larsson's elbow.

He smiled at Nilda, and her cheeks turned pink. "My aunt thinks you are going to be a perfect aide. She praises your mastery of English highly. So do I."

Her cheeks turned rosier. "Thank you. I am learning about a whole different world. Culturally, I mean. A different culture. I am doing some simple writing tasks for her, and I learned the words 'diacritical marks.' English doesn't have any."

He laughed out loud, obviously delighted. Signe wondered if something serious was brewing there.

"I am even taking piano lessons now," Nilda continued.

"That's wonderful! Who is your instructor?"

"A Mrs. Potts. She is elderly, but she is very patient. She makes it easy to learn."

His voice softened. "Oh my. Mrs. Potts was my first music teacher, and she is still the best I've ever had. And I studied music in university too. I'm so glad for you." He cleared his throat and turned to Signe. "Now, about the boys."

Some hours later, when Nilda and Ivar returned from accompanying Mr. Larsson a good way to Benson's Corner, they clambered in the back door, grinning and exhilarated. Signe and Rune met them in the kitchen with hot tea and bread.

Ivar exclaimed, "Rune, these skis are excellent. Enough camber to flow smoothly, and the length is good. Great job."

"Takk. I mean, thank you."

"The beauty of the moonlight and shadows on the snow-covered land! I can't get over how glorious it is out there." Nilda spread her arms to encompass the land she had seen. "Sure it was cold, but no wind, so we kept warm enough just by moving. Rune, your skis glide like any others I've had. Now I can truly tell Mrs. Schoenleber that she will not go wrong buying from you. It will be interesting to see how they do on a steep downhill."

"I have no idea where you will find that around here." Rune folded his newspaper. "I guess we better get on home. Knute, you want to bring Rosie and the sleigh up here?" They had just finished building runners for the cart that Rosie pulled several days earlier.

"Come on, I'll help you and then bring Rosie back to the barn." Ivar clapped Knute on the shoulder. "At least I won't feel like a third wheel this way."

"What does that mean?" Knute asked.

"Someday you'll understand."

Chapter 26

"We will be attending a board meeting also."

Nilda looked across the white linen tablecloth in the dining car to see Mrs. Schoenleber smiling and nodding at the same time. She knew there had been a possibility of this, but the thought of meeting Mrs. Schoenleber's brothers at supper one night had already made her stomach knot. "B-but why do you want me to attend a board meeting?" Nilda had put off asking this question ever since it was first mentioned. Going shopping in St. Paul was bad enough.

"Nilda, as Jane has reminded me, I need to explain my motives more completely." She smiled at the waiter who set cups and a teapot on the table. The sun glinted off the silver rims of the saucers.

"Your order will be here in a short while," he said.

"Thank you, Mr. Alders. Your service is always impeccable."

Impeccable. Another word to add to her vocabulary. Nilda wished she had a pad of paper and a pencil with her. She had a feeling there would be a lot more to write down. A board meeting. *Do not shake your head nor mutter.* Giving herself instructions did not make her feel any more secure.

"As I have said, I am training you to be my assistant. Perhaps we need to define that more fully," Mrs. Schoenleber said.

Miss Walstead nodded. "That's a good place to start."

"Ever since I first met you, that night you spent at my house, I have had strong feelings that God has sent you to me, an answer to prayers of some time ago. Years, in fact. You have a fine brain that learns quickly, your curiosity knows no bounds, you like adventure, and most importantly, you are dependable and committed to doing your best."

Nilda stared at her. Where was all this coming from, and where was it going?

Miss Walstead reached over and patted Nilda's hands, which were clenched together on the table.

"How—I mean, where . . ." Nilda shook her head. "How can you know all that?"

"Because I recognized myself in you. Not the me of now, but the me of former years." Mrs. Schoenleber poured the tea as if she'd just remarked on the weather. "I am getting older—I refuse to say old—but I want someone who can act in my place as needed. You had to learn the language first to be able to understand business and society and whatever else we need to do. I really want you to help me spend and invest my money wisely. I don't mean invest in railroads and banking. I mean invest in people, in my community, to help make a difference in other people's lives." She smiled. "I know this all sounds overwhelming, but we won't be doing it all at once and not immediately. This trip is a first step."

"But . . . but I dreamed of meeting a good man and getting married here in America, probably living on a farm and raising a family." Her words tripped over each other. Her teacup rattled when she set it back in the saucer without taking the sip she intended.

"Preferably not a lumberjack, I hope," Mrs. Schoenleber said.

Nilda cocked her head. "That thought had entered my mind before I came here."

"And now?"

Thoughts of Dreng and Petter zipped through her mind. "I think probably not."

The waiter stopped at their table with a smile and set plates before them. "Our chef said this fish could only be fresher if he had gone out and caught it himself. He is known for serving excellent food in general but fish in particular, depending on the season."

"I have to agree with you. Eating on this train is always a good experience."

He bowed slightly. "Thank you, Mrs. Schoenleber. I will tell him."

Could all this be real? Nilda replayed her employer's words in her head. What if she really did not want to do this? Was this fear or excitement she felt? Did she need to make any decisions right now? How could she turn down an opportunity like this? Why would she want to? But what about her family? What would they say? She could hear Rune and Ivar first of all in awe, just like she was, and second accusing her of having lost her mind to hesitate. Signe would be ecstatic for her, and Mor? Mor might think she was making it all up, but once she'd thought on it, she'd smile and nod. And remind them all to thank God for whatever it was He was doing.

She would not see them as often. But think of the people they would be helping—whoever they were. And whatever plans were yet to come.

"You can ask me any questions you want," Mrs. Schoenleber said.

Nodding, Nilda wiped her mouth with her napkin and laid it back in her lap. "Could we have a new pot of tea, please?"

"Of course, miss. Right away." The waiter beckoned to someone else to pick up the plates. "And would you care for dessert, any of you? I'll bring the tray when I return with the tea."

"Thank you, Nilda." Miss Walstead's smile added to the approbation. "Well done."

Back in their compartment in the parlor car, Mrs. Schoenleber laid her leather journal on the table. "We need to make shopping lists, and I have here the minutes for the board meeting I would like you to read through. Then perhaps I will read while you and Jane continue your lessons."

"Is everything ready for the social next Friday?" Miss Walstead asked.

When no one answered, Nilda looked up from the pages she was reading. "Are you asking me?"

"Yes." Both women answered at the same time, making them smile at each other.

"Oh. Not everyone has responded to the invitations, but we'll have enough to have a good time again. Since everyone had such fun with charades, I thought we would start with that again. Cook and I talked about the menu, and she said she would order what was needed. Mr. Larsson said he would be glad to play for singing after supper, and he is choosing the music. I'm afraid I do not know many of the songs people sing."

"Ah, we should have thought of that earlier. Put that on your education list."

"At least now I know more about the keyboard. Good thing reading music in Norwegian and English is the same."

By the time the train pulled into the station in St. Paul, the sun was sliding near the horizon. As the conductor assisted them down the stairs, a man in a greatcoat and top hat met them.

"Good to see you, David." Mrs. Schoenleber pointed at their luggage. "Oh, and by the way, this is my new assistant, Miss Nilda Carlson. David is my brother Heinrik's driver."

"Pleased to meet you, miss." His slight bow included Miss Walstead. "And good to see you again. Welcome to St. Paul." He snapped his fingers, and a redcap brought over a barrow of luggage. "The carriage is in front of the main doors."

"Yes, sir."

David guided them through the crowds, leaving Nilda with the distinct feeling that without him, they would have been lost, or at least she would have been. Mrs. Schoenleber never appeared to be confused or overwhelmed. Or did people automatically make way for her? While they walked, she was asking David about the family news and other questions. Nilda gave up trying to see everything.

Once they were in the carriage, Mrs. Schoenleber pointed out various buildings on one side of the carriage, and Miss Walstead the other. They seemed to know St. Paul as intimately as they knew Blackduck.

"I hope you do not expect me to remember all this," Nilda said.

"Not really."

When they were helped down from the carriage at the stately hotel, David motioned to a young man in a uniform to take their bags while he escorted them to the front desk.

"I will be here at nine to take you to the board meeting," he said.

"Yes, I know. Heinrik insists on the meeting starting at ten. We will be waiting here in the lobby. Thank you." Mrs. Schoenleber turned to the man behind the desk. "Good evening, Mr. Blaine."

"How good to see you again, madam. It's been some time

since you were here. Your suite is ready. Would you prefer supper in your room or in the restaurant?"

"Our rooms, I think." She looked to Nilda and Miss Walstead, who nodded.

Nilda kept smiling and doing what the others did, all the while trying not to look shocked at anything. Not the elevator with a man pushing the buttons that made the cage go up, nor that the suite was bigger than most houses, with an office, a living room, and four bedrooms that each had a private bath. All that was lacking was a kitchen. Women were in each room, unpacking and hanging up garments. Those that needed pressing disappeared out the door with them, and they promised to have them back before bedtime.

Supper arrived some time later on tables with wheels and floor-length white cloths. The waiters set the platters of food on the dining room table, and one stayed to serve them, a folded towel over his arm.

Signe will never believe all this, Nilda thought when she climbed up into the canopied bed that had been turned back for her. She had planned to read for a while, but sleep claimed her immediately in spite of herself.

Persistent knocking at the door woke her the next morning. "Come in."

"Sorry to have to wake you, but you don't want to be late for your meeting." Dressed in a black uniform with white apron and hat, the maid smiled. "My name is Sonja, and I will be your maid while you are here." She crossed to the armoire and pulled out the black jacket and skirt with a white waist. "Mrs. Schoenleber said this is what you will wear today. I started a bath for you. It should be ready by now."

"Do I have time for a bath?"

"Not a long soak, but I'm sure that will feel really good tonight."

Nilda bundled her hair on top of her head and stepped into the half-filled tub. As she sank into the warm water, she felt like she could float away. "I'll hurry."

She washed, dried, lotioned, dressed, and then sat in front of the dressing table mirror so Sonja could brush and arrange her hair.

"Will you be wearing this hat?" Sonja held up a black hat with jet beads.

"I, uh—where did that come from?"

"It was on the shelf in the armoire."

"I see. Then I guess I am." She promised herself she would mention this to Mrs. Schoenleber, but in all the hurry and hustle, it slipped her mind until they were in the carriage and moving. "Where did this hat come from?" She touched it with the tips of her fingers.

"I ordered it from a milliner down the street to be delivered. I had originally planned to go shopping first, but since Heinrik set the meeting for today, and I have learned to pick my battles with my brothers, I ordered the hat."

"'Pick your battles'?"

"Yes, we do not always see eye to eye."

"Yes, I understand having brothers." Nilda remembered Johann's refusal to tell her how they planned to deal with Dreng. Whatever they did had been effective, but . . . She snapped her mind shut on any thoughts that had to do with Dreng. Right now he was exiled to the lumber camp, and please God, he would stay there and perhaps grow into a real man.

"Let me give you some background on my brothers," Mrs. Schoenleber said. "You remember that I am the eldest of five children, and our father, unbeknownst to the boys, appointed me as chairman or president of the board that oversees all the different enterprises. He was a very successful businessman and went against the strictures of the day by appointing me as the head. Jonathon, next in line, is in charge of our railroad enterprise. Jacob handles the business associated with the lumbering, and our youngest brother, Heinrik, oversees it all. My sister, Elizabeth, had no interest in the businesses, but she married Brett Cullen, who also works for us. He is excellent in sensing new fields to be explored, like the forests near the Canadian border."

"They all live here?"

"No, Brett and my sister live in Rochester. He was a doctor before he married into the family. Well, he still is and he is associated with the Mayo brothers, who have built a hospital there."

"I see. How often do you all get together?"

"Usually once a month."

David drew the carriage to a stop in front of a brick building with a portico in front and two flags flying, one the red, white, and blue of the national flag, and the other the Minnesota state flag. A man wearing a navy and gold uniform greeted them and held open the door. "They are waiting for you in the boardroom, Mrs. Schoenleber."

"Thank you, Joseph." To Nilda, she said, "Interesting. We're not late, but they are already gathered. Hmm."

Nilda returned the doorman's smile and made sure she kept up with her employer. Another elevator, and the doors opened onto a walnut-paneled hall and a double door of carved walnut with an arch above it. The elevator man stepped out and crossed to open the doors for them.

"Thank you. Come, Nilda." Mrs. Schoenleber dropped her voice. "We will breast the bears."

Nilda swallowed. If Mrs. Schoenleber could smile, so could she. She straightened her back, and they strode into a paneled room with tall windows along one wall that filled the room with light.

"Good morning, gentlemen." Mrs. Schoenleber smiled and nodded. "I'm glad to see you are all gathered." She stopped at the chair at the head of the table, and a woman lifted away her coat to hang it up. "You sit there, Nilda." She pointed to the chair on her right. "This is Miss Nilda Carlson, my new assistant that I told you about. I will have each of you introduce yourself when we are seated."

Nilda nodded and smiled and said thank you over her shoulder as her coat disappeared also.

"Let's be seated, and then we can have introductions while the coffee is served. I see, Jonathon, that you made sure we have a treat, Irish scones. Lovely." She smiled up at him as he held her chair for her. Once she was seated, she clasped her hands on the table. "It's good to see you all. One of these months, we are going to have this meeting in Blackduck so you can see where some of your investments are."

"Are the logging camps back in business?" a gentleman asked.

"Yes, ten days or so ago. A bit early due to severe cold and early snow. The camps have moved farther north and west, as the pine trees are growing more scarce."

"How long will they last?"

She nodded to her brother Jacob. "Ask him, not me." A chuckle rounded the table. "We'll begin as I said. Miss Nilda Carlson emigrated from the Valders region of Norway six months ago with her younger brother to help on a farm owned by distant cousins. She spent her first night on American soil at my house due to the train schedule. They came via Duluth. Even as tired as she was, I was impressed and followed her accomplishments as they adapted to life here. A few months ago, I invited her to come work for me. Since then, she has undergone and is continuing intense schooling in English, history, deportment, and social graces, and now business and economics. I present to you my assistant, Miss Nilda Carlson. Please stand so they can see you. Thank you. Now, Jonathon, let's begin with you as the elder brother. Introduce your assistants too."

As they went around the table, food was served, and people began eating until their turn to talk. While their smiles said welcome, Nilda had the feeling that it was politeness, not enthusiasm, that prompted them. She smiled and nodded in return, all the while writing their names on her pad of paper so she would remember.

When they finished, Mrs. Schoenleber stood again. "I would open this up for questions, but I know we have a lot to cover, so let us begin with the reading of the minutes of the last meeting, and then reports." She nodded to a young man who had a sheaf of papers at hand.

He stood and read aloud the pages that Nilda had read on the train.

"Any questions or additions?" Mrs. Schoenleber asked. Several questions were raised and dealt with, and the minutes were approved. "Jonathon, your turn. You did bring copies of your report for everyone?"

"Of course. So I shall summarize."

Nilda quickly realized that she needed to learn to abbreviate. Good thing she would have a copy of the full report.

When he finished, Mrs. Schoenleber announced, "We will have fifteen minutes for questions, and then fifteen minutes for a break. Questions, anyone?"

Jonathon's usual answer was, "You'll find that in the report." One question about the railroad moving beyond Bemidji caused some discussion, especially regarding if there were enough goods to be shipped from there to make the extensions worthwhile. Nilda was grateful that Miss Walstead had schooled her in geography so she knew about the region they were discussing.

"How are you doing?" Mrs. Schoenleber asked her in the women's restroom during the break.

"Learning a lot. Do they always challenge each other like that?"

"Oh yes. That is a major part of my job, keeping the anger levels down so we can get work done. Each one feels their department is the most important, so when budget time comes, the meetings can get terribly obstreperous." She smiled in the mirror. "I am not in charge of any one section but over everything to keep business running smoothly. The amazing thing to me is that we have all learned to leave the fights and arguments here in this building, and when we go home, we leave the feelings behind too. I have not seen this happen in any other company we have worked with."

"It sounds to me like your father chose well."

"He was wise beyond his years and his experiences. He always said that wisdom comes from God and we must seek it diligently, or we would become like other companies and let rancor take over."

Rancor. Nilda repeated the word in her mind. More words to look up.

The meeting was adjourned at one o'clock so dinner could be set up on that same table. The discussions continued through dinner and the afternoon, until Mrs. Schoenleber dismissed them all at four thirty.

Heinrik smiled at his sister. "Supper will be at seven, so David will take you back to your hotel now and pick you up again at six thirty, unless you would just as soon go straight to the house."

"Thank you, but we need to pick up Miss Walstead too, and I would like a bit of a lie down. If you don't mind, that is."

"Not in the least." He turned to Nilda. "My youngest son, Jeffrey, is looking forward to meeting you. He is in his final year of college here in the Twin Cities."

Nilda nodded. "Meeting you all was indeed a pleasure. I will see you this evening, then."

Had she needed to describe herself, *limp rag* would have sufficed. When she lay down on her bed, sleep rolled over her like an ocean wave. She woke again to a tapping on the door and Sonja offering her assistance.

Supper at the Schmitz estate passed by with one bright spot. Jeffrey. He was seated next to her, had a fine sense of humor, and made her face flush several times until his mother came to her rescue.

"Now, Jeffrey, Miss Carlson is not used to your banter, so be gentle with her."

"Yes, Mother."

Mrs. Schmitz rolled her eyes. "He means well."

"I have brothers, ma'am. This is not new to me, and I can usually keep up with them." She turned to the young man. "Now, if we were speaking Norwegian . . ."

He nodded. "You would cut me off at the knees."

"See, you did it again. Why would I want to cut your knees?"

Heinrik Schmitz roared. "You have met your match, son. I warn you, your Aunt Gertrude might get after you."

"You think she needs me?" Mrs. Schoenleber gave her brother an arch look. "I think not. However, this has been a rather taxing day, so I plead an early evening."

"And what are you doing tomorrow?" he asked.

"Shopping."

"All day?"

"Most likely."

He turned to Nilda. "I fear you will think today easy after a full day of shopping."

"I found some of the things you were asking for," his wife said to Mrs. Schoenleber. "If you would like, I will go with you and show you which stores carry them."

"Yes. We would appreciate that."

Heinrik shook his head. "Good Lord, deliver us."

On the way home on the train two days later, Nilda still smiled at Mr. Schmitz's comment. He had been right. The business day was far easier than the shopping day. The three women had dragged her from store to store, made decisions as to what was best for her, and promised her they would do this again the next time they came to the Twin Cities.

Nilda could hardly wait.

Chapter *27*

T here's a letter for you, Miss Nilda," Charles announced Thursday morning.

"Thank you. That must be my first letter here." She stood up from the breakfast table where she had been reading the section of the newspaper that Mrs. Schoenleber had already finished.

"Did you see those two acceptances on the hall table?" Mrs. Schoenleber looked up from her reading to ask.

"No, but that's good." Nilda read the front of the letter Charles handed her. "From Petter."

"Are you surprised?

"Yes and no." *Had I been looking for a letter? No, I didn't even think about it. And now that I am thinking about it, I've not been thinking of Petter at all and Dreng less and less.* That thought made her smile as she slit the envelope open.

Dear Nilda,

I thought I would write more often, but by the time supper is done, most of the time I go directly to bed. The noise does not bother me at all. I thought I would be getting stronger by now, and I guess I really am, but I need every minute of sleep I can find. If anyone ever tells you that being a lumberjack is a good way to make a living, take it from me, it is one of the hardest. Even worse than on the fishing boat in the North Sea. I know I could return to Blackduck to the lumberyard, but I said I would do this, and I am going to stick it out.

The only other news is that Dreng is gone. The foreman, Mr. Nicholson, sent for the sheriff, but Dreng was gone when the law arrived. I do not know the situation.

Nilda coughed to clear her throat.

"What is it?" Mrs. Schoenleber asked.

"Dreng has disappeared."

"Mark my words, he will be back here soon, if he's not here already."

Nilda rubbed her forehead. "The nightmare has finally gone, and now this."

"He knows about the social. I would not be surprised if we hear from him today, asking if he can attend."

"Can we say no?"

"If you want. You are in charge of the socials."

After such an invigorating trip, to come back to this. Nilda picked up her coffee cup, but it was cold.

"I'll get you more." As always, Charles was standing by the door, ready to serve. She'd forgotten he was even there.

"What is on your list for today?" Mrs. Schoenleber asked.

"Miss Walstead will be here about ten, and before she comes, I want to have piano practice out of the way. I have not finished reading all those reports yet either." Nilda sipped her refreshed coffee. "I've been thinking, do you have reports and minutes from past board meetings here?"

"Yes." Mrs. Schoenleber nodded with a wide smile. "I was

hoping you would ask me that. I have the minutes from this year in the cabinet in the library, and more are in boxes in the storage room. Charles can get those for you."

"When I need them."

Late in the day, Nilda was reading the reports from the previous month's meeting when she heard the knocker on the front door.

"Come in, come in," Charles greeted someone. "Miss Nilda is in the morning room."

"Ivar!" Nilda stood so quickly that the pages snowed to the floor. "In here. Come in, get warm." She met him at the door and stopped. "Oh, you two came together. You didn't ski, then?"

"Good evening, Miss Carlson." Mr. Larsson nodded. "We decided the horse and sleigh might be wiser."

"Well, look who is here, my nephew who might as well be living in Canada." Mrs. Schoenleber crossed the room to them.

"I saw you just a couple of weeks ago, remember? You said I did a fine job playing the organ for the wedding."

"I know, and you did. Tonight you will have to put up with a lowly piano." She kissed him on the cheek and shook hands with Ivar. "I am delighted to see you again. I hope you have felled as many trees as you wanted."

"We are doing well, especially since Oskar Kielund is trading work with us."

"Nilda just received a letter from Petter. He says he will survive the lumber camp only by sheer willpower, it sounds."

"I know I have far the better situation. There is no one yelling at me to work harder, faster. That's normal, Oskar Kielund told me. He took his team out to the lumber camp one year and swore never to do that again."

"Take your things up to your rooms. Fritz, I put Mr. Carlson in the room next to yours."

"Do I have to be mister here?" Ivar asked.

Nilda chuckled. Her brother sounded like a young boy again, not like the broad-shouldered, powerful man she now saw before her.

"You can be Ivar if you would rather." Mrs. Schoenleber patted his shoulder. "You just help entertain the ladies tonight, and I will call you anything you desire."

"Are we playing charades again? That was a good time. I was shocked by how good Dreng was at it."

Nilda tried not to let on what they'd heard regarding Dreng, but her brother knew her too well.

He frowned. "What has happened?"

"Petter wrote that Dreng has disappeared."

"I hate to even think this, but a snowbank might have taken care of him."

Nilda heard him say *permanently* but knew that was not so. "Tonight we will not mention him. All the others know he and Petter will not be here, so we just shrug if someone asks."

"We'll get changed and come back down." Mr. Larsson picked up his satchel. "Come on, Ivar. We can catch up on the news later."

Nilda checked the clock. "I better go up too."

"We'll have a bit to eat right away, since supper will be later, so hurry down," Mrs. Schoenleber urged them.

The social that night seemed calmer than the previous one, especially during charades. They numbered off again, and this time Ivar and Mr. Larsson were on the same team, not with Nilda. She gathered her team together and whispered, "We are going to beat them, agreed?" The others nodded, and the girls grinned at the one man on their team. "You agree?"

"Of course. I like to win. It's a shame that Dreng isn't here, but we can do it without him."

By the time they finished the game, Nilda could hardly believe what she had seen. Mr. Larsson had left his scholarly teacher self somewhere else and carried his team to victory. She was the first to offer a handshake and congratulate him.

"Supper is served," Charles announced, and the group laughed their way into the dining room to heap food onto their plates.

"Are you positive that laughing fellow over there is truly Mr. Larsson or only someone who looks an awful lot like him?" she muttered to Ivar while they stood in line for food.

"He sure knows how to play charades."

When they finished eating, Nilda announced that card games were set up in the parlor and after that, their guest this evening, Mr. Fritz Larsson, would be playing the piano for a sing-along.

"Then what if we skipped the card games this time?" one of the girls asked. "I've not been to a sing-along in ages."

When the others agreed, Fritz shrugged. "If that's what you want, all I need is someone to turn the pages for me."

"Nilda will do that," Ivar volunteered her.

"Ivar!" The look on one of the other girl's faces said disappointment. Nilda leaned closer to her. "Why don't you turn the pages? You know the songs far better than I do."

"Thank you." She tried to hide her giggle behind her hands.

Nilda had not heard any of the pieces that everyone knew. "When It's Moonlight on the Prairie" instantly became her favorite. Or maybe "Shine on, Harvest Moon." Several of those present knew the harmony. It was just beautiful. They finished with "Goodnight, Irene," whoever Irene was.

As the guests prepared to leave, Nilda saw them all out the door while Charles and George assisted them into the sleigh. Another successful social. Relief that all had gone well and pleasure with a dash of pride teamed up to keep her smiling.

Saturday morning, Nilda and Mrs. Schoenleber were already in the dining room when their two guests wandered in.

"I guess all that entertaining last night wore him out." Ivar motioned to Fritz over his shoulder.

"I always sleep well here," Fritz replied.

"You know your room awaits whenever you decide to come," Mrs. Schoenleber said.

"And I eat well too. I suppose Cook has outdone herself as usual." He took the chair across the table from Nilda.

"You never did hire a cook?" his aunt asked.

"It seems a waste of money for one person. Besides, when I take the time, I'm not a bad cook." He raised a hand. "I know, you offered to pay the cook, but . . ."

"She could clean house, do your wash, all the things that need doing."

"I often eat at students' homes when I do my visits. Some, like Nilda's house, have superb cooks, and some are not so good. The Skarsteads often invite me over, and the Bensons too." He looked at Ivar. "Just tell Charles what you want for breakfast."

"I'll have whatever everyone else has," Ivar said, looking nervous.

"He'll have ham, eggs, toast, and fried potatoes." Nilda grinned at her brother as she placed his order. "Cook does the best fried potatoes."

Charles exited to the kitchen.

"Now, may I make a suggestion on how you could spend your morning?" Mrs. Schoenleber said.

Fritz nodded. "How did I know this was coming?"

"Because I always have something for you to do, that's why.

If you would come more often . . ." She laid her hand on her newspaper. "Since it is so perfect out, I think you might enjoy skiing, but we have one problem—only two pairs of skis." She looked to Ivar. "How soon might your brother have my order ready?"

"I think he has the first coat of wax applied, so fairly soon."

"Good. Nilda really enjoys skiing, and because I am such a failure at it, Charles goes with her."

Nilda shook her head. "As if I could get lost in Blackduck."

"Going alone is just asking for gossip."

"So Miss Carlson going with me would be proper?" Fritz asked.

"You know the best trails, and I have something else for Ivar to do."

Fritz turned to Ivar. "I should have warned you."

"Cinnamon rolls!" Ivar stared from his plate to Nilda's when Charles brought them in a few moments later. "You didn't tell me that."

"I forgot. You turn in your order, and Cook adds whatever specialty she has for the day."

"She always makes cinnamon rolls when I come." Fritz inhaled the aroma. "This always says home to me."

"You lived here?"

"Most summers when I was attending school in Minneapolis. Aunt Gertrude let me play the piano as much as I wanted. And read—oh, the hours I spent in the library or outside in the shade."

"I was hoping he would follow his heart and draw too," Mrs. Schoenleber said. "He is quite an artist when he allows himself to be."

"Don't believe everything she says. She is a bit prejudiced."

Fritz smiled at Nilda. "So according to her plan, we ski first and then have piano lessons."

"See what a good boy he is?" Mrs. Schoenleber patted his hand.

Nilda felt like shaking her head. This was not what she had expected. "Is Miss Walstead coming today?"

"No, she is going to visit her sister who lives on a lake south of here. This was the perfect opportunity. George will drive her out, so Ivar, if you would like to see more of the country?"

Ivar nodded with enthusiasm.

"Have you been on the other side of the river?" Fritz asked when he and Nilda were strapped into their skis and ready to leave.

"No, the river was not fully iced in the middle."

"When did you go out last?"

"Over a week ago."

"Good, then we'll go that way. I asked George, and he said one of the older men was out drilling holes for fishing, so the ice is thick enough now." He set his poles and pushed off. "We should have brought Ivar's skis along. They're at my house."

Nilda kept up with him without much effort. Should she suggest they go faster? Thoughts of Dreng crept back into her mind, making her sure she was seeing a man with a black hat behind every birch tree. A grove of maple trees provided even more lurking spots.

"Do you ever ice skate?" Fritz called back after they crossed the river. He shushed to a stop and pointed to a pond off to the right, where benches lined the banks and people of all ages were skating.

"Oh, that would be so much fun. We used to pump enough

water to make a pond at our farm in Norway, back when we were children. I've not skated since then."

"Aunt Gertrude has skates of various sizes out in the carriage house. I can ask George to find and sharpen them, see if any fit you."

We never had time to play, Nilda thought. *Doing anything we could that raised money was far more important, as we needed food on the table.* "That would be delightful."

The wind was picking up, blowing ice bits in their faces, so Fritz curtailed the rest of the trek he'd planned and led them back to the house.

"Thank you." She bent over to unbuckle the straps and rammed her skis in the snowbank against the carriage house wall. "This was grand, but that night when Ivar and I skied you halfway home was beyond description."

He smiled at her and nodded. "Yes, it was. The shadows on the snow were almost black. By the time I got home, my fingers were itching to draw what I had seen."

"I didn't know you liked to draw."

He looked into her eyes. "I have a feeling there are a lot of things about you that I don't know."

She could feel heat rising from her neck, and it wasn't the scarf she wore. "Most likely that goes both ways."

That old adage *time stood still* became real to her as they gazed at each other.

He broke the spell first. "We better get to those piano lessons in case Ivar and I need to head home earlier than we planned."

She nodded. "Yes, we better." She headed for the kitchen door and kicked her boots against the step, unwrapping her scarf as she dragged each foot over the boot brush. Cook would not be happy if they tracked snow inside.

"Thank you."

She looked up at his face and nodded. "Thank you."

After warming in front of the fire, they sat on the piano bench, and she clenched and stretched her fingers.

"Show me what you have learned," he said.

She tried, she really did, but for some strange reason, her fingers did not want to perform. They usually did these exercises well—because she practiced every day—but not this time. Could it be the man sitting beside her?

Chapter 28

Nilda woke up feeling as if she'd been screaming. Perhaps she had been. Even her throat felt sore—and tired.

Not wanting to be greeted by Gilda, she dressed in the dim light from the window and made her way down the stairs. Only one gas lamp lit the stairs, so she kept a hand on the railing. Somehow the smoothness of the banister made her feel grounded in reality rather than still stumbling along in the dream world.

The man in the black hat—again. She'd been so relieved to sleep through the nights in peace, but now he was back. She never had seen his face.

From the dining room, she could hear Cook moving about in the kitchen, so she pushed open the swinging door and went in.

"Oh, my goodness, you scared me half to—" Cook paused. "Something is wrong, Miss Nilda, I can tell. You sit yourself down at this table, and I will have tea ready in a jiffy. The water is already heating. Coffee will take a bit longer."

Nilda did as instructed. "Tea will be fine." Even her fingers twitched. "Is there something I can help you with? I could bring in wood or . . ."

"This is a gas stove, and Charles keeps the wood full for the fireplaces. But here, you can fold napkins." She set a pile of them on the table. "You know the way he does it?"

"Yes." She set to folding, pressing the creases in with the heel of her hand.

When Cook set the teapot and cup in front of her, Nilda heaved a sigh. She needed something to do that involved moving around more.

"Would you like some toast with that?" Cook asked.

"Yes, please, but you know I could do that myself."

"I know, but that is really not proper. Mrs. S would be offended if she knew you were slaving in the kitchen."

"Slaving in the kitchen?" Nilda's eyes widened. "Folding napkins or buttering toast is slaving?"

"There, that's better. You are more like yourself now." Cook pulled a packet out of the cupboard. "One raisin bun left. I could heat that for you."

"Oh yes." Nilda poured the tea into her cup. "Did you use cardamom in those buns?"

"I did. A Norwegian friend of mine gave me the recipe." Cook slid the lone bun into the oven. "Won't take but a minute."

When the stack of napkins was folded, Nilda set them in the butler's pantry. Picking up the teapot and cup and saucer, she took them into the morning room, where Charles was building a fire in the fireplace.

"Good morning, miss. You're up early. Can I get you anything?"

"No, thank you. I'm just going to sit here and read until breakfast."

He nodded and left.

The report could not hold her attention. The library was

too cold. Her bed had already been made. If she got caught polishing the banister, who knew what would happen?

At last it was time for breakfast.

"You're restless as a bird in a trap. Whatever is the matter?" Mrs. Schoenleber laid her paper down. "I hear you scared Cook in the kitchen and folded napkins. I've never seen you like this."

"I have got to get out and move. Fresh air will help. I think skiing will top this off."

"I'm sorry, but Charles has other commitments for this morning."

"I will go by myself. If he asks, please tell him I will follow the route he laid out. I'm praying that some fast skiing will take this away." She remembered a better phrase. "Vigorous activity. Mor says weaving, especially slamming the shuttle, is one of the best ways to deal with restlessness and anger. That and kneading bread. Since we have no loom and Cook might be offended if I made bread, skiing will have to do. I'm just grateful for the sun. Had it been stormy today . . ." She shook her head.

"Please do not cross the river."

"I won't. When I get back, I will settle in." Nilda bit back the words "I promise." How could she know, when she'd not felt like this for who knew how long?

Mrs. Schoenleber frowned. "Are you angry?"

"Possibly, but I doubt it. Restless seems a more appropriate word. I could run up and down the stairs a few times, but I think fresh air and the cold would work better."

Mrs. Schoenleber shook her head. "Ah, the perils of being young."

"Did you ever feel this way?" Nilda tucked the ends of her scarf into her coat and pulled her knit hat down over her ears.

"Most likely, but I don't remember skiing a lot. I sometimes walked fast in the spring."

Outside, Nilda buckled her skis on, rammed the poles into the snow, and shot off toward the trail. She pushed as hard as she could and went as far as she could short of crossing the river, until she was panting. It was much colder than she had anticipated when she looked out the window. And the wind . . . Her breath would have looked like a steam locomotive's, but the strong breeze whipped it away immediately. But the fresh snow was so beautiful. Perhaps the glory of this morning was part of what took her breath away.

It was early enough that she didn't see a lot of people out of doors yet. There was only one set of tracks through the snow near the house besides hers. They appeared to be those of a person in a hurry. She hoped that person would pause long enough to savor the beautiful day, the crisp snow, and the blue sky.

She stopped by the back stoop, resting on her poles, until her breaths came evenly again. She decided she would go around the route one more time. This time she would not rush. She would relax and enjoy the lovely countryside.

She looked toward the kitchen window. Cook was waving enthusiastically, so she waved back. She took off again.

Skiing smoothly, settling into an easy pace, she had drawn even with the maple tree orchard when a noise behind her made her look over her shoulder.

A man in a black hat threw himself at her from behind a tree, screaming, "It's all your fault!"

"Dreng!"

He knocked her to the snow and pressed her neck down, nearly choking her. He was laughing! A horridly evil laugh. "I searched for you, asking about Einar Strand. He has a wide reputation. All over. You don't know how happy I was to find you in Blackduck! I had it so good in Valders, and you spoiled it. Now you are going to pay! I've thought of nothing else, ever since I came to America. You will pay!" Holding her with one hand, he ripped off his coat, threw it to the side, and fought through her wool petticoats. "I am going to enjoy making you pay. I will enjoy this so much! Go ahead, fight me. I love it when girls try to fight me off."

Nilda bucked against his weight and thrashed from side to side. She fought to breathe, to overcome the dizziness.

He laughed and pulled at his trousers, undoing the buckle. In that moment, Nilda's hand closed over a ski pole. She grabbed the bottom end of it and, with all her waning power, stabbed upward at his face.

He screamed. Both of his hands clamped his face, and blood squirted from between his fingers.

Nilda bucked again and twisted to the side, throwing him off. She surged to her feet. She was still in her skis, but the left was broken off just behind her boot. She had only one ski pole, but one was enough. Leaning into the fierce wind, she sped off toward the house, toward home, pumping that pole with both hands.

Behind her Dreng was screaming, "You blinded me! I'll kill you for this!"

She glanced back to see him, one bloody hand covering his eye, his trousers open, his coat cast aside in the snow. He lurched forward, yelling, coming toward her, running in the snow, pursuing her. No!

She knew how to get the most speed from her skis—long, smooth glides, not choppy thrusts. The icy wind blasted her. No wonder the wind chilled her body—her clothes were torn. She could not afford to stop and fix them.

As she approached the house, Charles came toward her, running. Cook stood on the back stoop, jumping up and down and shouting. And George was running from the carriage shed, skis in his hand and the tails of his greatcoat flapping.

Charles stopped Nilda by engulfing her in a powerful hug. Her face was numb, her throat burned; her teary eyes could barely see.

He asked simply, "Dreng?"

She bobbed her head, grateful he was holding her up.

"Cook saw him running back up the trail and waved at you, trying to get you to stop. Then she became worried and called me from my duties. Madam is calling the sheriff."

George was buckling into his skis.

"The maple grove," Nilda gasped and bent over her skis, trying to get her breath.

Gilda and Stella crowded in against her, holding her up. She could feel Charles releasing her ski bindings. Then they steered her toward the house. She stumbled on the steps, but they held her steady. She heard Charles say, "Let's go!"

Mrs. Schoenleber stood in the doorway. "The sheriff is on his way."

The maids guided Nilda into the kitchen and set her near the warm, welcome stove. Cook had turned on the oven and opened the oven door. The warmth flowed over Nilda.

Mrs. Schoenleber gave orders firmly, with confidence. "Hot chocolate. Cream, not milk. And bring her some crackers, something to settle her stomach. She's not breakfasted yet. Warm a quilt by the stove and wrap her up. Nilda, did he, ah—"

"No," Nilda interrupted before Mrs. Schoenleber could say that horrible word. She looked down at her front. What a mess. Her dress was torn, and the buttons were missing from her coat. Cook handed her a mug of tea to tide her over until the hot chocolate was ready and set a plate of crackers on the table beside her. Nilda's hands were still trembling violently. She sipped some tea just to keep it from sloshing.

Now the danger was past, but Nilda could not stop sobbing. She had only partly pulled herself back together when Gilda ushered an imposing uniformed man into the kitchen.

Hat in hand, he nodded at Mrs. Schoenleber. "Good morning, ma'am."

"Good morning, Sheriff Gruber. Cook, bring him coffee. Cook? Where is she?"

Stella replied, "Out telling his deputies what happened."

"I'm sorry, my deputies are on snowshoes; they won't be as swift as your men on skis. But they'll get there."

Nilda felt comforted by the sheriff's voice. Like Mrs. Schoenleber's, it was strong and authoritative. Listening to him, you just knew everything would be all right.

"Mrs. Schoenleber, your maid says your two men have gone after him. I'm afraid that wasn't wise, putting themselves in mortal danger." The sheriff swung a chair around to face Nilda and sat down, watching her closely.

Mrs. Schoenleber sniffed. "Miss Carlson is very special to us all, and my employees are not people to simply sit on their hands when a wrong has been committed. They know the fellow, and they are competent. It is not they who are in danger, but he."

The sheriff turned his attention to Nilda. "Miss Carlson, I am Sheriff Daniel Gruber. Did your assailant show you a knife or gun?"

"No. He choked me." Nilda's voice was thin and reedy, not like her at all.

"And Mrs. Schoenleber, are your men armed?"

"No."

"Miss Carlson, did he succeed in forcing himself on you?"

She had not heard that phrase before, but she could guess

its meaning. Mrs. Schoenleber replied, "It was an attempted rape." She emphasized the *attempted*.

"Good. Is the assailant on skis or snowshoes?"

"No. I mean, neither." Nilda was grateful that Gilda wrapped a warm quilt close around her, both for the warmth and for modesty.

The sheriff asked, "Do you know the man?"

"Dreng Nygaard. It's a long story." Her sobbing had eased, and now her face burned, actually a good sign. She was warming up at last, however painfully.

"Tell me."

She explained as briefly as possible about Dreng's attack on her back in Norway. She used English, but when she could not remember a word, she used Norwegian and Cook, bless her, translated. She told the sheriff about Dreng's boast that he searched her out in this country and found her. She did not mention that Einar Strand's name helped him locate her. She told of his threatening letter and his insistence that everything was all her fault. "When I stabbed at his face with the ski pole, trying to get away, I may have put out his eye. He said he would kill me for that. He chased me, ran after me, and screamed threats at me."

"I see." The sheriff pushed himself to his feet. "I will need a written statement from you, of course, but we will do that later. If you think of anything else relevant to the incident, please call and tell me."

Relevant. Yet another word to learn.

He smiled. "Mrs. Schoenleber, thank you for your part in this. And thank you too for the socials you've been hosting. They are a real addition to our community, something our young people need. My niece says they all have had a grand time."

"Glad to hear that." She walked with him to the door, and

once he went out, she returned to the warm kitchen. "I wish Fritz were here to play for us this evening. I so enjoy his music, and we could use something soothing and lovely tonight."

Hours later, Nilda, Miss Walstead, and Mrs. Schoenleber were sitting comfortably beside the fire when Charles and George returned. Mrs. Schoenleber motioned to two side chairs. She said simply, "Inform us."

Charles sat down. "You look much recovered, miss. Did he injure you?"

"No. I'm well." Nilda was glad her voice was getting back to normal.

George moved his chair closer to the fire and held his hands out toward the flames. "We found the place of the attack easily from the ski tracks. His heavy coat was still lying in a heap at the site, as was the tail of your ski that had broken off. Your other ski pole was broken as well. Why he did not go back for his coat, we cannot say."

"He was terribly furious, insanely furious. He chased me."

George nodded. "We saw that from the tracks in the snow. We debated pursuing him and decided to wait for the officials."

Charles picked up the story. "When the deputies arrived, we followed his tracks. He ran after you for nearly a quarter mile, but he was wading in the snow. He gave it up, finally, and turned toward the river. He seemed to be headed for the Cantwell farm, but he was obviously in extremity. He started dragging his feet. He fell a couple of times. Then he stopped, sat down, and leaned against a tree. That is where we found him."

"Did he say anything to you? I mean, about me?"

"No, miss," said George. "He was no longer breathing."

Nilda gasped. "Oh no! I killed him!"

"No, you did not!" Charles insisted. "We believe he died of hypothermia."

Mrs. Schoenleber translated, "He died of the cold."

George said gently, "It was his own foolishness that killed him, miss, not you. Certainly he should never have attacked you. But he should at least have gone back for his coat. The wind was especially fierce on the river. Hypothermia only takes an hour or two to kill you."

Nilda stared into the fire. "He said he had changed, he begged me to forgive him. And I did. He proved himself otherwise, but I would never want to hurt him or kill him."

"You were protecting yourself from madness." George frowned. "He must have been watching this house, but I never noticed him. Did you?" He looked at Charles.

"No. We can leave it to the law to sort that out. Surely someone saw him."

Nilda's head was whirling. "What will happen to him?"

"You and your family know his family. That will make it much easier. We cannot bury him here until the ground thaws anyway, so there is time to make arrangements."

Nilda turned to her employer. "Could I please go home for a few days?"

Mrs. Schoenleber squeezed her hand. "Of course, dear. Whatever you need."

The next afternoon, Nilda and her family were gathered around the kitchen table. When she finished telling them all that had happened, she looked around at their faces. "The sheriff reminded me several times, as did Mrs. Schoenleber, that this was not my fault. No matter what Dreng screamed at me, his death, even though I injured him, was not my fault either. I did not kill him—the cold and his fury did that. Still, I feel twinges of guilt sometimes. I hope that passes."

"He should have died in Norway," Ivar murmured. "We were too easy on him."

"Then you would have had to live with that responsibility." Gunlaug laid her hand on her younger son's arm. "Guilt is a horrible thing to live with. This way, he brought it on himself. His own actions caused his death."

Nilda continued. "I had to prepare a written statement for the sheriff. At that time, the sheriff revealed to me that the foreman of the lumber camp where Dreng worked had written to him asking him to lock Dreng up if he saw him, and the foreman would press charges. The letter said that he attacked a girl who works in the camp just like he had attacked me. He slipped into the cook shed early one morning when she was preparing potatoes for breakfast. Others heard her screams and came to her rescue, but he got away."

"We will give the sheriff the addresses for his parents. That we can do." Rune nodded as he spoke. "This is out of our hands."

Nilda nodded. "I feel better now that you all know. I've been having those terrible dreams of a man in a black hat." She looked at her mor. "But last night, nothing woke me. I slept until the maid woke me for breakfast so we could get on the road out here."

"How long can you stay?" Rune asked.

"Two more days. George will pick me up on Thursday morning."

"Good. So let's all get back to work. Work eases sorrow and pain; it will lift us up. You say you broke a ski. Bring it to me the next time you come, and I will make another of the same weight and length. I will send the two pairs of skis we just completed back with you. Ivar and Bjorn can go back out and finish limbing those trees and bring in a load of wood. Knute will help them, and I will work in the shop." Rune looked around the table.

310

"And life goes on." Gunlaug smiled sadly.

Rune nodded. "Yes, tragedies happen, but life goes on. Many losses, many blessings. One season after another."

"I would say we have been in a season of grace, with God watching out for us." Gunlaug returned her son's smile. "No matter what time of year, we will remain in His season."

Nilda nodded and shuddered. Far, dead and gone. And even Dreng, dead and gone. But there was a beautiful new baby in this home, and lively children.

A sudden thought seized her. It wasn't just birth and death. The families were changing in other ways. Here were two prosperous farmsteads where one struggling farm used to be. No, there were three farms, for Oskar and his children, with Selma, were now part of their world. She thought of the boisterous Petter, the quiet Fritz. They were a part of her life as well. So many losses, so many blessings.

This was why she had felt the need to come home. To be with her family who took things as they came, the good and the bad, and kept on going.

A season of grace indeed.

Lauraine Snelling is the award-winning author of over 70 books, fiction and nonfiction, for adults and young adults. Her books have sold over 5 million copies. Besides writing books and articles, she teaches at writers' conferences across the country. She and her husband make their home in Tehachapi, California, with basset hound Annie and their "three girls," big golden hens.

Sign Up for Lauraine's Newsletter!

Keep up to date with Lauraine's news on book releases and events by signing up for her email list at laurainesnelling.com.

More from the UNDER NORTHERN SKIES Series!

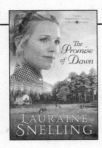

In 1910, Signe, her husband, and their boys emigrate from Norway to Minnesota, dreaming of one day owning a farm of their own. But the relatives they stay with are harsh and demanding. Can she learn to trust God through this trial and hold on to hope for a better future?

The Promise of Dawn
UNDER NORTHERN SKIES #1

More from Lauraine Snelling

Visit laurainesnelling.com for a full list of her books.

Miriam Hastings intends to complete her training to become a nurse in Blessing, North Dakota, and then return home. But her growing attachment to local Trygve Knutson soon has her questioning all her future plans. . . .

To Everything a Season
Song of Blessing #1

After she is called home due to a family emergency, will nurse-in-training Miriam Hastings find a way to support her loved ones and return to Blessing, North Dakota—and the man who is never far from her thoughts?

A Harvest of Hope
Song of Blessing #2

When widow Anji Baard Moen returns to Blessing, North Dakota, with her children, two men enter her life. As she moves forward from her loss, who will capture her heart?

Streams of Mercy by Lauraine Snelling
Song of Blessing #3

◊ BethanyHouse

You May Also Like . . .

After getting left at the altar, Kenzie Gifford determined never to love again. But when an earthquake devastates the life she's built in San Francisco, Kenzie finds herself facing a hidden danger—and two men set on winning her heart. With her life on the line, who can she trust?

In Times Gone By by Tracie Peterson
GOLDEN GATE SECRETS #3
traciepeterson.com

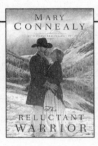

Newly reunited with his daughter and nephew, Cameron Scott wonders if they will ever love him again. When he's hurt protecting them, he finds himself under the care of the stubborn but beautiful Gwen Harkness—and he sees why the kids love her so. As she helps him win back their hearts, he finds himself wanting to win hers as well.

The Reluctant Warrior by Mary Connealy
HIGH SIERRA SWEETHEARTS #2
maryconnealy.com

Zanna Krykos eagerly takes on her friend's sponging business as a way to use her legal skills and avoid her family's matchmaking. But the newly arrived Greek divers, led by Nico Kalos, mistrust a female boss who knows nothing about the business. Yet they must work together to rise above adversity when confronted with the mysterious death of a diver and the rumor of sunken treasure.

The Lady of Tarpon Springs by Judith Miller
judithmccoymiller.com

⬧BETHANYHOUSE